I0713708

PAINTING THE EARL

Marrying a Mabry, Book 2

Lexi Post

© Copyright 2023 by Lexi Post
Text by Lexi Post
Cover by Kim Killion Designs

Dragonblade Publishing, Inc. is an imprint of Kathryn Le Veque Novels, Inc.
P.O. Box 23
Moreno Valley, CA 92556
ceo@dragonbladepublishing.com

Produced in the United States of America

First Edition June 2023
Trade Paperback Edition

Reproduction of any kind except where it pertains to short quotes in relation to advertising or promotion is strictly prohibited.

All Rights Reserved.

The characters and events portrayed in this book are fictitious. Any similarity to real persons, living or dead, is purely coincidental and not intended by the author.

ARE YOU SIGNED UP FOR DRAGONBLADE'S BLOG?

You'll get the latest news and information on exclusive giveaways, exclusive excerpts, coming releases, sales, free books, cover reveals and more.

Check out our complete list of authors, too!

No spam, no junk. That's a promise!

Sign Up Here

www.dragonbladepublishing.com

Dearest Reader;

Thank you for your support of a small press. At Dragonblade Publishing, we strive to bring you the highest quality Historical Romance from some of the best authors in the business. Without your support, there is no 'us', so we sincerely hope you adore these stories and find some new favorite authors along the way.

Happy Reading!

CEO, Dragonblade Publishing

Additional Dragonblade books
by Author Lexi Post

Marrying a Mabry Series
Stealing the Duke (Book 1)
Painting the Earl (Book 2)

Acknowledgments

For my wonderful husband, Bob Fabich, Sr., who values my sisters' and grandmother's artwork as much as I do.

For my amazing sister Paige Wood, a fantastic artist, a great friend, and the best beta reader I could ever ask for. Thank you for all your help on this story.

A big thank you to my critique partner, Marie Patrick, who encouraged me and wouldn't let me lag too far behind. Her faith in me is truly humbling.

I also want to thank Heidi Manzone, who was pivotal in helping me get the opening scene just right. Her insight was spot-on.

A special thank you to Lexi's Legends, Marina Bauman Leonard and Denise Hasund Sherman, who helped me find a name for Andrew's brother, and to Becki Lowe whose research into classic artwork was absolutely invaluable. Lastly, I want to send a huge thank you to my editor, Amelia Hester, my publisher, Kathryn Le Veque, and my agent, Jill Marsal. Without these wonderful ladies, the Mabry sisters wouldn't have their happily ever afters.

Author's Note

The Marrying a Mabry series was inspired by one of my favorite books of all time, Louisa May Alcott's novel, *Little Women,* published in two volumes in 1868 and 1869. This was an American coming of age story about four young ladies in New England. They were Margaret, Josephine, Elizabeth, and Amy March, or Meg, Jo, Beth, and Amy respectively. Each tries to live up to their mother's expectations of them, which were to become good people and respectable women.

Painting the Earl is specifically inspired by Amy March and her journey to womanhood. For Amelia Mabry, it is a journey from dreamer to accomplished artist. Basically, what if Amy March lived in Regency England and was the daughter of a marquess? How would a young woman of significant artistic talent fulfill her destiny within the norms of her society? What can she do when faced with a proposal from the one man she's longed to paint, but not marry? Is it possible to be both an artist and a wife, or must she choose?

On a weather note, it should be explained that 1816 was denoted as the Year Without a Summer. This was due to exceedingly cold temperatures and torrents of rainfall, freezing rain, and snow in the northern hemisphere causing catastrophic loss of life. The reason for this was unknown at the time. However, our current science is quite confident this event was caused by one of the largest volcanic eruptions on Earth during mankind's existence. The volcano was Mount Tambora in the Dutch East Indies, or present-day Indonesia, which erupted in April, 1815. Its ash cloud was so extensive that it changed the weather causing crops to fail in all countries affected, including England. The fallout, no pun intended, would cause famine, riots, looting, soaring prices, and believe it or not, due to the cost of feeding horses, possibly even the invention of what became the bicycle.

CHAPTER ONE

London
June 1816, the end of the season

"MY LADY. THE Earl of Sommerset has come to call and your mother has requested your presence in the garden."

Lady Amelia Mabry gritted her teeth before taking a deep breath and setting down her paintbrush. It wasn't the butler's fault that she couldn't get her male figures right. Nor was it his fault that a peer of the realm chose an inconvenient day and time to call. She couldn't quite muster up a smile, but she did keep her irritation out of her voice. "Let Mother know that I have been painting and will need a few moments."

"Of course." Channing gave her a nod and turned on his heel, exiting her studio room on the third floor of Craymore Hall.

Once his footsteps faded, she turned back to her painting of two men conversing in Hyde Park. Studying it, she then looked at the sketched image in the book her sister Joanna had lent her. Why did the male figures seem accurate to her? She'd used the same sketch for her painting of three men after a hunt, but they had been so flawed that gentlemen at her exhibit remarked upon it. Picking up her brush, she changed the shading on the shoulder of the tailcoat and hat of one of the men. Stepping back she frowned.

Dropping the brush onto her palette in frustration, she turned away. It was useless without a male model. She was doomed to painting flowers and women. The thought had her whipping off her apron, too angry at her own incompetence. "And now I'm to play happy hostess to some earl?"

Despite her best efforts, there was paint on her hands, and she moved to her water basin to clean it from her fingers. Her fingers remained a light violet color, so she didn't make any extra effort with them. It wasn't as if she wished to impress the gentleman below. What was his name? Lord Saunders? Selkirk? Summer? No, that wasn't it. Oh, Sommerset. She'd met him, hadn't she? Yes, they'd danced once, and if he was who she was thinking of, there had been a reason she'd avoided him most of the season.

Wiping her hands on the towel, she added a few more coals to the fire so it would be warm when she returned. It was critically cold outside. Whyever would her mother wish them in the garden?

Not a little irritated with both her mother and Lord Sommerset, she stalked down the stairs and waited as Channing helped her on with her blue spencer. Pulling on her gloves, she turned to the man. "Are they at the front walk?"

"No, my lady. They are at the dolphin fountain awaiting you."

That one was outside the ballroom. She glanced up the stairs wishing herself back in her studio. There was no help for it. If her mother requested her presence then she had to go.

"Excuse me, my lady, but you may have a bit of paint on your cheek."

She grinned. At least she hadn't stained her pink dress. "I do believe that is quite acceptable. I am a painter after all." Feeling a bit rebellious, she walked past the mirror in the entryway without looking into it and proceeded back to the empty ballroom and out the French doors into the cold and cloudy late June afternoon.

Descending the four steps to the path, she walked briskly

toward the dolphin fountain. Just as she caught sight of it, the sun peered through the clouds casting its dappled light upon the tawny hair of Lord Sommerset. She halted. His tall form all in browns and tans set against the cold patina of the dry fountain sparked a vision of him replacing Neptune atop the Trevi Fountain in Rome, the sun illuminating him as the quintessential male being pulled not by winged horses but lions. Her pulse raced. If she could capture him in a painting, it would be breathtaking.

"Ah, here she is." Her mother noticed her and waved for her to proceed.

She forced herself to move forward gracefully despite her wish to be back in her studio painting the image in her head, not that being in her studio would help. Her artistic abilities were such that painting was almost impossible without the object before her, and it wasn't as if she could run back and bring her easel down to the garden.

"Amelia, Lord Sommerset tells me that you two have met before?"

She nodded. "Yes, we have." She turned toward the man. His eyes filled with shades of gold and brown like his hair. "I wasn't aware you were still in Town."

He smiled, showing very white teeth. "I am, and will be for a fortnight or so."

"Then will you be attending Lady Dulac's ball? It is truly the final one of the season."

Her mother started down a path, a clear indication that they should follow.

He held his arm for her, and she placed her hand upon it. From what she'd heard whispered, he never called upon anyone, which begged the question, why was he here? They were barely acquainted.

He moved them forward. "I do. My mother would be much displeased if I did not."

That sounded like he'd prefer not to go. "If you enjoy dancing and a very good dinner, you will have a lovely evening. Have you attended her balls before?"

Lord Sommerset halted, allowing her mother to continue a bit farther down the path.

"Lady Amelia. Would you do me the honor of becoming my wife?"

She sucked in her breath at the surprise proposal. They hadn't exchanged more than a few sentences to each other all season. And for good reason. As handsome as the man was, in her private thoughts she'd dubbed him the Golden Adonis, he was far too tempting a subject. Though he had made an impression upon her, it was only in her need, perhaps obsession, to capture his appearance on canvas, but most definitely not him in marriage. She had far too much to accomplish before she could marry.

Unfortunately, turning down a third suitor in one season just wasn't done. Her parents might request that she give up her painting. She couldn't do that. Her mind raced with possible options. What if he rescinded his offer? Then her parents would be none the wiser.

Holding back a sly smile, she looked at her would-be suitor and didn't blink. "I will marry you, but only if you agree to pose nude for me, so I can create a masterpiece painting."

Lord Sommerset's eyes widened in shock.

Good. He deserved to feel as equally off balance as she did after such an unexpected proposition.

Recovering from his initial surprise, he frowned, his dark brown eyebrows accentuating his confusion. "I'm sorry. Did you say you wished for me to be your model for a painting after we marry?"

Oh no, that wouldn't do. She doubted any husband would allow her to spend hours a day refining her talent when there was so much time needed to run a household, entertain, and mother children. Absolutely not. It was why she'd turned down the last two offers she'd had. She must reach the pinnacle of her talent *before* marrying.

Scanning the garden to make sure her mother was far enough away, she shook her head. "Not after, *before*. And not simply model, but pose without any clothing. I would, of course, need to do a few paintings with clothes and numerous sketches with and without, but to paint the scene I envision for you, I would need you to pose nude. It will take many sittings."

To give the earl credit, he did not run straight to her mother, nor politely retract his offer and leave. Instead, he studied her, obviously trying to decide if she were jesting. But this was no jest. This was how she would avoid having to turn away another offer of marriage. She needed more time.

"I see." As he spoke, he ran his gloved hand through his thick hair on the right side of his head. "Would that not put your reputation at risk?" He glanced toward her mother before lowering his voice, "or would you be chaperoned?"

To be fair, she hadn't expected him to continue the conversation beyond his initial reaction, and so she hadn't thought through the details. The idea had simply sprung to mind once she'd caught her breath after her initial surprise. What would he find more offensive? "No, there could be no chaperone. In fact, no one must know." She paused as she searched for particulars on how the arrangement could work if she were actually willing to marry. "Of course, that would mean while in the company of each other at any public setting, we would pretend no specific relationship to avoid any hint of impropriety." That should send him off in a huff. What man wanted his betrothed to appear available?

His eyebrows raised at that. "But it is improper."

To pretend to not be spoken for? Oh, he meant the unchaperoned sittings. She sighed. Of course he would think it improper. No one in the *ton* could understand that the human form sans clothes, was the same as a horse, or a church, or a dinner plate, to an artist. Though, it was far more complex than a dinner plate, and one of the reasons she struggled with the male form. "I understand that many would think so, but from an artist's point of view, it would be no different to me than painting a bowl of fruit."

He straightened his rather broad shoulders, obviously insulted by her comparison.

She quickly grinned. "Please excuse me, I forget sometimes that others do not appreciate how an artist's mind works. Let me make a better comparison. It would be no different to me than painting the Tower of London."

His stance didn't relax. "And when would this secrecy end?"

Horse feathers. She hadn't expected to still be discussing her offer. He should have been too shocked by her terms. He was supposed to leave off immediately. She lifted her right shoulder. "Until the painting is complete, of course."

He appeared to be contemplating her offer seriously. "And where would you create this painting?"

Her stomach tightened. Did he inquire because he didn't believe she meant it and wished to see how much she truly wanted to paint him, or did he believe her and wished to know how to fulfill his part of the bargain? Either way, she could feel excitement starting to ignite in her chest right beside her greatest fear. "I have my own studio, both here at Craymore Hall and at our country estate in Bedford."

"I see." He moved to the left to stand before a tree trunk which he promptly leaned against. He crossed his long, muscled legs which were revealed by the fall of his brown great coat before they disappeared into his black boots. His thick multi-toned hair, not mussed in the least from his hand, seemed to capture the sun's rays in specific strands, adding a bit of warmth to their spot in the mostly dead garden.

What did he see? There was nothing to see. She'd asked him to pose nude, unchaperoned, in her studio. He should be appalled. Or did he think her a woman of easy virtue? She frowned. "Of course, such sittings would be innocent at all times." It was the closest she could bring herself to discussing her virginity. "And after the painting is complete, if you prefer not to wed, no one would be the wiser."

His lips quirked up. "But then you would have a painting of all of me. Would you keep it or would I become the owner of said piece?"

Her heart thudded in her chest. He was clearly considering her proposal. Half of her was elated. She would finally discover what she'd been doing wrong with her male figures and do so with the very man whom she'd wanted to paint since Lord Harewood first introduced him at the theatre at the start of the season. The other half of her was terrified. What if this didn't result in her masterpiece? What if after finishing the painting, he insisted on marriage and she hadn't accomplished her goal?

"Lady Amelia?" He pushed away from the tree and stepped closer to her.

She grasped the thick folds of her rose-madder spencer to keep her fingers from twitching. The thought of painting him was quickly becoming a craving too hard to dispel. "Would you wish to have it?"

He cocked his head. "If it was well done, then yes. I am after all, an art collector."

She hadn't known that. Obviously, he wished to add an artist to his collection as well. Could she allow him the painting if it resulted in her masterpiece? At the thought, her decision came quickly. She could. Her need was to create, not covet. The tension left her. "Then I would gladly relinquish it to you." She held up her hand to forestall any comment. "But only when I determine it is finished."

"We would want at least one witness each to our bargain, to protect both parties." He glanced behind her, no doubt looking at her mother.

She shook her head. "No, this would be far too much for my mother to keep private. My eldest sister is the keeper of all secrets in our family."

"And my good friend, the Earl of Harewood, who has impeccable integrity, has kept many a secret of mine over the years."

He spoke as if he'd already made his decision and she found herself growing breathless, so she simply agreed with a nod. Could this truly occur? It was a serious risk to her painting, her reputation, and her future, but it gave her everything she wanted, except a husband. But she'd learned a few difficult lessons from Aunt Mabry, and one was that a husband was a requirement no matter how much artistic talent a woman had, and no matter how much she didn't want one.

He offered his arm to her. "Shall we walk a bit more? You have given me much to contemplate."

She linked her arm through his, resting it on the wool of his coat. Disappointment crept up her spine that he hadn't agreed, but then again, he hadn't dismissed her proposal out of hand. Would it be worth agreeing to marriage for the opportunity to paint him? The answer came swiftly. *Yes.* Though they'd hardly spoken all season, she'd sought his visage at every public event. It was as if he'd been created for the purpose of a painting. He was far too perfect to ignore.

His features were sculpted like Corradini's *Adonis* sleeping, giving him a youthful appearance. He even had wavy hair reminiscent of the Italian marble but with less curl and with multi-golden tones that made her fingers tingle with the need to grasp a paintbrush. It didn't help that his whisky-colored eyes and tanned skin reminded her of a lion. He was the perfect animal for her artwork.

"Have you been painting long then?"

His innocuous question startled her. "I have. I exhibited at the London Art Academy just last week."

"You exhibited at the London Art Academy? I didn't know they had opened to female artists." He halted them next to the smallest fountain in the garden, the one with a mermaid, her own nude torso covered by her flowing locks.

"We were the first." She could feel him studying her, but she kept her gaze on her mother who was just ahead on the path.

"I'm sorry I missed the opportunity to see your work."

She lifted one shoulder and dropped it. "The exhibit had mixed reviews. There were three other female artists there. I'm not sure how they felt, but I know I could have produced better works if I'd had more notice." She paused, thinking back to the negative comment she'd overheard about the male figures in the foreground of her "After the Hunt" painting, which in her mind trumped all the complimentary reviews she'd read.

She finally looked at him and rolled her eyes. "My sister, the Duchess of Northwick, says the fact that I was asked to exhibit is a great step forward. She is a champion of anything that appears to place women on equal footing with men."

He moved them forward again. "And you don't believe your invitation to exhibit met that criteria?"

She chuckled. "Hardly. I believe it was more that we were an oddity, like a monkey paraded about at court." She felt his arm tense beneath hers.

"Now I wish I could have viewed your work, so I might comment on your interpretation of the invitation."

She appreciated that he didn't dismiss her opinion out of hand nor agree with her too quickly. "It's of no matter. I exhibited and it's done. I know I'm no DaVinci or Rembrandt. I studied the masters extensively while abroad. Reaching that level of skill could take a lifetime."

"But not with natural talent." He looked at her as they strolled through what just last summer had been a haven for butterflies, but all the stems were simply leafless sticks pointing to the sky now.

She met his gaze, though she didn't wish to since his eyes were such a warm brown with flecks of gold and spots of dark brown that would make a wonderful study. "My mother tells me I have talent. My Aunt Mabry, though, would tell me talent without discipline is simply dreaming. So she took me about the continent to see all the great works."

His gaze drifted from hers. "I have collected great artwork for years, or rather what I thought was the masters' works. I wish I had someone with me at the time who could tell the difference between the authentic and a forgery." His gaze snapped back to hers, a new tension in his chin. "Can you distinguish between the two?"

At his tone, she studied him, sensing her answer meant more than simply polite inquiry. "I can."

He didn't immediately speak, instead he seemed to be contemplating something of great import. He looked forward as he guided her along the pathway. "I recently discovered one of my paintings was a forgery. It was a complete surprise."

Immediately empathy filled her. Forgeries were common and quite acceptable as long as the purchaser was aware that was what they were buying. Her good friend Lady Spencer had been very embarrassed to discover she'd bought a forgery when assured it was authentic. "I wish I could have prevented you from such an experience. It is one of those practices that I find quite upsetting."

"I'm pleased to hear you say so. I admit I was shocked. I have a rather large collection and was thinking of selling a few pieces. I'm not one for turning my entire home into an art exhibit, despite my appreciation for it. Now, I am unsure if any of my paintings are originals."

Seeing they had almost reached her mother who strolled a polite distance ahead, she stopped, pulling her hand from his arm. Clearly, he was more than a little put out by the discovery. She understood that those who truly collected artwork did so with a passion that rivaled the artist's passion to create it. "Did you purchase them all from the same person?"

He ran his hand through his hair again. "No. I rarely acquired two works from the same seller. My collection is from all over Europe and a few paintings from even farther afield. Each one means something to me." He paused as if he'd revealed too much. "I never sought to acquire forgeries. Now, I know not what I have."

Despite knowing she should simply sympathize with him, his

emotion at the betrayal connected to the one she'd experienced at the will of Aunt Mabry, though for a completely different reason. Torn between propriety and the desire to help him, she sought a solution that would accomplish both. "Have you had anyone review your collection?"

He shook his head. "I have been unsuccessful in finding an expert who is willing to take the time without the benefit of a possible purchase."

Of course, that hadn't occurred to her. Experts would want to buy, and for a lord to be told he had a forgery would be embarrassing at the very least and could damage his reputation, preventing any further sales, never mind becoming fodder for gossip among the *ton*. She understood his dilemma.

"It troubles me enough that I'm having all my paintings taken down at my country estate until I can verify their authenticity." His eyes seemed to have turned darker with his emotions, now almost the color of the oak tree trunk nearby.

She grimaced. The idea that beautiful works of art would be sequestered in storage until reviewed sent a sharp pain through her heart.

He looked away as if unwilling to let her see how deeply this incident had affected him, but she knew. And there was nothing she could say to ease that burden. This brief insight into Lord Sommerset had her feeling unsettled, like the time she'd rushed out to skate on the pond, ignoring her sister's warning, and felt the ice shift beneath her just before it gave way. Knowing more about Lord Sommerset than simply his appearance was not in her best interest. It was best to keep any future conversation to the odd weather or the last ball.

Her mother waited for them at the entrance into the house through the library, where her father would no doubt be. It wasn't hard to discern that her mother hoped Lord Sommerset would wish to see her father.

Before they reached the house though, the earl halted. "It has been a most enlightening afternoon. I have much to think upon, so I will take my leave now. Please tell your mother that I have enjoyed my visit."

Surprised, but pleased by his decision not to extend his time with her, she smiled and gave him a nod. "I will await your response."

Tipping his hat and bowing, he then turned on his heel and headed back down the walk the way he'd come, his step brisk.

Needing time to consider the afternoon's turn of events herself, she continued toward her mother, who now stood with furrowed brow.

"Did Lord Sommerset not wish to come inside for tea?" Her mother looked past her, most likely watching the man in question walk away.

"No. He has other plans." As in he planned to think about her proposal.

Her mother's gaze moved to her. "You do know he hasn't called upon a single woman all season."

She hooked her mother's arm with her own and opened one library door. Oddly enough, her father was nowhere to be seen once they stepped inside. She untied her bonnet and unbuttoned her spencer. "Yes, I'm aware of the gossip, and he would prefer no one know he visited here." At least, that was what she preferred, so it wasn't an outright lie.

Her mother, who walked across the room, stopped. "Whyever not?"

That was a good question. Moving past her mother, she exited the library into the corridor. "Because it wasn't *that* kind of call." She looked up half expecting her deceased sister Belinda to strike her down for lying to their mother. "He only wished to relate his concern about a forgery he'd purchased unknowingly." *I'm sorry Belinda. I'm just never going to be as good as you.*

Her mother caught up to her just as she handed her outerwear to Channing.

"Oh dear, that is quite unfortunate. I'm to guess that he learned of your expertise in that area?" She handed her cloak off to Channing as well.

Not before he'd arrived, but she nodded anyway. "Yes, and he requested advice. I'm surprised he didn't simply consult his friend, Lord Harewood. That man likes to pretend he's an expert on every subject."

"The son of our neighbors in Bedford?" Her mother's pretty blue eyes softened. "They are lovely people. Though I haven't seen young Harewood for many years." She paused as she thought. "He went off to Oxford and then shipped to Europe for a few years. His parents are quite pleased with him. He's already taken on management of one of their estates."

The last person she wanted her mother to be thinking about was Lord Harewood. It was no secret that she had longed for one of her daughters to marry the man. And with the season coming to a close after Lady Dulac's ball at the end of the week, they would be headed back to Bedford when visits to the Harewood estate would no doubt ensue.

"I am quite happy keeping Lord Sommerset's call to myself, especially since he simply sought my expertise." Maybe not simply, but she wasn't beyond a small lie to keep her life moving in the direction she wanted, especially since her mother was still a champion of her painting. That would change in a year or two when she was in her second or third season and at the risk of becoming a spinster. She must create her masterpiece as soon as creatively possible.

Her mother jumped upon the change in subject. "What do you think about the earl now that you have spent some time with him?"

"I think he is a passionate art collector and a rather liberal minded thinker."

Her mother grasped her arm. "But what do you think about his appearance. I have to say that even though I haven't lifted a paintbrush in over twenty-three years, I was wishing I had one today. I do believe the sun came out just to shine on that young man's handsome features."

She grinned. If anyone knew how difficult it was to be a female painter, it was her mother. "That's a bit fanciful, but I agree. In fact, if you don't need me, I'd like to run up into my studio and do a few sketches."

Her mother laughed, releasing her arm. "Please go. If you can draw from memory, I won't delay you. I was never able to develop that skill."

Giving her mother a kiss on the cheek, she ascended the stairs as quickly as possible. She hadn't actually developed the skill either, but she hoped she could get something done in the next few minutes. Maybe, just maybe if she could, she could withdraw her ill-conceived proposal.

CHAPTER TWO

ANDREW CRAUFORD, EARL of Sommerset, strode down the street fighting his need to whistle. He could still smell the light violet scent Lady Amelia wore that gave the impression the garden had flowers. She even sported a splash of lavender paint on her cheek.

After avoiding being alone with any woman all season, he'd finally agreed with his closest friend, Harewood, that he would need to choose one to marry and quickly. He'd never expected to receive a proposal in return, and possibly an alternative option.

He tipped his hat to a young woman and her mother whom he'd met during the season. Edith? Eleanor? Elsbeth? One of those was her name. She, like many others, had not intrigued him in the least. To be fair, neither did Lady Amelia, who though quite pretty with pale blonde hair, blue – almost violet – eyes, and a pert nose, had not piqued his interest during the season. Despite her constant pleasant disposition, he'd found her unsettling. She reminded him of a fairy like the ones in the watercolor done by William Blake, almost unearthly in appearance and disposition. She wasn't untoward, exactly. If pushed to explain his impression, he would say she was impish. It always seemed as if she knew something no one else knew and found it amusing. Though she followed a conversation perfectly, even adding a witty remark on occasion, the topics she chose were unusual and unimportant.

It was his closest friend, Felton Enderly, Earl of Harewood, who had revealed that Lady Amelia might be of interest due to her ability as an artist. She had never brought that to his attention in their meager interactions, and considering she'd been invited to exhibit at the London Art Academy, he found that unique. Did she not think her talent was worthy of notice? It was as if she found herself as amusing as everyone around her.

A carriage pulled up beside him and halted. He glanced at the coat of arms and grinned. He should have guessed. When the door swung open, he didn't wait for a footman and bounded into the conveyance. "You couldn't wait." Dropping into the seat opposite of Harewood, he shook his head, stifling a smile.

"Of course I couldn't. It's not every day I have a good friend proposing to a woman he knows little about." The Earl of Harewood looked down his nose as if it was to be accepted that he be entitled to knowing all. The man's coloring was the exact opposite from himself with almost black hair, and eyes the color of spring leaves. The fact that he always dressed in dark hues gave him the appearance of being quite a somber individual, but Andrew knew better.

"*You* suggested Lady Amelia. I would never have considered her." He crossed his arms, curious as to why Harewood suddenly appeared to have what could only be called cold feet. Had he discovered something about the lady's character that would not bode well for marriage? He could understand that after the bargain she'd just proposed.

Harewood knocked on the ceiling of the carriage with his cane before answering. As they lurched forward, he waved his hand. "Of course I did. Anything to keep you from considering one of the Worthington sisters. I don't think my wife and I could stand to call on you then."

"Wife. You have no wife."

"Not yet, but I will soon and I feel it necessary to at least be able to stand in the same room with the woman you marry."

He shook his head. Only Harewood would think so far into

the future. That was his strong suit, looking ahead foreseeing possible outcomes. He was rarely wrong. They'd met their first week at Oxford, where they'd discovered they had similar interests in rowing and trifle, among other enticements. His friend knew more about him and his motives than even his own sibling.

The man raised his brows. "I'm assuming from your step that she accepted. Did her father also agree?"

He smirked. "She did not say yes."

Harewood nodded, satisfied that he had predicted correctly. "She said no."

"No, she didn't refuse me either."

"You're not making sense. Out with it, man."

It was much too fun to frustrate Harewood. It wasn't often that the man didn't foresee a scenario, and in this case, he'd been completely wrong, having reasoned that she would refuse an offer of marriage as she had with the two others before him. "She made a counter proposal." He barely held in a laugh, enjoying the surprise on Harewood's face.

Harewood's gaze grew shrewd. "What could she possibly have proposed? I mean, she is a lady with a perfect reputation."

Not quite sure why he found the whole situation amusing when his future, and that of so many others, hung in the balance, but he couldn't help drawing out the suspense. "That is why I told her I must think upon her proposal."

"Bloody hell, Sommerset, what did she propose?"

He laughed. "If I tell you, you must keep it in the strictest of confidence."

Harewood crossed his arms and glared at him.

He thought about prolonging the inevitable, but he did need the man's counsel on the subject. His own anticipation of Harewood's reaction was too tempting to deny himself any longer. "She will marry me on the condition that one, I pose naked for a painting, and two, that until said painting is done, we let no one know we have any relationship whatsoever, so as not to ruin her reputation before we marry, which we will do after the painting is completed."

Harewood's mouth dropped open, his stare almost catatonic in his shock.

He, on the other hand, couldn't stop grinning. He didn't know if it was because Lady Amelia unwittingly opened another path that he might take, or because he was extraordinarily pleased to find her far more interesting than he'd ever imagined. Or it could possibly be that he was excited by the prospect of posing for her.

"She…you…" Harewood gave up, closing his mouth tight.

"Didn't expect that, did you?"

"No." Harewood shook his head, then stilled. "Are you sure you spoke to the right Mabry sister?"

"I'm not daft, of course I spoke to the correct Mabry. The oddest one married the Duke of Northwick."

"Oh, right. I'd forgotten." Harewood's brow furrowed. "That was last month, wasn't it? I remember thinking the man should have kept to Lady Caroline as was rumored."

"Maybe the duke preferred an interesting wife as well."

Harewood frowned. "Why did you say you would think upon such an outrageous proposal?"

"Because I'm intrigued. I did not expect such a surprise from her. Perhaps an off the subject remark, but not a full counter proposal like she'd thought of this idea for a while. Either she has a very fast intellect or—"

"Or she's thought about you and painting you specifically for quite some time."

Harewood's conclusion had also been his own, which made Lady Amelia all the more a puzzle. If she'd thought about him so frequently, why had she never shown any interest in him? Actually, she had almost gone out of her way to avoid him. *Of course, that would mean while in the company of each other at any public setting, we would pretend no specific relationship to avoid any hint of impropriety.* Her words echoed in his mind. "I believe it is the former. She has shown no interest in me and even if I accept her proposal, she will continue to show no interest in me while in a public setting."

Harewood gave him a sly grin. "Yes, but in private, it appears her interest in you is quite strong."

Harewood's insinuation had his body reacting and his anger surfacing, a combination he'd never felt before, especially not with his good friend. He stifled his emotions and shook his head. "I don't believe she has an interest in me in that way either." Though his body obviously had an interest in her. "No, she sees me like she sees a bowl of fruit."

"A bowl of fruit?" Harewood's grin disappeared. "Maybe she sees you as ripe and easy for plucking?"

The man never was good at admitting he was wrong. It was a pathetic attempt. "No. She sees me as an object to paint like a bowl of fruit. Those were her actual words."

Harewood pulled his head back to rest against the seat cushion as he studied him. "I suppose you do have a certain classical appeal. She has studied the masters, so I can see why your Apollo-like appearance would be of interest to her as an artist."

He tensed. His appearance was both an advantage and a curse as he'd discovered. At least Lady Amelia was interested in it for an artistic reason, which made it much more palatable. "It's rather ironic. The one woman I finally propose to is more interested in me as an *objet d'art* than as a husband."

Harewood grunted. "When are you to give Lady Amelia your answer?"

"I didn't say."

"You don't have much time left."

He gave Harewood a piercing look. "I'm well aware of my time constraints."

"If it weren't for this ungodly weather, you would have been fine."

"I know." He sighed. He'd never planned on a love match, but he had wanted to find someone who had some depth of character. All the young ladies he'd conversed with had been, at best, uninteresting. That was, until this afternoon.

Harewood leaned forward. "You could try selling more paintings. Just because that one was a forgery doesn't mean they all are. It could provide the income you need until the spring."

"I have thought of that. In fact, I learned today that Lady Amelia can tell the difference between a forgery and a true masterpiece."

Harewood looked askance at him. "So if you could manage to have her review the paintings you have here at your London house, you would know which you could sell, and then gracefully decline her proposal." Harewood pulled in air through his nose. "That's brilliant."

"I thought so as well."

"Braggart."

He laughed. Now all he needed was to create a way for Lady Amelia to review all his paintings before her family left for the country. If he didn't have as many authentic pieces as he thought he did, he could accept her proposal. And if he did have plenty he could sell, that would sustain those who depended upon him until spring. Then his new investments could take over from there, and he wouldn't have to marry so quickly. There was only one problem. Lady Amelia's counterproposal had done what no woman in two years had been able to do. She had caught his interest.

Lady Dulac's ball

ANDREW SCANNED THE dancers for Lady Amelia. She was to be his next partner. He found her at the front of the line just about to make her way down the center of two rows of couples. Earlier in the evening, she'd been surprised at his request for her supper dance. He had yet to accept her proposal, so dancing with her was still perfectly appropriate as they had no bargain yet, if ever they would.

At that moment, she moved gracefully down the middle of the room with her partner, her smile wide as the wisps of hair about her face swayed with her movement. Her small breasts and lithe form added to her fairy-like mystique.

"I understand her to have a substantial dowry." Harewood stood next to him, dressed in all black except for his white shirt and cravat, the opposite of himself as usual.

"You were discreet in your inquires?"

A snort was all he received in reply. While marriage was a pressing need, it did necessitate a woman with a significant dowry. Yes, she was the daughter of a marquess. She was also the epitome of beauty in the eyes of the *ton*. Wearing a lavender dress that brought out the color of her eyes, she looked particularly striking in the light of the ballroom. And after last week's counterproposal, he also found her intriguing, but none of that mattered if she didn't come with the dowry he needed to sustain his mother, younger brother, Christopher, and his tenants through to next summer. Their needs took precedence, no matter how he felt personally.

"I admit my suggestion was quite brilliant. She fits your needs and she's pretty in the typical fashion." Harewood was obviously still smarting from having missed his prediction about Lady Amelia so thoroughly. He only touted his own intelligence after being off the mark.

As the dance continued, he faced Harewood. "I hope she understands the responsibilities of life. There are heirs to beget and social obligations to be met. I'd much rather a lady who is pleasing in other ways beyond appearances."

Harewood frowned. "Not every woman you meet is a Lady Frederica."

Even though it had been three years past, the mention of that particular lady still gave him a chill. "True, but I must assume every woman is exactly like her until I know more."

"I understand." Harewood looked past him then returned to their conversation. "I don't think you need concern yourself with

Lady Amelia manipulating you into any particular situation. I haven't heard a word about you calling on her earlier this week, so she obviously has not mentioned it. You also have already proposed and since she didn't exactly say yes, it does appear like she won't make your decision for you. This is her first season, and she's turned down a couple of offers. It appears she is enjoying herself too much to consider marriage. I should have noticed that before. I'm quite surprised she even entertained your offer."

He studied his friend. "How do you know so much about the lady? I thought you said you avoided your neighbors in Bedford."

"I simply know more than you do because Keighley was smitten early in the season before he married."

That made sense. The Earl of Keighley was an art collector like himself, and Lady Amelia was an artist. Keighley was a cold fish. No doubt he'd display his wife like he displayed his art: arrogantly.

The dance was nearing its end. His next conversation would have to be broached carefully. If any of the *ton* sniffed out a hint of his inherited financial troubles, he could find himself an outsider. That would be uncomfortably limiting if he wasn't able to get the lady in question to review his collection, or if need be, to the altar.

Harewood gave a nod toward the center of the ballroom. "I will see you after supper. I expect to hear of your success or failure then."

"Of course. I wouldn't have it any other way. Would you care to predict what she will say?"

Harewood straightened his shoulders and lifted his chin. "No." He turned on his heel and went in search of his own partner.

Andrew smirked before turning back toward the center of the room. As the dancers bowed and curtsied, he pulled down on his white cashmere waistcoat, then made his way to where Lady Amelia had completed her dance. Harewood was correct, she was much sought after. He hadn't seen her sit out a dance all evening.

Her partner escorted her back to the Duke and Duchess of Northwick, the duchess being the lady's sister and chaperone for the evening.

It would be a few minutes before the supper dance commenced, so instead, he walked by the table with punch and poured a cup before weaving between the crowd. He watched her, his stomach tightening, hoping she hadn't forgotten he was her next partner.

She spoke to her sister then turned back toward the dance floor scanning the crowd.

He quickly stepped forward and bowed. "My lady, I believe I am your partner for the next dance."

She turned at the sound of his voice and a smile lit her face. "Lord Sommerset, I was just looking for you."

There was something about her that made a person smile, of that he'd been aware in the past and it was no different now. It could be the wisps of pale blond hair that framed her face. Or perhaps it was simply the ever-present twinkle in her uniquely colored eyes. "And so you have found me." He turned quickly to acknowledge the duke and duchess. The duke appeared bored, but the duchess seemed thoroughly entertained by the event.

Catching Lady Amelia's eye again, he lifted the punch. "I thought you might like a bit of refreshment before our dance."

Appreciation shone in her gaze as she reached for the small glass. "How did you know? I was just telling my sister that I haven't participated in so much activity since before my art show."

Seeing an opportunity for extended conversation, he pounced on it. "If you would like, we could forgo the next dance."

She finished taking a sip and gave him a grateful smile. "I would adore that." She pulled out her fan. "Perhaps we could venture out onto the terrace?"

He tensed. He never went outside with an unmarried lady. Lady Frederica had cured him of any such inclinations. Then again, this was possibly his future wife.

Amelia made her voice louder. "I'm sure the duke wouldn't mind accompanying us."

Her ploy worked. The duke moved forward instantly. "It may be too cold to stay long, but I, for one, would enjoy a breath of cooler air."

Lady Northwick rolled her eyes. "You'd enjoy anything but standing here."

The man's expression changed, softened, actually. "That's because I'd rather be waltzing with you."

Lady Amelia waved her hand at them. "Don't pay them no mind. My sister and her husband are quite…unusual."

He silently agreed with her observation. "I would enjoy some cooler air as well."

With that decided, he offered his arm and the four of them moved toward the open doors as the dancers took their positions about the floor. The familiar scent of violets filled his nostrils as they walked together, which was far better than the heavy perfumes he'd been exposed to earlier in the evening.

The duke and duchess moved to the right of the terrace, and he steered Lady Amelia that way as well. He halted near the other couple.

"Oh, look." Lady Amelia disengaged her gloved hand from his arm and pointed to the sky. "Is that not breathtaking?"

He moved his gaze to find a very bright moon hiding behind clouds. "I think it would be far more pleasing if that celestial body showed itself, would it not?"

She shook her head, but didn't look at him. "Absolutely not. There is no subtlety in that." Her hand moved to the right. "Look. See how the light filters through the thinner clouds and exits in a soft wash of white? Yet, there." She moved her finger, still pointing. "There, where the clouds are thickest, the light escapes the sides in bright streaks that reflect on the clouds nearby."

She was quite serious in her observation, so he studied the light as she described it. He'd never looked at the moon in quite that way. "I see what you mean." He paused as another cloud attempted to obscure the moon all together, but seemed to think better of it. "That new cloud, instead of dimming the scene, is actually reflecting more light, thereby brightening the sky." He wouldn't have noticed such if she hadn't pointed it out.

She dropped her hand and spun around to look at him. "Exactly."

Her smile was wide and her eyes, in the limited lantern light, sparkled with excitement. "Moonlight itself is far more subtle than sunlight."

The duke interjected. "That's because the moonlight is simply reflected sunlight. Moonlight, per se, does not exist."

"James, I don't think Lord Sommerset needs a lesson in astronomy right now." The duchess pulled her husband further away from them.

Lady Amelia shook her head. "Don't mind the duke. He's quite intelligent, as is my sister, but they cannot appreciate true beauty." She sighed. "They subscribe to some ancient philosopher's definition of beauty."

He watched the other couple, hoping they wouldn't move too far. "I imagine that would be Aristotle."

"Why yes, I do believe that was the name. Do you agree?"

He turned back to face her, not wishing to be rude. "I understand Aristotle's concept of symmetry, but I often find vistas that are not symmetrical quite beautiful."

"Yes!" Her eyes practically glowed. "That is what I have tried to tell them, but they will hear none of it." She leaned in and lowered her voice. "What would some old, dusty, philosopher know about beauty anyway?" She cocked her head before spinning about to gaze at the sky again.

Did he just see light freckles sprinkled across her nose? He couldn't be sure because her blue, almost violet eyes had completely distracted him. He felt an odd sense of privilege that she had included him in what seemed to be her secret observation.

"Already the beauty is fading." Her voice was sad, as if the scene in the sky had been what she'd hoped to see all evening.

He lifted his gaze once again to find she was correct. More clouds had joined ranks and seemed determined to shield the moon from their view. He didn't care for the disappointed sound of her voice. "That may be true, but isn't that what makes the beauty of the moment that much more special?"

This time when she turned back to him, she appeared to study him. "You are correct. I have often thought that. The first time it occurred to me, I had just set up my easel by the River Seine when the sun began to rise upon the flying buttresses of Notre Dame. I was so spellbound by the play of light that I failed to capture it with my brush."

So she had traveled to Paris. That made sense if, as she'd mentioned, she'd traveled abroad to study art. Perhaps that was why she was so well-versed in the artwork of the masters. "I too have seen the sunrise on Notre Dame, but from the opposite vantage point." He had been about all night drinking with friends and had yet to go to bed, but she needn't know that. He felt far older and wiser now. "It was a rather symmetrical experience until the light reflected off the Rose Window."

She nodded sagely. "Yes, I have witnessed that view as well. I was able to capture it in paint until that exact moment happened."

"Do you think not capturing such a sight makes it more personal?"

"I do. I call it the mystic moment. It's that happening that speaks to your soul and can't be replicated or even shared unless witnessed with another."

Surprised that he knew exactly what she meant, he couldn't keep silent. "I would call it a moment beyond human comprehension. It's less that you understand it, and more that you feel it."

Her eyes widened for a moment in shared understanding before she looked away, as if embarrassed.

He understood because he felt similarly. Better to steer their conversation into other avenues. He offered her his arm again so they could stroll closer to her sister. As they approached, a half-smile played upon her lips, which was not how she'd appeared while looking at the moon. Though nothing changed in her visage now, he sensed her withdrawal as if she had retreated back into her shell, much like Botticelli's Aphrodite may have if she didn't wish to be seen. Had the moon's appearance behind the clouds invited the lady artist to reveal herself, and could it be that now, like the moon, the profound woman scurried back into hiding, only she did so behind smiles?

It was a curious thought. As Lady Amelia conversed with her sister, nothing changed. She was much like she had been every other time he had danced with her. But he had seen something else. Had it been a single moment of thoughtfulness, or did she indeed have other weighty observations? Or were they only in relation to art like her counterproposal? If so, he should be more flattered that she wished to paint him.

"Lord Sommerset, do you have any thoughts as to why we have had such a dreary, cold summer?" The duchess held both hands out as if to indicate the chilliness of the air about them.

"I have not. I have been more concerned about the results of this cold on my tenants, and their ability to survive the winter. Not much has grown, and I fear food shortages in the coldest of months."

The duke nodded. "As do I. I have been making alternative plans and would be happy to share them with you."

To have the Duke of Northwick share his ideas would indeed be a boon. "I would be very interested. This is my first year not having my father to discuss such matters with, and I appreciate any experience you can share with me."

The duke's eyebrows rose. "I doubt I have as much experience as the late earl, but I may have read a bit more about the subject than you."

"Of course." He held back a grimace. He'd just intimated that the duke was as old as his father when he was no more than maybe eight years his senior.

The duchess gave an exaggerated shiver. "I do believe I'm growing quite chilled. I'm sure the supper dance should be ending soon."

Lady Amelia grinned wickedly. "Are you sure it's not your penchant for sweets that calls you in, Joanna?" She turned to him to explain. "Lady Dulac makes my sister's favorite trifle."

"I was not aware." Nor did he find it of grave importance. She had returned to trivial topics.

Her grace answered. "Oh yes. If you haven't tasted Lady Dulac's cook's Citrus Trifle, then you must be sure not to eat your fill at dinner. It is well worth the wait." She shivered. "And as much as I love it, I really am quite chilled."

The duke's brow furrowed. "Then let us return to the ballroom posthaste." He did not wait for anyone's agreement as he guided his wife toward the brightly lit open doorway.

Andrew followed with Lady Amelia on his arm. "Are you also chilled?"

She waved off his comment with her hand. "Not at all, but I was dancing most of the night. I can't imagine how boring this must be for them. They only serve as my chaperone when my parents or oldest sister cannot."

How the many debutantes' chaperones enjoyed, or not enjoyed, the evening had never occurred to him. He congratulated himself on having a younger brother and not a younger sister. "Is it only your sister and the duke who grow bored?"

Lady Amelia let out a soft chuckle. "I can't comment on others, but my sister and brother-in-law are far too intellectual for the frivolity of a ball." She looked askance at him. "I find these events invigorating, don't you?"

He wouldn't describe his feelings about a ball in quite that way. Riding the hunt or taking a brisk walk in winter were more his definition of invigorating. "I find them enjoyable in many ways."

"You do?" Doubt flitted about in her pretty round eyes before she faced forward again. "I suppose in addition to dancing, I do enjoy watching everyone at dinner."

He found that an odd comment. "Watching?"

"Yes. I like to observe people's expressions and mannerisms, and guess at what they are discussing and thinking. My sisters and I used to make a game of it when we were younger. Now they are all far too old for such nonsense." She made it sound as if her older siblings missed so much by not playing the game anymore.

He would think it frustrating and rude to engage in such a game, so he kept silent. What possible purpose could there be in such an endeavor? Where had the observant artist disappeared to?

They entered the very warm ballroom and halted as the dance finished and the dancers bowed to each other. A bell was rung at the wide opening between the room and library, indicating it was time to stroll through to the dining room.

His curiosity as to whether he would catch another glimpse of the thoughtful Lady Amelia was strong. Discourse with her was proving to be both captivating and frustrating the more time he spent with her. She definitely looked at things differently. Could there be more relevant viewpoints yet to come?

As he escorted her into their host's dining room, his attention was caught by a forgery of the painting of *Juno* by Rembrandt Harmenszoon van Rijn. In his fascination with the multifaceted Lady Amelia, he'd almost forgotten his purpose in asking her for the supper dance. One that could help him make his decision regarding her counterproposal. He would remedy that in due course.

CHAPTER THREE

THANKFUL FOR LORD Sommerset's arm, Amelia felt as if her very balance had deserted her the moment he'd been able to appreciate the beauty of the moon. That she often remarked on such scenes was not unusual, but no one had ever responded with understanding before. It excited her and made her uncomfortable all at once, more the latter.

If the earl were like every other eligible gentleman of the *ton*, his reaction would not have affected her in the least beyond a bit of curiosity. But he wasn't. His very countenance enticed her to paint, making her far more susceptible to his charms. But for him to understand, no, to have felt a mystic moment made him too tempting as a husband and very dangerous to her artistic plans.

She'd never wanted to be more acquainted with him beyond a dance, knowing that her artist's eye might sway her towards a more familiar relationship, which she could not pursue yet. Thanks to her aunt's sudden change of heart, she had but little time to find the pinnacle of her talent. At the reminder of that betrayal, her heart constricted.

She forced herself to focus on the moment and not the past. Until now, she'd only appreciated Lord Sommerset aesthetically. Unfortunately, tonight he wore his usual lighter colors than the typical gentlemen, eschewing classic black for a light brown that made him all the more unique in his handsomeness. Her attempts at sketching him from memory had failed miserably. She simply could not see him well enough in her memory to produce a reasonable image. Her best recourse was to forget she'd ever met him, but that was impossible now.

The only way to avoid him was to not attend balls, but not only did she enjoy them, she'd promised to participate in her first season when she'd begged for her own studio at both family residences. She enjoyed flirting and playing her part. Her favorite activity of the evening was dancing. Though she preferred contemplating her next brush stroke or daydreaming about future paintings, night was rarely conducive to her work, so a ball was the perfect pastime. Someone like Lord Sommerset, with his broad shoulders and sensual smile needed to be painted in the light with full sun glowing on his—

"May I get you a plate?"

His question jarred her thoughts as he brought her to a table where her sister had already seated herself. "That would be lovely. Anything but the lamb. Thank you."

He acknowledged her instruction with a nod and walked with the duke to the long table laid out with the usual feast.

"I have not met Lord Sommerset before. He's quite stunning." Joanna gazed past her.

She pretended a nonchalance she didn't feel. "He does have the makings of a great painting." Smirking, she eyed her sister. "Does he fit your Aristotle's view of beauty?"

"I did not study him that closely." Joanna finally met her gaze. "I'm no artist, but I think the two of you are aesthetically pleasing."

"And we both know what a terrible judge of that you are."

"True." Joanna chuckled. "Where did you say you met him?"

She thought back to the night three months ago when she'd first been introduced. "We were at the theatre. Lord Harewood was there and introduced us. I understand they have long been friends. I've seen him twice since."

Her sister leaned forward. "Do you find him personable?"

"Joanna, you know I'm not looking for a husband at the moment. I have too much to accomplish first."

"Yes, but didn't you say last month that a husband would help you with a particular area of your work."

At the mention of her rash words about needing a nude man to paint, she blushed. If her sister knew what she'd proposed, she'd be put under lock and key. "I was frustrated. I doubt very much that a husband would be patient enough to sit for me, never mind allow me the time away from my wifely chores to paint in my studio." She stilled at the thought that once married, she may have no space where she could paint. It sent a chill through her that she couldn't explain to anyone. It just proved that her counterproposal to Lord Sommerset had been rash and ill-advised. Her only hope now was that he declined. Even at that thought, she found her fingers curling into her palms in frustration.

Joanna patted her hand. "I did not ask to make you uncomfortable. I, of anyone, understand. Though I will say that my wifely chores are much more enjoyable than I had anticipated."

She ignored the gleam in her sister's gaze. She was happy for Joanna, truly happy for her, but was not interested in wedded bliss until she'd achieved her masterpiece.

The men returned to the table with plates for each of them. She smiled her thanks to Lord Sommerset and reviewed her plate. He'd given her healthy helpings of all her favorites as if he knew what she liked. Glancing at his plate, she smirked. It appeared they had similar tastes. "You enjoy the blancmange, too."

He gave her a sheepish smile. "I have a certain weakness for it. I'm not sure if it is truly the flavor, or the fact I enjoyed it so much in Marseille."

"The confluence of memory and flavor is also my reason. I cannot think of a better one." She quickly took a bite of the soft and savory dish to keep herself from saying more. Best to stay with things mundane and polite, not personal.

"Did you travel much when you were on the continent?"

She finished swallowing and took a sip of the wine he'd poured for them from the decanter on the small table. "Only France, Greece, Holland, and Italy. I traveled with my aunt as her companion, but she encouraged my painting." She grimaced. "I believe she thought if I saw the great masters that I would be inspired. But to be honest, they stifled my creativity for a very long time."

"Why?" He took a spoonful of blancmange himself.

"Why? Because they were so talented. I spent far more time studying them than practicing my own art. Once I recognized their brilliance, it made it hard to even attempt such a feat."

He gave her an encouraging smile. "But you did attempt, and I have to guess with some success if you exhibited at the London Art Academy."

"Yes, eventually." Only because her aunt had forced her to take up paint and brush with a strict tutor, keeping her dream alive even when she'd abandoned it. She'd been very thankful for such stalwart support, but her gratefulness had dulled considerably after reading the letter left for her upon Aunt Mabry's death. Swallowing the betrayal, she glanced at her dinner companion.

He took a sip of wine, his Adam's apple rising and falling in his corded neck. He set down the glass, and she quickly averted her gaze.

"It sounds as if your time spent studying the great artists helped you achieve some success of your own and a talent for recognizing forgeries of said artists. Have you ever been asked to determine if a painting is authentic?"

"I have, usually by my friends or my mother's friends. It's not a talent I want to make known since it's not necessarily smiled upon."

His brows furrowed then lifted as understanding must have dawned. Men rarely had to worry about their reputations, yet women must watch every word spoken and every act undertaken. It was this simple fact that had her understanding Joanna's need for equality between the genders, though to undertake to change it was far braver than she could ever be.

He set down his fork. "Would you consider..." His gaze moved away as he eyed the duke and her sister before returning to her. "Would you consider examining the paintings I have here in London?"

Before she could respond, he continued in a lowered voice. "My mother is hosting a small dinner party this Friday before we leave Town. If you would deign to attend, you could perhaps arrive early?"

What a creative solution to his dilemma regarding his collection. That he sought her expertise had her filling with pride, but she quickly set it aside. He was simply being practical. Who else could he find to review them without the promise of a purchase? "I would be pleased to see what you have and give my opinion."

His lips formed a brilliant smile that had her envisioning him as Apollo in his golden chariot pulling the sun across the sky. She grasped her fork to keep her fingers from noticeable movement as the need to paint him struck hard.

"I am in your debt." He gave her a nod. "I will have my mother send an invitation to you in the morning."

Forcing her mind back to the room filled with people took her a moment. She gave a nod of her own before turning to her food again, wishing she were in her studio where she could sketch the vision that had burst upon her. It would no doubt fade as it always did, leaving her frustrated.

She was spared further conversation as the duke engaged the earl in the latest bill that passed in parliament. It gave her time to refocus on the evening and her purpose for being there, mainly to enjoy herself. In her opinion, her intensity about her artwork had no place in polite society and after two conversations with the earl that dove deep into her personal feelings on the subject, it was difficult to find the lightness in the evening.

"Amelia, I thought you liked salmon." Her sister nodded toward her plate where she'd not yet touched the cold fish.

She raised her right shoulder. "Oh, I do. I was just enjoying the conversation."

Joanna glanced toward her husband. "I never thought I'd see the day that the weather and politics would be equally valued."

She gave her sister a chuckle, hiding how out of sorts she felt. "I'm sure there have been stranger bedfellows. Didn't you mention Lord Bromley is courting Lady Warren's daughter? Now who would have expected that? I doubted very much that she would give him any time at all, considering his lack of wealth, and yet they are expected to announce a betrothal any day."

As her sister launched into the many reasons the two would hardly do, Amelia half listened. Who would be her next dance partner? That is what she should be thinking about, not painting her dinner companion. It would be hours before they arrived back at Craymore Hall and by then the images of the rest of the evening would wipe away any thoughts of the Greek god bursting with sunlight.

"Amelia, please accompany me."

At the sound of her name, she blinked before giving Joanna a smile as she rose. "Of course."

The two men rose, and her sister linked their arms as they made their way to the retiring room set aside for the ladies of the ball. After attending to necessities, Joanna sidled up to her as she pinned up a wayward curl.

"You do not seem yourself this evening." Joanna eyed her in the mirror. "Is it the Earl?"

She loved her sister, but their relationship had not been one of sharing confidences. Joanna was the one she went to for nonconventional issues. Her oldest sister, Mariel, was the one she went to when she needed a secret kept. And Belinda, kind Belinda, now buried in her cold tomb, had been the only one to see her heart and her unrealistic dream. So she lied. "No, it's not the Earl. I've been contemplating a problem with my background on my current painting, and it keeps nagging at me."

"I should have guessed. Well, do try to focus on your companions for the rest of the evening, even if you ignore all that I say." Joanna winked before giving her a fond smile and heading for the door.

It was good advice. Now if she could just follow it. Checking her appearance one more time, she followed her sister from the room. Maybe tonight, once she was home, she would stay up and attempt again to sketch the man who understood mystic moments and might become her unwanted husband.

CHAPTER FOUR

ANDREW FOUND HIS mother in the drawing room adjusting the flowers in a vase on the pedestal to the left of the fireplace. He stopped in the middle of the room and surveyed it. "A fitting space for our guests this evening."

She turned at the sound of his voice, her hand to her chest just above her midnight blue dress, which accentuated her pale wrinkled face with eyes too far apart. "Andrew, I told you not to startle me like that. If I didn't know better, I would think you part cat." She shivered.

"I apologize. I thought the heels of my boots on the entry floor would have been enough to announce my presence." He wasn't surprised she hadn't noticed. His father's death had taken a great toll on her in many ways. He'd found her unaware of her surroundings more than once.

She put her fingers to her greying temple, a common movement for her of late. "I didn't hear you. I'm just too worried about this evening. When I first planned this dinner, it was only a few friends, but hosting a Marquess' daughters without Lord Sommerset has my nerves quite rattled."

He didn't correct his mother on the fact that he was now Lord Sommerset. He understood her feelings as he too missed his father on a daily basis. While he empathized with her, he could not very well tell his fragile mother that the main purpose for

Lady Amelia's presence was to determine if he could save their comfortable style of living by selling his paintings instead of by marrying her. He was sure his mother would take to her bed until her death if she even heard a hint of their financial troubles. "You will find Lady Amelia quite easy to contend with. I'm sure her eldest sister will be accommodating as well. Perhaps you can speak to Lady Mariel about events such as these. I understand she is widowed as well."

Though he'd meant to assuage his mother's nerves, water filled her eyes. Damn. The word "widow" always sent her into tears. Scanning the room, he quickly made to distract her. "Do you think that chair should be moved next to the settee? It seems a little out of place over there."

His mother's attention instantly switched. "I'm not sure. Let me stand where you are." She glided over to him, the strong scent of roses filling his nostrils. "Oh yes, I see what you mean. I will get Mr. Pratt to move it. Thank you, dear."

As she exited the room, he moved to the window. Lanterns lit the short walk from the road to the front door of the house. The butler, Mr. Pratt, knew not to tell his mother that all the paintings had been moved into the study.

He'd taken the precaution of locking the door. So much of his future course depended upon this evening and the woman he'd hardly given a passing thought to until barely a sennight ago, and now found himself thinking about continually.

Like his mother, he wished his father were with him this evening. In truth, he'd wished for his father's presence much over the last nine months. Mostly in the first days after the earl's death when he'd discovered the many bills not paid, the ledgers an undecipherable mess, and their coffers sorely depleted. He'd wanted to know why, but had soon pieced together what had happened.

The disease had taken his father's usual attention to detail and possibly even his memory. Though he'd known his father had mistresses over the years, and even indulged in a night at a brothel now and again, he hadn't realized to what extent those activities had sickened him until it was too late. Luckily, after seeing his mother's red rimmed eyes many a morning when his father had not arrived home, he had determined as a young man to be very careful about his bed partners. It was his goal to remain monogamous with the woman he married, which was, in part, why his search had been taking so long.

He grinned as Harewood's coach came to a halt in front of the house. His friend had helped him avoid complete financial collapse after he'd paid all the debts and now the investments were starting to improve, but mother nature's odd behavior had him trapped in an unfortunate situation. Everyone was calling it the year without a summer, which also meant a year without crops and tenants unable to pay rents or even feed themselves.

As Harewood strode up the walk, he moved out into the entryway where Pratt was already opening the door. Pratt was the only person in the household who knew about their financial issues besides himself, and he planned to keep it that way.

He waited for Harewood to remove his great coat and hat before stepping forward. "You are the first to arrive. Thank you. Mother will be very pleased."

His friend's smile was genuine. "I would not want to disappoint her."

Moving to the side to indicate the parlor, he waited for Harewood to join him, and they strode in together. "How was Tattersalls? Did you buy that stallion you spoke of?"

Harewood moved to the fireplace, his dark clothes and coloring in stark contrast to the white mantel. "No. Melbourne was all too happy to steal it from under me. But I did find a gentle mare to my liking."

From the smirk on his friend's face, he understood he wasn't speaking about an animal. "You did? Do I know her?"

"I hope not." Harewood chuckled. "I have yet to ascertain if she prefers the light or the dark."

"That's fair." He grinned. At school they had played off each other's looks with pranks and with the ladies. The habit of Harewood dressing dark, and he light every time they were aware they would be in the same place, had limited both their wardrobes, so what started as a bit of fun became habit. Even tonight, Harewood's deep blue coat was in stark contrast to his own beige one. He moved to where he could see out the window while still conversing with his friend. His plan was to whisk the ladies into the study as soon as they arrived.

"Do you need me to distract your mother while you escort Lady Amelia in to view your collection?"

Harewood's question led him to divulging his quandary. "I would like your thoughts on that. Though the Lady Amelia is coming with her widowed sister, I do not know if said sister would be truthful if anything were to be assumed."

His friend shook his head. "Will you ever overcome Lady Frederica?"

"Of course. Once I've married a lady of *my* choosing."

"If that is the way of it. I will accompany you to the study. Perhaps you can have Mr. Pratt interfere if your mother comes to seek you out?"

He should have thought of that. So much rested upon what Lady Amelia told him tonight that he'd failed to think of Pratt. "I will take care of that right now." Striding out of the room, he quickly spoke to his waiting butler before returning to the drawing room where he found his mother fanning herself. Once again, he was grateful to Harewood for being so accommodating. Though the truth be told, he'd rescued Harewood from more than one untenable situation in the past. Now, it was second nature for them to help each other.

"There you are, Andrew. You really must teach Felton that he shouldn't compliment an old woman so dashingly." She blushed, bringing color to her far too pale face.

He strode up and crossed his arms as he faced Harewood. "You must not compliment my mother so dashingly."

His mother laughed before hitting him on the forearm with

her fan. "Truly Andrew?"

The sight of a carriage pulling up had him dropping his arms. *She* had arrived. "I believe our first guests are here."

His mother moved quickly across the floor. "Oh my so early? Whatever will we talk about?"

Harewood followed her. "Lady Sommerset, I do believe it is the Lady Amelia and her sister. She is an artist, so perhaps we could show her some of your family's paintings until your other guests arrive."

His mother halted. "What a wonderful idea." She locked over her shoulder at him. "You must show her the Rueben." She turned back to Harewood. "It was Lord Sommerset's favorite."

Andrew followed them to the door, his chest tightening at what he might learn tonight. If he was lucky, there were no other forgeries in his Town collection and he could sell them, except for his father's favorite, which he highly doubted was an original. And if there were more forgeries, would he accept Lady Amelia's improper proposal? More to the point, would he have a choice?

He was saved from thinking further upon that by the opening of the door and the entrance of Lady Amelia and Lady Beaumont. As Pratt took their cloaks, he strode forward to make the introductions. "Lady Amelia, Lady Beaumont, may I present my mother, Lady Sommerset."

As his mother expressed her pleasure, he took in the sight of the sisters. They reminded him of himself and Harewood. While Lady Amelia's pale peach dress seemed to give her skin and hair a warm glow, Lady Beaumont's dark grey accentuated her paleness, leaving her chestnut hair to fade away. He didn't know much about the oldest Mabry sister beyond the fact that she was a widow and served as a chaperone to her younger sisters when needed.

He motioned to his friend. "And I believe you know my good friend Lord Harewood?"

"Indeed we do." Lady Beaumont nodded. "We are neighbors in Bedford."

He was aware of that because as young men, he and Harewood had stayed far from the home of the four Mabry sisters, too focused on enjoying their youth, though Harewood's parents were quite social with theirs. "I do recall something to that fact."

"I'm surprised you remember." Harewood gave him a telling look. "You haven't been to visit my parents there in years."

"I promise to remedy that this winter."

"Do you?" Harewood looked askance at him. "I will be sure to inform them that you will."

His mother stepped to the side of him, and grasped his arm, though she focused on the Mabry sisters. "I hope you will excuse me as I must check on preparations as I did not expect you so soon."

Lady Amelia threw him a questioning glance.

He laid his hand gently over his mother's. "I'm afraid that was my oversight. I will take the ladies into the study to see Father's favorite painting as you suggested. Lady Amelia is a talented artist and recently exhibited at the London Art Academy."

His mother's eyes rounded. "Oh my. How I wish that Lord Sommerset could have met you. He just adored art almost as much as my son."

Though his father did collect art for about a year, it was nothing more than a passing fancy, but he didn't correct his mother.

Lady Amelia stepped forward. "I'm sure I would have enjoyed meeting your husband as well, Lady Sommerset. I'm already charmed by you." The smile she gave his mother surprised him as she seemed to genuinely care about his mother's feelings, despite having just met her. It could be Lady Amelia would refrain from her usual frivolousness this evening. If so, it would be far more interesting than he'd anticipated.

His mother blushed for the second time that hour. "You are too kind." She looked at him. "You do have such wonderful friends. Now I must see to my last-minute preparations." As she hurried off, showing far more energy than he'd seen in a fortnight, he breathed easier.

"I don't imagine there is much time before your other guests arrive. Should we proceed?" At Lady Amelia's words, his stomach tensed. "Yes, please." He forced himself to offer his arm, leaving Harewood to escort Lady Beaumont.

The walk to the study was too short yet seemed to take forever. Disengaging his arm from his companion, he pulled a key from his waistcoat and unlocked the door.

Lady Amelia's eyebrows rose, but she didn't ask the obvious question. Instead, she preceded him into the room.

"I have taken the liberty of having all the paintings I'm interested in selling brought in here so as to make it easier for you to view them." He glanced at the myriad paintings secretly pulled from walls throughout their London home so his mother wouldn't notice. While dinner commenced, Pratt would have the important ones rehung. If she discovered what had transpired, he would simply explain that they needed a good dusting.

Lady Amelia strolled to the left side of the room to halt in front of a large painting called the Feast of Venus by Peter Paul Rubens that usually hung in his father's bedroom.

He couldn't seem to make his legs move to join her, remaining where he was to watch her reaction.

Harewood moved past him toward the other side of the room, Lady Beaumont on his arm as she exclaimed at the amount of artwork.

As Lady Amelia moved to the next piece of art, he found the will to move.

When he approached, she turned toward him. "That is not an original, but I'm guessing you surmised that." She didn't point to the Ruebens, assuming correctly he would know which she referred to.

He simply nodded. That particular bawdy work had been suspect in his own mind. His father had purchased it for the subject, not the artist.

The next one she viewed carefully, even bending over to inspect it closer. Upon rising she sighed. "Though this one is quite good, it is also a forgery."

She kept staring at it as if impressed with the painter, but his chest tightened. He'd acquired that painting while in Paris and had been assured it was authentic. This did not bode well for him. "Are you sure?"

She nodded before pointing to what was supposed to be a Francoise Dubois. "I noticed an odd shading here. It does not work with the light coming in from this direction, which is why I checked the color of the cloth on the figure. Dubois used carmine in his paintings not rose madder for color. It is a very well-done imitation. I wouldn't be surprised if it was someone who studied with him."

That was not what he wished to hear. He wanted to have options, but his own hubris at knowing good artwork may have limited them.

She moved to the next as if she hadn't just dashed his highest hope. The following painting, which he thought could be a forgery proved to be authentic, which gave him some relief. However, the next five were of no use to him, three he'd obtained and two his father had purchased. The only difference was that his father's were obviously forgeries. Had he purchased them knowing they were copies because he didn't wish to expend his funds on his brief hobby?

"Now this is beautiful." Lady Amelia lifted a small painting from the table it lay upon. "The colors, the lighting, the strokes themselves are magnificent."

Something in her voice caught his attention far beyond wondering if the artwork was authentic. He stepped forward to view the pastoral scene that had been hanging in his mother's sitting area adjacent to her bedroom. He'd forgotten about it, having not noticed it since he was a child. It should not have been brought down. Just as his father had his favorite painting, so too did his mother have hers.

He stood next to Lady Amelia to view the piece again. Now that she had pointed out its artistic merits, he could see beyond the simple baby lamb and mother sheep he remembered from childhood.

She studied the signature on the back. "I do not recognize this name."

"I don't imagine you would. It was painted by my mother's sister."

Her gaze left the painting to stare at him. "Your aunt painted this?" She turned back to view it again, then faced him. "Does your mother have such talent? Do you?"

The excitement filling her voice made him loathe to disappoint her, but there was no help for it. "Alas, neither of us can paint."

"But have you tried?" Her gaze had turned intense, causing her eyes to darken to a breathtaking violet.

He'd had many of those mystic moments she'd spoken of while they had viewed the moonlight. So many, he'd attempted to capture them. "As much as I hesitate to disappoint you, I have picked up a paintbrush to disastrous results, and so I have instead spent my life collecting great artwork." He couldn't hold her gaze. "Only now, I find, my discerning eye for great art was not as keen as I'd thought it."

"Lord Sommerset."

When she didn't continue, he finally looked at her.

"From what I've seen thus far, I see two types of forgeries in this collection. Those that barely pretend to be the artist, and those that are so close it takes someone with significant expertise to recognize them as such. I would even hazard to say some art collectors wouldn't know the difference."

He raised his brows, not sure why that would have any significance. "How is this important?"

Her lips quirked up. "I apologize, I seem to have forgotten to make the connection between what I was thinking and what I said. What I mean to say is that your eye, your selection, your appreciation is stellar. I would not doubt that."

He gave her a nod. It was a compliment from an expert, and

he took it to heart, even if it did little to change his situation.

She cocked her head, a wisp of hair falling forward which she brushed back with the back of her hand. "My question is, who chose the other forgeries. It cannot be you."

He grinned at that, both relieved and pleased that she had discerned that fact after only reviewing less than half of what was laid out before her. "It was my father. He grew interested in art one year and set out to purchase whatever took his fancy."

"Ah, so it was the subject of the paintings that attracted him, not the talent."

"I must admit that is true."

Her smile turned devilish. "Your father had a rather..."

He chuckled. "Mundane, common, plebeian taste?"

She shook her head as her smile widened. "Rakish."

Heat filled his face at his father's obvious interest in subjects far more sexual than his own, and he quickly turned to look for Harewood and Lady Beaumont. The pair had taken a seat near the fireplace, seemingly engrossed in conversation. Seeing no way to distract Lady Amelia from her thoughts, he turned back to find she'd already returned her attention to the next painting.

They continued down the line of artwork. For every four or five forgeries, there was an authentic piece. His chest tightened at every pronouncement good or bad. It was quickly becoming obvious that his art collection would be of little help to his current situation. When they reached the final painting, a pastoral scene with a couple, Lady Amelia studied it carefully, once again bending over to examine it.

"This is by Catel. I saw him in Paris."

Relieved that she acknowledged it as authentic, he let out his breath. "Yes, I acquired this while there."

Her brow furrowed as she stared at it. "I was unaware that Catel had painted any shepherd scenes at all. This could be quite rare. What is it called?"

It was his favorite piece and it hung in his bedroom. "According to the seller, it's called True Love, but on the back its title is

Italienischer Hirt und Mädchen."

"That's German, correct?"

"Yes. It means Italian Shepherd with Girl."

She nodded absently. "The simplicity of life for the shepherd and girl in such an idyllic setting makes for a peaceful scene."

"Yes." His word came out in a whisper, surprised that she saw what he had seen.

She finally looked at him. "This is expertly done. Catel had to have felt this single moment in time to make it so obvious. It is very close to capturing a mystic moment."

He agreed, but the feeling of connection between them was so strong that he failed to utter a word. Staring into her eyes, it was as if he touched something beyond human comprehension.

Blinking, she stepped back as if she'd felt it too and feared it.

He understood and turned to view the artwork. "I also found it unique for the softness of the lines. I'm pleased it's authentic."

Having returned them to polite discourse, he offered his arm. "Thank you for reviewing these pieces. Now that I know so few our authentic, I think I'll forgo selling them."

She placed her hand on his arm. "And the forgeries?"

He grimaced. "Until I have a chance to replace them with better work, I will return them to their locations. My mother is used to them being about the manor, I would not want to take more from her than she's already lost, since most of those were my father's."

They strolled toward Harewood, who rose as they approached. "Did you see anything of great value, Lady Amelia?"

She smiled politely. "I did, one of which was done by Lord Sommerset's aunt."

Harewood's eyes widened. "I didn't know artistic talent ran through his veins."

"It doesn't." He glanced at Lady Amelia. "But I may have to acquire another piece of artwork before long."

Lady Beaumont, having risen, joined them. "I would highly recommend my sister's. She is quite talented."

Lady Amelia's arm tensed on his. "Lord Sommerset has an excellent eye for artwork. I do not believe that mine would quite reach that high, but I appreciate the sisterly support."

Harewood and he exchanged a look, surprised by her humility. Many a young woman had sung her own praises to them about her skill at the pianoforte, riding, singing, sewing, or even painting. Harewood recovered first. "I imagine our hostess will be looking for us soon. Shall we repair to the drawing room?"

They immediately agreed and moved into that room in no particular haste. Lady Amelia walked with him in silence. He didn't feel a need to fill the quiet, quite content to contemplate what he must do now. He had two options left. The first was to determine if the artwork at Lyonsmere Hall was authentic or false. That would require finding another expert he could trust who was willing to travel to his estate there and review over a hundred pieces.

His second option was to accept Lady Amelia's proposal. Of the two, the second was the most intriguing and easiest, but it did have life-long ramifications, which he'd fully intended to pursue just last week. At that time, he'd thought Lady Amelia was typical of the rest of the single women of the *ton*, though perhaps a bit less interested in marriage.

Now, he was far more interested in her as a wife. The question was why? Was it because he had seen a depth of character he hadn't expected? Or was it her unusual view of herself? Or could it be that in her he saw something he'd thought impossible, something only created as an ideal on canvas, a woman of equal sensibility?

His only hesitation was the very issue that caused his interest to rise...her counterproposal. It was scandalous to the extreme that she would want to paint him nude. Not quite the woman he imagined for the mother of his children. Though to have such a one as a wife did have its benefits. Then again, if she looked upon his naked body as she did upon a bowl of fruit, it could become awkward. After their conversation at the ball and here in his own home, he found himself far less shocked and more understanding of her artist's view. Afterall, had she not studied the masters who had painted many a nude form?

No, it wasn't that she wished to paint him nude that gave him pause. In fact, he was flattered by her interest far more than any other woman who had fawned over him. At least Lady Amelia made it quite clear her interest was for art and not for him as a husband. No, it was her insistence that they pretend not to have any relationship until after the painting was complete. He understood why, but a part of him, one he didn't know he possessed, balked at the idea. That and the fact she allowed that he may not want to wed when all was finished. In all honesty, he'd like to wed before, so as to rest easier about the fate of his family and tenants.

As they entered the drawing room, his mother greeted them, her happiness radiating from her. "Ah, there you are. And how did you like my husband's artwork?"

Lady Amelia slipped her hand from his arm and moved toward his mother. "It was a varied collection. Tell me, do you have a favorite?"

As the ladies moved to the settee, Lady Beaumont joined them, so he moved to stand near Harewood who had halted in the doorway.

"What was the conclusion?" Harewood spoke quietly without looking at him.

He answered in the same way. "That avenue is not worth pursuing. There is nothing I'm willing to sell that will bring any relief."

Harewood turned to face him at that. "My offer stands."

"No." He would not accept a loan from his friend. To do so would be to admit he could not be the master of his own estates.

"Then what will you do?"

He finally met Harewood's gaze. "I believe I'm going to accept her counterproposal."

"Will that be expedient? I'm sure a proposal to another

wealthy young woman would bring you to the altar much sooner and the dowry in your hands." He raised his brows as a sly grin formed. "Or is it that you look forward to lounging on a settee with no clothes while she ogles you." He cleared his throat, "I mean draws you?"

"I admit to anticipating such sittings; however, that is hardly a reason to wed her. No, I actually think she will fit me reasonably well and be an acceptable wife."

Harewood's eyes widened. "Really?" Then his gaze grew shrewd. "I was under the distinct impression that you needed a woman who actually paid attention to what is important in life." He glanced at Lady Amelia meaningfully.

"I've discovered that she does. I simply hadn't asked the right questions." And he planned to ensure he had plenty of time with her to ask many more questions. He no longer wished to avoid the pretty artist. Instead, he wanted to uncover every layer of her, probably more so than she wished to uncover him.

Harewood suddenly faced the ladies and took a couple of steps toward them. "Did you say Lady Hester is to marry Lord Blanford?"

At his friend's sudden interest, he moved closer as well, surprised that Harewood would care about such matters. The only time he took an interest in such trivial events was when he had money on the outcome. Ah, that had to be it. He kept his voice low. "White's?"

Harewood barely nodded, his focus on the women.

It was rare that his friend placed a bet in the book at White's Gentlemen's Club. In fact, he only did so when the odds were highly improbable, but he anticipated otherwise.

His mother brightened at Harewood's interest. "Oh yes. I understand that he not only charmed the young lady into accepting, but also persuaded her father there were benefits to the match. Though what benefits, I can't imagine."

She turned to the Mabry sisters. "Lord Blanford squandered his money at the gambling hells and desperately needed a rich dowry if he was to save his estate." She lowered her voice as if someone else listened. "His father had cut him off completely."

Harewood grinned, obviously having bet the man would marry by a certain date or a certain lady.

Though his own situation was different, Andrew didn't care for the way his mother gloated as if their life could ever be similar. She had little knowledge of what her husband had done to them, and as angry as her worship made him on occasion, he wouldn't reveal the truth.

Lady Amelia's eyes widened. "Whyever would she marry such a man? Why, she is asking for her own ruin. I, for one, would never marry a man who needed my dowry." She shuddered, as if the idea truly horrified her.

Harewood glanced at him before rejoining the conversation. "Perhaps she had good reason. Mayhap her life at home was less than satisfying."

Lady Beaumont interjected. "Or perhaps she fell in love. I would marry a man who needed my dowry if I loved him."

Andrew noticed Lady Amelia squeeze her sister's hand. There was a story behind the lady's suggestion, and Lady Amelia knew it. Could she then be persuaded perhaps if she were to fall in love?

His mother waved her hand. "Oh, I have no doubt that rake charmed that poor innocent woman. I'm sure once they marry, she will rue the day she ever met him."

He couldn't allow the comment to hold sway. "And maybe Lord Blandford fell in love with Lady Hester."

"Doubtful." His mother shook her head. "You obviously have not been introduced to Lady Hester. She's long in the face, her hair a mousey brown, and she has a slight limp." His mother shook her head. "It had to be her dowry."

"I would beg to disagree."

At Lady Amelia's response, he found himself anticipating her reasoning. "What do you think?"

"Lady Hester is the sweetest woman I've met all season. She's kind, patient, and is truly interested in others. She reminds me a bit of my deceased sister." Lady Amelia's gaze softened. "I could easily see a gentleman falling in love with her. She has a beautiful heart."

At her defense of the unfortunate Lady Hester, he found himself responding. "Then you would agree that beauty is subjective and in humans it is part of character as well as appearance?"

Her gaze refocused on him and her eyes seemed to light from within. "Yes, that is exactly how I feel, though I don't believe I've ever articulated it so perfectly." Even as she explained herself, her cheeks flushed. She quickly turned to her sister. "Does not Lady Hester remind you of Belinda?"

As the two conversed, his mother frowned, but his thoughts were on Lady Amelia's revelation. Once again, she had mildly critiqued herself and grown uncomfortable when he understood her. His instinct was telling him, despite her beauty and talent, she didn't see herself as worthy, but by what standard and why?

"What are you thinking?"

Harewood's low-toned question brought him out of his reverie. "I'm thinking I need to accept Lady Amelia's conditions forthwith."

"Then I highly suggest you do not inform her of your financial situation."

He frowned, turning his back toward their guests. "If she's to be my wife, she should know."

Harewood gave a solemn nod. "I agree, *if* she is to be your wife. But until the banns are read, I strongly caution you not to even hint at it. After her reaction to Lady Hester's betrothal, it's best that she knows you well before you admit the condition of your purse. Only then, when you are sure of her, should you tell her."

He didn't like the idea of omitting such critical information, but Harewood did have a point. Also, he trusted Harewood above anyone else. They had depended on each other ever since they'd discovered they were far better together against the upperclassmen at school than alone. Finally, he nodded. "I will refrain from any comments that may have her questioning my ability to provide for those in my care."

"Good. Now, I suggest you escort the lady into dinner, I do believe I hear Mr. Pratt approaching."

At the mention of Pratt, he also noticed the sound of footsteps. Following his friend's advice as he was wont to do, he took the next step in securing his wife.

CHAPTER FIVE

"IT'S JUST WRONG." Amelia crumpled the paper into a ball and threw it across the room. Her upstairs studio, now littered with similar crinkled white balls, looked like it had snowed inside, which fit her mood and the gray skies outside perfectly.

She rose and strode to the lit fireplace, her body stiff from sitting for several hours and her mood foul. She should have known better than to try to sketch Sommerset on a dreary cold day more than 12 hours after seeing him. If she hadn't been able to do it after he'd visited the week before, there was no possibility she could do it now, yet here she was attempting the impossible again. She should have braved her cold studio and come up straightaway after dinner last night, but she'd been overconfident in her memory of his face when he explained he could not paint. There had been something akin to pain in his eyes as if he'd been told what he desired most, he could never have.

Dropping more coals into the fire, she set the tongs aside before holding her stiff fingers over the warmth. It didn't help that her dreams had been a mixture of Michelangelo sculptures, angels, the acropolis, and Sommerset leaning in to speak to her as he had at the ball more than a sennight ago. She'd woken up multiple times which left her tired and cross. Not wanting to be around her family, she'd sequestered herself to sketch, but that had been a study in frustration.

She turned away from the fire and observed the sky. The clouds were various tones of gray, and the smoke from the many London chimneys melted into them. Despite it being not much past noon, it appeared quite late in the day. She lit the lantern closest to her, trying to dispel the bleakness and melancholy that seemed to have taken hold. There was only one more lantern to light, but the flames did not dispel the grayness of her mood.

She moved to the desk in the corner and opened the drawer, taking out the miniature she'd painted of her sister Belinda not long before she died. To this day, she considered the small painting her best piece, even though she'd known so little of painting at the time. It had been as if her subject had inspired some muse inside her who guided her brush. She held the miniature in both hands. "I'm out of sorts today, Belinda. I feel restless and anxious. Tell me why."

Though she could often hear Belinda's voice from years past in her head, no words came through clearly. She had not expected them to, but sometimes talking to her sister helped her find her own way. Belinda had taken a piece of her heart with her and seeing her made her feel whole again...sometimes. But not today.

Gently, she laid the miniature back in the drawer and closed it. Maybe she just needed to work on something else, something stormy and dark. Something she would never show a soul. Pulling a new paintbrush from her box, she scanned her paints for just the right color for her mood. Bitumen or ivory black might do.

A knock at the door made her jump before Mariel strode in wearing the very color she needed, a pale gray to start the background.

"I'm painting."

Mariel gave her an understanding smile. "I know, but you have a caller."

She opened the bitumen. "Tell Lady Spencer I'm not at home."

"It's not Lady Spencer. It's a gentleman caller. Unfortunately, Mother is not at home so I will join you."

It was Mariel's tone more than the words that caught her attention. Still refusing to look at her sister, she spoke to the blank canvas. "Who is it?"

"It's both Lord Sommerset and Lord Harewood."

Her heart constricted. No. Dropping the paintbrush, she fell more than sat on the stool behind her, trying to get her lungs to work.

"Amelia, what is it?" Mariel's skirts brushed against the furniture in the crowded room as she approached.

Her older sister grasped her arm, just as she pulled air into her lungs. "It's nothing. No, it's everything." She turned her head to find worry etched in Mariel's brow.

"Tell me. Has Lord Sommerset come to ask you to be his wife?"

She stared wide-eyed for a moment. "Why would you ask that?"

Mariel cocked her head, her emerald gaze softening. "There was something about the way he looked at you at dinner. It was as if your every word fascinated him."

Shaking her head, she rose unsteadily to her feet. "If you're thinking he's in love, it cannot be. We have had only two conversations of any worth."

"Then why has his presence here upset you so?"

She couldn't look at her sister. There was only one reason. He was here to accept or reject her proposal. She crossed her arms over her stomach and moved back toward the fireplace. *We would want at least one witness each to our bargain, to protect both parties. And my good friend, the Earl of Harewood, who has impeccable integrity, has kept many a secret of mine over the years.*

She gripped the back of the wooden chair near her to keep from falling. If he was here with Lord Harewood, he planned to accept! What had she been thinking? She looked to her sister who remained patiently waiting for an explanation.

Already Amelia could feel the disapproval that would come once the specifics of her proposal were revealed. If Belinda was an angel, Mariel, after the man she loved died in battle, had become a saint, sacrificing herself for her family, living to make others' lives better.

"Amelia? Whatever it is, we can make it right. But you must tell me if I'm to help." Mariel's kindness just made her feel worse. She always was the worse sister. The most selfish, the most unaware, the most rash.

"Are you with child?" Mariel's soft-spoken question finally freed her of her shock.

Shaking her head, she frowned. "No, I am untouched."

"Oh good. Then what is it? I'm sure we can do something."

She wasn't so sure. Still gripping the chair, she took a deep breath. "Lord Sommerset asked for my hand in marriage. I told him I would marry him under…certain conditions. I never thought he'd accept them, but if he's here today, I believe he has decided to accept."

Mariel moved toward the stool before the easel and sat. "Poor dear. You want so much to create a masterpiece, but you knew if you turned down another offer that Mother might balk, despite how proud she is of you."

She nodded, astounded once again by her sister's insight.

"But now he has come to accept, and you must agree."

"Must I?" She strode to the window once again, searching the greyness for an answer to her troubles.

"I'm not as intelligent as Joanna, but I imagine it depends upon what you said."

She fisted her hands in frustration, silently cursing herself for making such a proposal and now having to admit it and possibly agree to it. She couldn't look at Mariel, so she spoke to the window. "I told him if he posed for me without clothes, and pretended we have no relationship until I finish the painting, that I would marry him when it was complete."

"You didn't…you didn't…Amelia!"

She swung around to face her sister. "I know, but I did."

"But why?"

Because she was weak. Because she couldn't resist the chance to paint the Golden Adonis. How could she explain it to anyone who wasn't an artist?

Mariel stared at her, her eyes unwavering until understanding dawned. "It's his appearance. It's not him you want; it's how he looks. You want him for your masterpiece."

She wanted to cry with relief but also to cry because of her situation. "Ever since I first met him, I've tried to sketch him, paint him. I think he could be the subject for my triumph." She looked away. "But I don't know for sure. I never thought he would accept, but if he's here with Lord Harewood that's why."

Mariel stood and walked toward her. "What does Lord Harewood have to do with this?"

"Lord Sommerset said that we would need two witnesses we trusted since they would be the only ones to know the terms of the agreement. He said he would have Lord Harewood and I said I would have you."

Mariel took her hand. "And I will be happy to bear witness for you, but I fear I can see no way for you to escape this."

"I know." She squeezed her sister's hand. "I must do what I promised."

Mariel gave her an encouraging smile. "Maybe this is exactly what you need. Maybe this will give you the inspiration you've been looking for to accomplish your dream."

A hopeful thrill cascaded through her at the possibility. Ever since reading Aunt Mabry's reason for bequeathing Silver Meadows to Joanna instead of to her, she'd been anxious to accomplish what burned inside her. Now, with this man, it might be possible. Then again, she may fail miserably. She looked at the white balls of paper littering the room. "But if I fail, I'll be married with no hope of ever reaching my destiny."

Mariel's body stiffened as she straightened her shoulders. "That is true, but I can attest to the fact that you will live beyond it. Mother has and is very happy." What Mariel didn't say was that she had lived after her dreams of marriage to Marcus Stratton had died, and she was happy, though that was not true even if she thought she was.

Sympathy for her older sister filled her and she firmed her resolve. At least she was being given a chance. She shouldn't be complaining. Impulsively, she wrapped her arms around Mariel. "You're right. I don't know what I'd do without you."

Her sister squeezed her back then set her away. "Now let me see how you look. You are about to accept your future husband."

Suddenly nervous, she looked down and realized she wore her painting apron. Untying it, she threw it over the back of the nearby chair. She'd chosen a pale-yellow morning dress in rebellion against the dreary day. She brushed at it with her hands. "Acceptable?"

Mariel smiled. "More than acceptable. Radiant."

Radiant? She didn't feel radiant. She felt like David facing Goliath, but that was ridiculous. Lord Sommerset was just a man, not a giant. He may not even want her after the painting was complete. It was that tiny hope that induced her to move toward the door, her sister following.

Just maybe, he was, as her sister said, the inspiration she needed. At the very least, she'd finally be able to give into the creative need that had been plaguing her since she'd first seen the man.

When Mariel's footsteps stopped before they reached the door, Amelia turned to find her sister's brows furrowed as she scanned the room. "Should we send the maid up to clear these away?" Mariel held her hand out toward the many balls of crumpled paper that littered the floor.

Viewing the scene through Mariel's eyes, she smirked. "No. I need them to give me the right atmosphere."

Her sister's brows rose. "Are you painting a back alleyway?"

Already feeling hopeful again, she grinned and grasped Mariel's hand to pull her toward the door. "No, but that's a wonderful idea. I was thinking of a snow scene."

"Ah, it does look a little like when we played in the snow as children at Thornwood."

They stepped into the upper corridor, and she pulled the key from her dress pocket. After locking the door, she faced Mariel. "We should do so again this winter. We can catch snowflakes!"

"We are far too old for such antics now." Mariel shook her head. "It's just not done."

She stuck her tongue out at her sister as she followed her to the stairs. There was so much more to life than being calm and well-behaved. She never understood why it was important to remain so in one's private moments. How did throwing balls of paper on her floor hurt anyone? Then again, there would have been no paper to throw if she could have sketched Lord Sommerset as he actually appeared.

At that thought, her pique returned. With no more events left in the season, she'd have to wait until spring before she could have him sit for her. That would strain her patience now that she knew she would finally have him as a model.

Mariel led the way and stopped just outside the closed double doors of the parlor to look at her.

Through the doorway, they could hear the low tones of the men's voices inside. Oddly, she could tell which was Lord Sommerset's though she couldn't hear what he said.

Excitement wrestled with her fear, and she ignored both, despite the imaginary mice running about in her stomach. Putting on a smile, she nodded to Mariel. Her sister opened the doors, and she strode in first.

"Lord Sommerset, it is lovely to see you again." And indeed it was, as the man looked resplendent in a brown tailcoat, tan pantaloons, a cream-colored waistcoat, and white shirt. *Lion.* The word whispered through her mind even as she fought the urge to run back upstairs and sketch him immediately. "I hope your mother is well."

"Thank you. She is a little tired from last evening, but she was very happy to have met you and your sister."

"I enjoyed meeting her and viewing all of your artwork."

"I'm pleased that you found my pieces interesting."

If she hadn't been focused on him, she would have missed the slight stiffening in his shoulders. Immediately, she understood that his artwork, so much of it forgeries, concerned him. Before she could think of something else to discuss to take his mind off his disappointment, Lord Harewood added his greeting.

When the pleasantries had been exchanged, she took a seat on the settee and Mariel joined her. If nothing else, it allowed the men to sit. Lord Sommerset took the chair closest to her, but Lord Harewood remained standing, like a forbidding raven ready to fly down and devour the dead carcass of a canary.

She blinked to remove the image from her head and looked at Lord Sommerset instead. If only she could memorize his face at the least.

"Lady Amelia, I have decided to accept your proposal. So I ask you again. Will you be my wife after all the conditions you put forth are met?"

Her heart skipped over a beat as Lord Sommerset smiled, a certain gleam in his eye she hadn't seen before. An uneasy shiver crawled up her spine as if she were staring into the eyes of a lion and she was the prey.

—

Andrew kept his gaze on Lady Amelia. Visions of them alone together disrupting his practical thoughts. When she looked away, he stiffened and glanced at Harewood. Had it all been a ruse, her willingness to marry? Had he wasted precious time simply because of his personal interest? His friend's lowered brow didn't bolster his confidence.

As Lady Beaumont placed her hand on her sister's lap, Lady Amelia looked at her. Neither moved, but something passed between them.

Finally, Lady Amelia faced him. "I will." She took a breath. "After you have modeled for me without clothes so that I might sketch and then paint you. During such time we will assume no relationship at all while among our peers, which includes our parents. If after the painting is completed, you wish to reconsider marrying me, you may."

He grinned as relief washed through him. "And I may have the completed painting if I so wish."

She nodded. "Yes."

Moving his gaze to Lady Beaumont, who also nodded, he then looked to Harewood. "You and Lady Beaumont are witness to this agreement."

"We are."

Though Harewood had started him on this path, he did not seem particularly pleased. It mattered not, since now he had a dowry forthcoming. His family would be none the wiser and his tenants could remain on his land. But his soon to be betrothed didn't appear as excited as he. If he could steer the conversation toward her art, she was sure to reanimate. "You mentioned you already had a vision for this painting. Are you able to share it?"

Her stiff posture relaxed and a smile tugged at the corners of her full pink lips. He hadn't noticed before what a perfect color they were.

"I'm afraid an artist never shares her vision with her model."

There it was, that secret amusement so often in her eyes, and he had no doubt he was the cause of her mirth. "Then I am anxious to begin."

She sighed. "As am I, but the season is over and we leave for Bedford in mere days. I suppose your sitting must wait until next spring."

He blinked in stunned silence. With the season over, his proximity to her in Town made much possible that would not be now that it was over and everyone left for their own estates. He should have thought of that since his own household was preparing for the long journey back to Lyonsmere.

Harewood cleared his throat. "Perhaps Lord Sommerset, you could spend some time with me at my parents' estate. You did say you owed them a visit."

Grateful that his friend proposed such a simple solution, he leaned back to look up at him. "If that is an invitation, I accept."

"Then it's settled. You can spend time at Sunnydale. This would allow you to pose for your betrothed." Harewood turned to Lady Amelia. "That would be acceptable, would it not?"

"I...I had not thought of such a possibility, but I suppose." She moved her gaze from Harewood to him. "I do have a studio on the grounds of Thornwood Park. I imagine we could begin once you have arrived in Bedford."

Before he could respond, Harewood interjected. "Excellent. I'm looking forward to having company and the painting can be completed. What do you think, by all Hallows' Eve?"

Lady Amelia's brows drew together. "I do not know. So much depends on when Lord Sommerset is able to join you. And creating is not a science. It does not listen to deadlines, but happens naturally. It cannot be rushed. Many pieces must—"

"Yes, yes." Harewood waved his hand. "I'm sure there are many particulars we would not understand, but I see no reason to delay the happiness of you both, so the sooner it begins, the sooner it can be accomplished. What do you say, Sommerset? Can you be at my parents in a fortnight?"

Not a little angry and quite puzzled by Harewood's sudden rude behavior, he rose to face him. "While I agree with your motivation, Lady Amelia knows best how to proceed with the painting. I have not seen her work, but we all know she has an expertise in this area."

Harewood raised one eyebrow. "Indeed."

Baffled by the man's actions, he turned back to Lady Amelia. "My Lady, though I am quite anxious to begin this...this adventure, I will not allow you to be rushed."

She rose and with her Lady Beaumont. "I cannot promise when the work will be complete, but I can be ready to begin it when you arrive in Bedford." Her countenance had closed to him, making it impossible to know what she felt. "Now, if you'll excuse me, the maid and I need to pack up my studio."

Damn Harewood and his rush. It was obvious she was in a pique. "Of course. I look forward to our next meeting."

She didn't reply. Instead, she gave a regal nod and strode from the room, her pale-yellow skirts swishing against her legs in her hurry to leave them.

He gave Harewood a scowl, but Lady Beaumont set her hand on his arm, gaining his attention. "Don't worry. She will meet the terms of the proposal if you do. I have no qualms that the outcome will be worth the wait."

Something in the woman's eyes had him wondering if she meant the painting or the marriage. "Thank you. I appreciate your willingness to bear witness. It is a most unusual arrangement."

Lady Beaumont grinned, and for the first time he could see the resemblance between the sisters. "My sister is a most unusual woman."

With those parting words, Lady Beaumont exited the room, leaving him with an uneasy excited feeling in the pit of his stomach.

"Well, that went better than I expected."

Throwing a glare at his friend, he stalked from the room, now furious with the one man he thought he could depend upon.

Collecting his coat and hat, he strode outside to his carriage, tempted to leave before Harewood joined him. Unfortunately, even in his anger, he wouldn't do so.

When his friend entered the carriage, he barely waited for the door to close before he knocked on the ceiling and they started to move.

"I'm feeling that you either did not think your call was successful or you are irked at me for some reason." Harewood pulled on the cuffs of his greatcoat to straighten the sleeves, a telltale sign he knew the answer to his own question.

"Irked would be understating the feeling." Now if he could just figure out why.

"I see no reason why you should be upset with me. I helped you tremendously." Harewood lifted his brows as if he were truly puzzled.

"Helped me? I'm surprised Lady Amelia didn't rescind her offer the way you pushed her to agree to start the painting this winter. When did you get so old that it became acceptable to be rude."

"If I hadn't pushed her as you so delicately put it, you'd be cooling your heels for another year before the banns were ever posted. Then where would you be? You're lucky I stepped in. That woman would have put off your marriage until the next century if she could."

He opened his mouth to rebut Harewood's accusation, but he had no defense. He had also noticed her reticence and assumption to prolong the inevitable. "Why do you think that is?" The words slipped out before he could take them back.

"That my friend is the question. She's turned down two men before you, but for some unknown reason has chosen to accept your proposal, only to try to put off anyone knowing about it for as long as possible." Harewood shook his head. "I fear you have a potential inmate for Bedlam as your betrothed."

"No, she is not unbalanced. She is very intelligent, but she looks at the world differently than most of us." In fact, that may very well be the key to his interest in her. No, he must know more. To not would be akin to having a spoon of blancmange and no more, ever.

"I, for one, am sorry I suggested Lady Amelia. Lady Susan would have perhaps been the best first choice after all."

That Harewood could suggest Lady Susan, a young woman with the personality of a candlestick, was in anyway preferable to Lady Amelia had his anger resurfacing. "You forget the woman I marry will be someone I will live with for the rest of my life."

"That doesn't mean you need to like her. Bed her a few times to produce a couple heirs then live your own life." Harewood's brows lowered. "Your father has proven that is perfectly acceptable.”

“Yes, perhaps. But he also found an early grave and left my mother a shadow of herself. You know damn well I plan on not following in my father’s salacious footsteps.”

Harewood’s eyes rounded. “I thought you’d given up that childish pledge.”

“That childish pledge was based upon facts that still hold true today.”

“Sometimes I forget how different we are.” Harewood turned his head away to stare at the buildings they passed.

“Yes, and in our differences, we find our strength.” Though his friend didn’t acknowledge his sentiment, they had long held their friendship was based on the fact that what one had as a strength, the other had as a weakness. Could it be like that with a wife, though obviously with different characteristics?

The rest of their ride continued in silence. Outside was another matter as the hawkers cried out their wares as many a coach headed out of the city. Soon they pulled in front of his London home. He bid Harewood farewell, and his coach took the man to his abode.

Andrew walked into the house to find servants running to and fro.

“Oh there you are, Andrew. Did you get your business finished?” His mother handed a maid a shawl and a small bust of Cicero. “Be sure to pack those with my things.”

Since he must keep his betrothal a secret for now, he linked his arm with hers and steered her into the parlor where the housekeeper was overseeing the packing of the writing desk. His mother’s face was flushed, and she appeared out of breath. “Mrs. Ridley, have someone please bring us tea.”

“But I must see to the packing.” His mother looked over her shoulder as the housekeeper bustled out of the room.

He led her to the settee, and holding her hand, he gently guided her to sit. “You know that Mr. Pratt and Mrs. Ridley have done this every year since I was born.”

Her lips puckered. "Yes, but I direct them."

"I know you do, but right now you need to sit with me and have some tea." He didn't like how warm her hand felt. "I wish your attention for a bit."

Her gaze finally left the servants and focused on him. "I'm sorry. Without your father here, I feel as if there is so much more to do, but there really isn't, is there? He never was here on packing day. He had too much business to attend to before leaving for Lyonsmere." She laid her free hand on his face. "You have taken care of everything, stepped into his role beautifully." Her gaze lost focus. "I remember when your father was your age. I first met him at Almack's. He commanded everyone's attention." She blinked then looked at him. "You will need to marry, you know." She dropped her hand. "Find a nice lady with a perfect reputation. That's why your father married me."

He didn't mention that he'd been looking for two years, since his father's health started to fail. "I know. It will be hard to find a wife who is as capable as you."

She gave him a proud smile before a footman entered with the tea service.

His mother immediately sat forward to pour their tea. There was a slight shake in her hand and as she fixed his, she hesitated over the sugar.

He quickly spoke. "I'll skip the sugar today. I had a few too many sweets at White's." It was the truth, but he never took sugar in his tea. That his mother had forgotten concerned him. His father drank his with quite a bit. She knew her husband was gone, but she still seemed to expect him to be there.

She quickly added a dash of milk, which he also didn't take, though his father did, and handed him the cup. "I always wondered why you men were off to your club so often. It's a wonder no lady of substance hasn't hired the cooks from those establishments just to keep their husbands home."

He took a sip to avoid commenting on her unrealistic expectations.

"We are still planning to leave the day after tomorrow, are we not?"

He put down his cup. He had been, but for her health he changed his mind. "I'm afraid we may have to delay that a couple of days. I still have a few business transactions to complete."

She visibly shrank, her posture usually so straight, curving as her shoulders slumped forward. "That's just as well. It will give us more time to get everything packed. It usually doesn't take this long, but this season we seem to have more than the usual."

They actually had less than the usual, but he wouldn't contradict her. It was simply too much for her now. He'd have his secretary make a note to bring less to London next year. Then again, if he were married, his wife would oversee the packing of the residence. Would his mother welcome that or resent it?

His mother's eyelids drooped.

Upset with himself for not realizing what a toll this took on her to be in London without his father, he searched for a solution. Yes, he'd tried to fill his father's shoes, but it wasn't the same. His mother needed a lady companion. He'd look into that straight away.

He took her hand. "Mother?"

She blinked, looking around in a daze. "Yes."

"Would you like to lie down? Since our departure for Lyonsmere has been delayed a few days, there's plenty of time to rest."

"Delayed? Oh, yes. That is a very good idea."

He motioned for his butler. "Pratt will escort you to your room so you can rest."

She nodded, still in a daze. "I'd like that."

Pratt helped his mother rise and sent a look of silent understanding his way. Then the butler escorted his mother out of the room as if she were the most fragile item in the house.

He rose, running his hand through his hair. Though he itched to be off to Lyonsmere and then to Harewood's, those in his care took precedence. With his mother ailing, having a new lady of the house would be of great benefit. He tried to envision Lady Amelia ordering about the servants, but the only image that came to mind was the lady sitting on the banks of the Seine painting Notre Dame.

Shaking his head, he headed for the study. Surely the Lady Amelia was well-versed in running a household as well as painting, but it couldn't hurt to start a search for a companion for his mother. Maybe a widow of similar years would be interested. Satisfied with his plan, he sent a footman to fetch his secretary and strode to his desk before halting abruptly.

A companion would need to be paid.

His gaze unconsciously landed on the Jan van Huysum painting between the windows. The flowers in the work fit the space very well, and according to Lady Amelia, was authentic. He continued to his desk. There was no help for it. If he wished to lighten his mother's burden immediately, he'd have to sell it. If he was lucky, it would be the only one he'd have to sell before marrying.

A flash of lightning lit the room before a boom of thunder echoed in the sky. The sound of hard rain hitting the windows followed, fulfilling the promise of the afternoon's gray skies. He glanced at the painting again. It had to be coincidence that the storm hit immediately after his decision to sell the flowers painting. Shaking his head at his own thoughts, he opened his bottom drawer to withdraw his ledger.

Still, as another flash lit the room, he determined to get to Lyonsmere and Harewood's as soon as humanly possible to secure the affections of one Lady Amelia Mabry and fulfill their bargain.

CHAPTER SIX

October 1816
Bedford, England

LADY AMELIA STUDIED the sketches she'd drawn then looked out the window of her studio. She used to complain that the old replica Grecian temple reconstructed into her studio was too far from the house, but at times like these, she was happy for it. It gave her uninterrupted quiet and a perfect view of the gardener who was overseeing the preparations for winter.

She watched his movements as he pointed, turned, and crouched. Then she studied her sketches. They appeared to capture him exactly. Looking over her shoulder at the painting that had drawn criticism for how she'd portrayed three gentlemen as they stood talking after a hunt, she compared their figures to the gardener sketches.

Horse feathers! She dropped her cedar pencil on the table and rose, rubbing her back. Why couldn't she determine what was wrong? The men she overheard talking about her painting during her one-week exhibit at the London Art Academy clearly found fault with it. She understood art was subjective and not everyone would be amenable to the subject or even the style in which she painted. But when one gentleman had chuckled and said the artist clearly had never seen a man's naked anatomy and his male companion laughed, she recognized it for what it was, a true flaw in her work.

Walking to the small table at the opposite window, she lifted the glass of water and drank. The now warm liquid slid down her throat, and she grimaced. Maybe she should switch to a landscape today. At least the sun was shining, albeit inconsistently, which did light up the dull brown leaves on the trees to a warm honey. She set down the water and moved to stand in front of her flawed painting. She didn't want to paint a landscape. She wanted, no, needed to create an accurate portrayal of a male figure. She cupped her elbow with one hand as she chewed on the nail of her other, her gaze moving to the sketches of the gardener then back to the two men most prominent in her painting. What could it be? Throwing her hands up in exasperation, she spun around and stalked to her supply chest.

The answer had to be in the book. Quickly, she opened the chest and pushed aside paint, brushes, rags, and other tools to reveal the book she'd borrowed from Joanna. Though the fake cover title was *The Education of the Feminine Species*, inside revealed the true purpose to be *The Illustrated Pleasures of Seduction*. She pulled the large tome from its hiding place and brought it over to the painting. She had to be missing something.

She sat on her stool and opened the book to a random page. She was rarely disappointed, since almost every page had a drawing of a naked man in some sort of position. Joanna had been hesitant to let her borrow it because she didn't realize that studying great art meant studying naked men and women. It was about the lines, shadows, and nuances, not the lack of clothing. Whoever had illustrated the book must have had a nude male model.

She stopped for a moment. *She* was supposed to have a nude male model this winter, but so far there had been no word that Lord Sommerset had arrived in Bedford. There was bound to be word because the village was not large and a new earl taking up residence would induce much gossip. Maybe he'd changed his mind. Disappointment filled her at the thought. She had so hoped to finally understand what she was missing instead of staring at other drawings until her eyes crossed.

With a sigh, she examined the drawing on the page she'd opened. The nude man lounged on his back while a nude woman sat on his pelvis. Maybe it was the position? Flipping through a few pages, she found a man standing. It was a back view that was almost unimpeded by the woman's dangling legs or her arms wrapped around his neck. Carefully, she studied every line, trying to find fault with what she'd painted since one man in her piece had most of his back to the viewer. The only difference she could find was that her gentleman was clothed.

Unfortunately, since the book was about what men and women did to procreate, there was only one full frontal view of a male without the woman hiding the male's body. She rifled back to the beginning pages and found the single page. She studied the legs, arms, torso, and neck then viewed her work again. It had been this very sketch that had emboldened her to attempt larger male figures. But she'd obviously failed. What if the sketch wasn't accurate?

That hadn't occurred to her before. The thought brought tears of frustration to her eyes. For the first time, she wanted Lord Sommerset to fulfill their bargain, even if it meant marrying him in the end. Anything to solve her dilemma. Slamming the book closed, she strode back to her chest, lifted the lid, and dropped it inside.

A knock at the door had her closing her chest with a thud. When her sister didn't enter as usual, she glanced out the window to see if it might be the gardener, but he still labored at his task. That meant it was either her mother or father. Quickly, she untied her painting apron and dropped it on the chest to keep it from becoming a topic of conversation.

Another knock sounded even as she walked toward the door. "You may come in."

The door opened just as she reached it, and Lord Sommerset

stepped across the threshold.

"You!"

He grinned, his eyes crinkling with mischief. "Me."

A strange leap of joy filled her before panic took over. Without further thought, she grabbed his arm and yanked him forward as she slammed the door shut. It was hardly a welcome, but after years of protecting her reputation, she wasn't about to hasten a marriage she hoped to avoid until the last possible brush stroke.

It was as if she'd conjured him into being there, and a shiver raced up her spine. She rounded on him. "What are you doing here? And dressed like that?"

The man had the audacity to smirk. "I suppose I could have skirted around your servants naked, but it is a bit chilly."

At the idea of him running across the garden without clothes, heat filled her cheeks, but she brazened it out. "No, I don't suppose having you arrive chilled to the bone would make for a good sitting." She gave an exaggerated sigh as if it were too bad that he couldn't have arrived naked, which wasn't the case. In fact, she was surprised to see him at all. "I had not heard that you had arrived at Sunnydale Manor."

He unbuttoned his burnt sienna greatcoat and hung it on a hook near the door next to her Prussian blue spencer before answering her. "I don't imagine you have. I just arrived, and since Harewood is under the weather and his parents are making calls, I decided to take the opportunity to let you know I'm ready to be your *objet d'art*."

He no longer smiled, but there was a twinkle in his warm crystal brown eyes that was difficult to ignore. She purposefully studied him like she would any scene she was about to draw. He wore his usual white shirt and cravat. Over it was a beige waistcoat that matched his pantaloons perfectly, not to mention set off the shade of his skin. The tan tailcoat he wore over it emphasized the medium tones of his hair. Finally she nodded. "Yes, I think you'll do."

One dark eyebrow rose. "I'll do?"

She gave a short nod, barely able to keep from grinning at his affront. "Yes, you'll do nicely." She pointed to a straight back chair set next to the small fireplace. "You can stand over there."

His brows lowered as if puzzled, but he moved to where she indicated.

As she pulled clean paper from her pile on her table, her heart started to race. Now she'd be able to discover what she had done so inaccurately that it made men laugh. To think the solution would be found because of an unexpected and unwanted proposal. She reached for her cedar pencil then halted.

Snapping her head up, she pierced him with her gaze. "How did you know where my studio was or if I'd be here?" Tension filled her. "Did you ask a servant?"

He stood behind the wooden chair, one large hand resting on the back. "Of course not. I'm far too clever for that."

Now he had her attention. "Clever, how?"

"It was quite serendipitous, actually. Before leaving town, I stopped in at Monsieur Armand's for a few macarons and the Duchess of Northwick was there with her husband."

That Joanna was at Monsieur Armand's was no surprise. He made her favorite ice cream, and she was probably once again pestering the man for his recipe. Either that, or arranging to have said ice cream transported to her new home in Peterborough.

His gaze, which had been taking in her studio, came back to meet hers. "We exchanged pleasantries, and I told her I would be visiting Harewood. She insisted that I call on your family, which I promised I would. Then she explained that you would spend the entire winter holed up in your art studio and she'd only see you at Christmastide when she arrived. I, of course, asked how it was that you had an art studio and she explained that this," he held both hands out to encompass the space, "used to be a Grecian temple that your mother had renovated into a studio for you shortly after you recovered from a severe illness."

It was so like Joanna to put the event in a positive light. Her severe illness had been her own fault. Rushing out onto an almost frozen pond had been a well-learned lesson. "But that doesn't explain how you found it or knew I would be here." Though he said he hadn't asked a servant outright, they were smart enough to figure things out.

"That was your sister as well. She explained to Northwick where your studio was and planned to show him. As far as you being here…" He shrugged. "I hoped it would be the case since the duchess said that you spend whole days in your studio."

"That's a bit of an exaggeration, but I suppose it's true when there's good light." She pointed to the windows to the right of him. "My mother designed this room so it would get the best light. She used to paint, so she knows what environment is best for painting." Now why did she tell him that? "Since you've finally come, then I suggest we begin. If you would, rest a hand on the back of the chair there and look out the window."

"Of course." His tone sounded disappointed. If he thought he was in her studio to court her, he'd soon learn differently. This was her domain, and she focused on only one thing here, her art. Putting aside the pencil, which was just too dark for him, she opened her pastels. Choosing burnt umber to capture him best, she placed it in her holder and started to sketch.

"Have you been painting long?"

She started with his broad shoulders. "Yes." Moving her hand quickly, she added his neck and chin. Having itched to draw him all season, her hand seemed to know exactly what to do.

"How long?"

Adding the outline of his profile took no time at all. The multi-tones of his hair though would be impossible to capture with just one pastel. Still, rather than take the time to switch out colors in her holder, she added the strands with the deep umber color she used, making them a bit longer than they actually were, but they only added to the effect. His nose was strait and blended in perfectly with the bone structure of his face. She smudged a short line around his cheekbone with her thumb. There was a slight shadowing beneath his nose and along his chin and cheeks which she added, his whiskers growing despite his morning shave, no doubt. It kept him from looking too young in her opinion.

"Lady Amelia?"

She added dark eyebrows, the same color as some of the strands of his hair. Drawing the outline of his eyes, she carefully stroked on the thick lashes. Looking back at him to capture his eyes, she found him looking at her expectantly. "You're supposed to be looking out the window."

"I asked you how long you've been painting."

"How long? Since I could hold a paintbrush I imagine, though I started with pastels at barely three." She held up her brass holder with the burnt umber rectangle crayon firmly in place.

"Three? You remember drawing when only three-years-old?" He fully faced her now, making it impossible to continue the drawing.

She dropped her hand on the table but kept a hold of her drawing implement. "Of course I don't remember, but it's what my mother told me. She painted before she married. As she tells it, I showed promise even at the age of five." She smirked at the memory. "By the time I was seven, I called myself the creator because I created art." She chuckled at her own audacity back then. "I fear my mother's indulgence led to an overly confident artist." She lifted one shoulder. "But to be truthful, we all carved out our own place in the family."

It was just that hers was the most frivolous and least needed. "Joanna is the knowledgeable one which was encouraged by our father. Mariel is the practical one and the one mother included the most in the daily running of the estate. Belinda passed before she could come out. She was..." Belinda was like a mystic moment, undefinable, unearthly, beyond human.

He set his foot on the chair and leaned his elbow on his knee. "You miss her."

At his words, she lifted her gaze to his. "We all do. She was the heart of our family. When she died, she took a piece of each of us with her."

As if he knew any words he might utter would be of no value, he kept silent. But his eyes spoke volumes. Sympathy shone clearly there, but there was something more. Something she didn't understand, probably because she didn't know him. Whatever it was, she found herself needing to explain. "Belinda cared about all of us, our friends, even strangers. She had a sympathy for all of humanity."

Her heart still hurt at the memory of the sister who was older than her, but the closest to her. "She died because she helped strangers. Mother liked to support charities with donations, but Belinda had a calling. She would bring food and medicine to those less fortunate. One of our tenant's babies had Scarlett Fever and she brought them food, but it was more than just the baby. The whole family had it. They could barely feed themselves, so she fed the baby." She swallowed hard, not able to continue.

"And she caught it as well."

His sympathetic voice had her nodding. She stared into his kind eyes and the tears that had welled up disappeared. Forcing herself to look away, she picked up her pastel again. "Now, you need to stay in your pose if I'm to finish this sketch."

He dropped his foot to the ground and moved back behind the chair. "And if I do, what will be my reward?"

She frowned. "Reward?"

"Yes. I understand that models for artists are usually paid well."

How did he know that? "So you want to be paid like a typical model?" It was hardly fitting for an earl, and she could only stare at him in disbelief.

He laughed softly, the sound seeping into her skin and causing a strange prickly sensation over it. "No, not paid in coin. Let's say for today, which must be a relatively short, uh sitting? Is that what you call it?"

She nodded, anticipating his next words too much to speak

herself.

"Sitting. That is a rather unusual term for one who might be needed to stand as I am now. And how could it be called sitting if I were to lie down?"

She opened her mouth to ask him to simply tell her what he wanted when she noticed a twitch at the corner of his right eye. If she had blinked, she would have missed it. Was he teasing her? Barely holding back a smile, she pretended to ponder his question. "I imagine the phrase sitting for an artist came from some ancient Latin word or other. I'm sure my sister Joanna could tell us. I will definitely ask her when she arrives." She gave him an innocent stare. "If you like, we can call it posing rather than sitting, if it makes you more comfortable."

He grimaced. "I'd rather not. That sounds like I'm in parliament where there's far too much posing and posturing going on."

She lifted her pastel. "Then sitting it will be." Immediately, she started to sketch on another paper. Since he looked at her, she attempted to capture his entire face, or at least the basic lines.

Then he turned his back to her to face the window completely. "This studio gives you a pleasant view of your family's eastern border."

She dropped the pastel in frustration. Obviously, he wasn't going to sit or stand still unless she agreed to whatever it was he wanted now. "You're forgetting that for me to complete this sketch, you need to remain still, and I can't sketch your face while looking at your back."

He looked over his shoulder at her. "Is this better?"

Now he was just being impudent. Purposefully, she lifted her pastel and stared at his backside. "I can always sketch another part of you."

Instead of being offended, he chuckled. "Well, I'm told that's my best side."

For some reason, her cheeks heated. She set down her pastel and gave him her undivided attention. "What do you want?"

CHAPTER SEVEN

Andrew turned to face her now that he had her attention, but he lifted his brows in pretended ignorance. "Want?"

She crossed her arms and gave him a stare better than any cook gave him when he'd been caught stealing Shrewsbury cakes. "You are perfectly cognizant of what I'm referring to." Despite her stern visage, humor danced in her eyes.

Pleased she wasn't truly irritated, he grasped the back of the chair with both hands. "What I would like for standing still while you sketch me is that you be present tomorrow when Harewood, his mother, and myself come to call."

She opened her mouth to object, but he held up his hand and she closed her lips tightly.

"I know we have an understanding of appearing to have no relationship. However, we also don't want to change any natural behaviors which might call attention to us, as in the gossip that there is a bad history between us." And if he was to bring her to some understanding of who he was and what their life would be like in the future, he needed to be in her presence as much as possible.

Her gaze shifted away from him as she thought over his words. She might think that sketching his profile was pleasurable, but he would as soon enjoy the sight of hers. The knowledge that he would be able to see her like this for the rest of his life pleased him. It had to be that he had begun to know the person beneath the pretty appearance that made him feel so.

Finally, she looked at him. "To be honest, it would be unusual for me to be about the house at that time of day, but I suppose I can complain about the greyness outside not being suitable for painting. Very well, I accept your terms. You will remain still and quiet for the next hour."

He'd never said anything about being quiet, but since she'd accepted his proposal, he'd be satisfied...for now. "Very good. Would you like me looking out the window then?"

She uncrossed her arms and leaned one elbow on her table. "No, I believe for my next sketch, I'd like you to sit in the chair and look at the curtains behind me."

He stepped around the chair. He liked challenging her. Every time he did, she revealed a bit more of herself. Sitting, he stretched his legs out in front of him and linked his hands behind his head. "Will this do?"

She didn't move for a moment as if she were seeing something beyond him and yet him at the same time. It was a bit unnerving.

Blinking, she sat up and lifted her pastel holder. "Yes, stay exactly like that, but focus on the painting behind my easel."

He'd rather watch her, but that was not the bargain, so he moved his gaze over her shoulder, past the top of an empty easel, to view the painting hung on the wall. It was hardly anything she'd paint as the scene appeared to be from the era of Henry VIII and included a Bishop and a royal entourage. He didn't recognize the style as any particular master, but most likely she was far more knowledgeable on that score.

It was her knowledge, her constant amusement, and self-effacing comments that had had him anxious to come to Bedford, but it had taken almost two months to accomplish. Finding a companion for his mother had been most difficult as she couldn't seem to make a decision on one person. Finally, a Mrs. Bolton was able to persuade her that she would do.

Though he'd chaffed at the delay, it had given him time to think, to plan his strategy in winning his betrothed's heart. He could see no other way to be assured she would marry him once her painting of him was complete and she discovered he needed her dowry as much as her.

But she clearly didn't wish to be courted. In her mind, it was obvious that they had made a contract, and she would fulfill her obligation if he filled his. Unlike other women, who wanted him for his appearance, like Lady Frederica, Lady Amelia appreciated his appearance only in that it could be used to create art. Somehow, he would show her they were quite compatible, but to do so he needed to discover more about her.

"You can stand now, if you like, while I finish."

Her voice brought his gaze back to her, and the fact that the light had shifted in the room. Glancing outside, it looked darker, but with the constant cloud cover, it was difficult to ascertain the time. Pulling his legs under him, he relaxed his arms and stood. Tingles started in his hands, and he wiggled his fingers to get them to stop.

"I have to say, you are an excellent model."

He caught her watching him before she returned to her sketch.

"That was fairly easy since I was thinking and that's how I sit to think." He smiled at her, but she didn't look up, too engrossed in finishing her sketch. Unable to contain his curiosity, he walked between another table and a chest, her studio a study in chaos, but it suited her.

He stepped around her to look over her shoulder and froze as he stared at himself. He half expected the drawing to move. Something shifted deep in his gut. Shaking his head at the ridiculous notion, he forced himself to study the sketch. The paper was not as large as a canvas, but far larger than that used for letter writing. She'd filled the page with his figure. Every proportion was perfect, but it was his face that had him staring. The look clearly showed he had been thinking. But how? No doubt, it was simply his imagination because he knew that's what he'd been doing.

She stopped shading and put aside her tool. "I think that's adequate for today."

Adequate? He couldn't allow such a minimal judgment. "That is far more than adequate. That's excellent."

She didn't look at him, but a slight flush covered her shoulders and neck. "It did help that you remained still." She looked up at him and raised one eyebrow. "Not talking helped as well."

Looking down at the slight smirk on her lips, he found himself tempted to kiss her. Abruptly, he stepped back. Her reputation was as important to him as it was to her. "I can see that my vast knowledge will go unappreciated on these visits."

She chuckled then stood, rubbing her back with the back of her hand, the side of her hand and two fingers colored from the pastel she'd used.

A memory of her brushing hair from her face with the back of her hand surfaced. It had to be a habit to keep from smudging her face or clothes. "Were you always so careful not to ruin your dress from your work?"

She stared at him uncomprehendingly.

He pointed to her hands.

"Oh, you mean this." She held them up so he could see her fingertips and palms. "No. It took years of Mother scolding me. When I was little, I didn't care, but as I grew older and came to understand that my pretty gowns were burnt instead of passed down to others, I finally made an effort." She took a few steps away to wipe her hands on a cloth. "It still took me months, and even now and again, if I don't have my apron on, I will forget. It all depends on how immersed I am in a particular piece." She dropped the cloth then glanced at him before looking over his shoulder. Her eyes widened.

He spun around expecting to see one of her parents, but no one was there.

"Oh, I must go. You must go." She brushed by him, knocking

over her stool in her rush.

Confused and not a little surprised, he reached out, catching her hand as she passed. The contact of skin on skin had him letting go as if burned. Though the touch had been mere seconds, the soft warmth of her hand traveled up his arm.

She halted, still facing the door.

He cleared his throat to break the awkward silence.

As if that was all she needed, she took another step away before facing him, the hand he'd clasped now held by her other. "I fear I forgot to make the connection for you once again. I noticed the time and realized I need to be back at the house to help my mother with a bonnet she wishes to change. If I don't arrive soon, she'll send someone out here—"

"And they would discover me. I understand." He bent to set the stool upright again before walking past her to help her with her spencer.

She shook her head. "No, you must leave immediately before someone sees you." She moved to a window not far from the door. "The gardener and his men have left."

He pulled his greatcoat from the hook, her urgency communicating itself to him now. "It's also growing darker and not because it's the end of the day." Though the daylight had been fading, a dark cloud mass had covered the sky, and he worried they would both experience a soaking if they didn't leave quickly.

"Yes, and you have miles to walk."

At the concern on her face, a hint of satisfaction filled him. If she worried already, perhaps her feelings would grow quickly. Still, he didn't wish to cause her undo distress. "Not so far. I left my horse in the woods at the edge of the Enderlys' estate."

She contemplated that. "So a mile or so." She glanced out the window. "You still best hurry."

He agreed and quickly fastened his coat. "I will call tomorrow. Should we plan my next sitting for the day after?"

She shrugged into her spencer and began buttoning it as she spoke. "No. I want to work with the sketch I have first. The day after that would be soon enough." She paused to look at him. "I suggest not wearing your typical clothing."

He widened his eyes. "Is it not appropriate for a portrait?"

She grinned, her nose crinkling just a bit. "It is, but I don't plan to paint your portrait. In addition, if you are seen in such quality clothing, rumors will be about Bedford within hours."

"Ah, you'd like me to be in disguise next time I visit." Her amusement over the situation had become contagious.

"Yes! That's it exactly. You'll find it enjoyable. I know. Joanna used to have us dress up and perform one of Shakespeare's plays at Christmastide every year." She rolled her eyes as if it was the worst possible pastime, but her smile never left her lips.

"Surely you must have liked at least one of them." At the mischief in her eyes, he was sure the skies could open up and he'd still stay to hear her answer.

"Oh, I did. Hamlet was my favorite with everyone dying here and there. By the end, the floor was littered with bodies."

He hadn't expected her to be so morbid. "You liked all the death?"

She chuckled. "I liked lying on the floor so I wouldn't have to say any more boring lines."

At that he laughed, too entertained to withhold it.

"Now, we must be off. I'll step out and make sure there is no one about."

He nodded before opening the door for her.

She took a few strides then halted. After surveying the area, she returned. "Everyone has sought shelter. You'd best go and quickly. The air is heavy with moisture."

Stepping outside, he silently agreed with her prediction. "I shall see you on the morrow." He gave a short bow then sprinted for the shrubbery not far away. Once somewhat hidden by any who would be about, he turned back to find her locking the door of her studio and walking quickly toward the stately home that was Thornwood. He remained where he stood until he was assured she'd be inside before any raindrops fell. Once more, he surveyed the area. Though he'd found his way across the Mabry land via gardens and shrubbery, with the impending rain, he started straight across open ground at a run, hoping against hope that he could reach his horse, Leonardo, before the skies spewed forth their heavy load.

He did not have long to congratulate himself upon finding Leonardo where he'd left him. No sooner had he mounted and settled into a gallop, then the rain began to fall. By the time he reached Sunnydale Manor, he was soaked to the skin and not a little chilled. Riding directly to the stables, he jumped from his horse once undercover and handed the groomsman the reins. After giving specific instructions for Leonardo's care, he sprinted to the house, entering into the grand foyer.

The swish of skirts was his only warning before his hostess emerged from the drawing room. "Andrew Crauford, Earl of Sommerset, is that really you turning my marble foyer into a pond only a duck would appreciate?" Despite her scolding, Lady Enderly smiled widely. "It has been far too long since I've set eyes on you, dear." She held her hands out then quickly clasped her hands before her. "Maybe you'd best change first, then join us in the drawing room."

He nodded. He'd forgotten how warm the Harewood's parents were and being back at Sunnydale had him feeling young again, before the responsibilities of his title had taken hold. "I will be but a few minutes. I'm anxious to see Lord Enderly as well."

His hostess waved away his comment. "You just wish to drink Scotch with my stubborn husband, but we have more guests and with you here, I am in great anticipation of the coming Christmastide."

Guests? Harewood hadn't said anything about guests when he'd arrived earlier. Probably because Harewood didn't keep abreast of his parents' friends, too preoccupied in his own activities. "I'll look forward to meeting them." He started toward the stairs that would take him to his room.

"Lord Sommerset? Is that truly you?"

At the sound of the woman's voice, he froze on the second step. Slowly, he turned his head and shivered. The black-haired, tiny-framed woman standing there in a pale gray dress was the one person with which he could not pretend politeness. "Lady Frederica."

She giggled. "Oh, no, not anymore. I'm Lady Garmoyle now."

At that news, he found it easier to speak. "Felicitations on your nuptials."

Lady Enderly put her hands on Lady Garmoyle's shoulders. "I'm afraid it is not so happy a story and condolences are best offered. Her dear husband died in an unfortunate carriage accident."

Though Lady Enderly spoke of sad tidings, Lady Garmoyle continued to smile. The juxtaposition chilled him far worse than the rainstorm outside.

As if finally remembering herself, Lady Garmoyle's face changed as quickly as the best actress on Drury Lane. "Yes, my darling Alfred was crushed when the coach rolled over him."

The hint of a memory tugged at the edge of his mind. Something about her mother and a carriage accident. He was saved from commenting by Lady Enderly. "Now I don't want you to think about it at all. Why don't you go back in the drawing room and continue your game with Rose."

Lady Garmoyle gave him a secret smile then turned around and disappeared into the drawing room.

Lady Enderly stepped to the bottom of the stairs. "The poor dear. When Rose discovered that Lady Garmoyle would be alone this winter, she generously extended an invitation to join us. I do believe we will have a very entertaining winter this year. Now, do go up and change. I want to know all the latest news about you and your family."

As Lady Enderly turned and reentered the drawing room, he forced himself to ascend the stairs. How could Lady Frederica, rather Lady Garmoyle, be at Sunnydale? And why hadn't

Harewood told him? If this was somehow supposed to be humorous, Harewood had missed his mark completely.

By the time he entered his room, he was practically stomping across the floor, sending water everywhere. At the sight of his valet's disapproving look, he growled. "Just help me out of these clothes and keep your thoughts to yourself for once."

Mr. Lambert pursed his lips, but he did nothing to hide his disapproval.

Thankfully, Lambert could do his job with or without commentary, and in no time, Andrew found himself soaking in a hot tub and sipping on brandy, which he was assured would keep the chills from setting in. The hot water and liquor did much to dampen his irritation, but did nothing to lower his temper.

They may be expecting him below, but before he descended into questionable company, he would be visiting one supposed friend, be he sick or simply in hiding.

CHAPTER EIGHT

"A MELIA, WHOEVER ARE you writing to?"

At her mother's question, she set the quill in its holder and swiveled in the high-backed chair. "Joanna. If she is to be delayed by a trip into Town, then I wish her to procure new oil paints for me." Going to the Western Exchange was a favorite shopping trip for her sister, so she was assured her request would be accepted with glee.

"Oil paints?" Her mother lowered her embroidery hoop to her lap. "But you prefer pastels or watercolor. Why would you wish to have oils? You know how difficult they are to work with. If I remember correctly your exact words were, they were damn impossible."

She grimaced at her mother's exceedingly good memory. "Yes, well, I'm older now and more accomplished. I feel the need to challenge myself and expand my skills." She smirked. "After all, I did exhibit in the London Academy of Art this year."

"Why do you say it with that tone?"

"What do you mean?"

Her mother cocked her head, brows lowered slightly. "Like it wasn't the honor it was. You always sound like you think it was amusing, like seeing the dancing dog at Vauxhall Gardens."

She couldn't tell her mother that's exactly how she thought of it. "I think you misread my feelings. I just think that since I have achieved that honor, I need to move further in my painting. I will need a husband soon, and my muse is calling strongly."

"Ah, I understand now. I never did follow my muse to the epitome of my talent, but as I discovered, creating live daughters, each so different than the other, was far more rewarding." Her mother's gaze drifted, no doubt thinking of each of them as a babe.

Amelia took the opportunity to return to her letter. After seeing how well the pastel sketch of Lord Sommerset had succeeded, she was anxious to try all mediums. It wasn't perfect, by far. It didn't capture his personality, but it did capture his likeness very well. Even she had been surprised at how easily it flowed, especially after trying so many times to draw him from memory. Of course, her success hadn't happened until he stopped moving about and talking. She had to admit, he'd been quite fun, once she realized he teased her purposefully.

The sound of Channing answering the main door had her and her mother looking at each other in question. Her mother glanced at the clock to indicate it was still a bit early for callers.

Setting the quill back into its stand, Amelia rose and walked to where her mother sat in a lovely sage dress that was just a shade darker than the pale green settee she sat upon. For herself, she'd chosen to wear rose, knowing she'd be seeing Lord Sommerset eventually and wishing to hide any blushes that may occur from pretending she hadn't just sketched him yesterday. Little lies were easy for her, since as a small child and the youngest of four sisters, she'd become adept at using them to stay out of trouble. However, this lie was far larger and more important. Both her reputation and her chance to fulfill her potential were at stake.

Channing stepped inside the room. "My lady, Lords Harewood and Sommerset are here to call. Are you receiving?"

"Lord Sommerset?" Her mother looked over her shoulder at her.

She lifted one shoulder and shook her head.

"Yes, my lady."

Her mother set her embroidery loop on the table next to her and clasped her hands together. "We are."

As Channing left to fetch the men, her pulse beat erratically at the performance she must execute. She was thankful Mariel had gone riding, her favorite pastime while not in Town. It meant she wouldn't have to pretend nothing was amiss.

"Amelia, come sit beside me."

At her mother's command, she walked around the settee on weak legs and sat just as the men entered. Sommerset was dressed darker than his usual with cocoa-colored pantaloons, a dark brown tailcoat, and a tan waistcoat with a beige shirt and cravat. Harewood wore dark blue, so the two still appeared opposites. They also appeared stiff as if not all was well between them. They lacked the easy camaraderie she'd remembered from when she reviewed Sommerset's paintings, though she hadn't thought on it until now noticing its absence.

Her mother held out her hand. "How lovely to see you both again. Lord Harewood, I dare say it has been nigh on three years, has it not?"

The man bowed slightly. "I fear it may be. It is, of course, my fault entirely."

"And so it is." Though her mother chided him, she did so with a warm smile. "And Lord Sommerset, what a pleasant surprise. I had not heard that you had come to our small village."

Sommerset bowed, not taking his gaze from her mother. "I just arrived yesterday." He glanced at Harewood then back. "Lord and Lady Enderly are hosting quite a number of guests as I discovered."

"Really, you must tell me about it. Of course, you remember my daughter, do you not?"

Sommerset finally moved his gaze to her. "Of course. Lady Amelia, it is a happy circumstance that I am in your presence again."

"I'm quite surprised, my lord. I thought you had planned

renovations at your estate. Have things changed?"

His eyes twinkled at her made-up story. "Indeed they did. When I informed my mother of my plans, she persuaded me to wait another year, and as I wish to make her happy, I've delayed any changes." He gestured to Harewood, but didn't look at his friend. "The decision did give me a chance to visit my friend and his family, who I had promised my presence to earlier this past season."

"Please sit, gentlemen. We had not expected anyone quite this early." Her mother focused on Harewood.

Sommerset took the chair opposite them, but Harewood continued to stand. "If you don't mind, my lady, I will allow my friend to accommodate you. We cannot stay long."

Amelia addressed her comment to Harewood. "You have arrived quite early, is there something amiss at Sunnydale Manor? Surely, your parents are well."

Harewood swallowed hard and glanced at Sommerset. "Everyone is fine. I will tell them you asked after their health. It is only that since Lord Sommerset has arrived, I must ensure that he is introduced to all our neighbors, but as you are our closest, I hoped you would be receiving."

Her mother set her hand to her chest. "How lovely of you to think of us first. We are honored. I saw your mother not more than two days ago. She didn't mention any guests."

Harewood brushed something off his sleeve before answering. "Lord Sommerset was actually expected last month, and my sister was not expected back until Christmastide, but she arrived early and brought a friend with her. My mother was quite surprised but also pleased."

She turned to Sommerset. "And how long do you plan to stay, my Lord?"

"Only a month. I must return to Lyonsmere for Christmas. My brother will be home from Oxford and my mother has been...anxious to have us all together to welcome in 1817."

Amelia purposefully spoke to Harewood. "You must have

Lord Sommerset to the Noells' masquerade after All Hallows Eve." She switched her gaze to him, his eyes seeming so familiar after staring at them so long the day before. "You really must attend. It is the largest ball in Bedford before the end of the year."

He smiled warmly. "Then I will be sure to have Lady Enderly include me in any acceptance of an invitation." He turned his gaze to her mother. "Does Lady Wakefield attend? Lord Harewood told me that you are good friends."

As her mother answered Sommerset's question, she watched his expressions, trying to pinpoint what was missing from her sketch. It could simply be that she didn't know him well enough to capture that part in her artwork quite yet.

Harewood had just begun an explanation of the purpose of the ball when Channing entered. "My lady. Lady Enderly, Lady Rose, and Lady Garmoyle."

Amelia glanced at the clock on the mantel. It was the perfect time for calling, so why hadn't Harewood waited for his mother?

As Lady Enderly entered, her mother rose to take her hands. "Lucinda, how simply wonderful of you to bring your daughter and guest. Your son was quick to have Lord Sommerset call."

Lady Enderly's gaze moved to her son. "So I was informed." Her smile did not quite reach her eyes as she glanced at him. "When I discovered he had called on you so early, I quickly gathered my daughter, and Lady Garmoyle to come call. I must apologize for my son's intrusion so early."

As they were all introduced, Amelia wished she could capture the awkwardness of the assembled people. Harewood hardly seemed contrite as he sniffed loudly while Sommerset was clearly angry at the additional visitors. Lady Garmoyle, a tiny woman of dark coloring and pale complexion, grinned as if very pleased with the situation. Lady Rose, whom Amelia was well acquainted with, had blossomed over the past year into a lovely young woman with pretty blue eyes and chestnut hair. The younger woman had her debut last season, though no offers of marriage had yet been made. She grasped her mother's hand once they were seated in what could only be construed as silent support. The entire scene would make an excellent tableaux for a canvas.

Her mother quickly ascertained the changing atmosphere and steered the conversation to Joanna's delayed arrival. A duke visiting Bedford was quite the thing and the ladies quickly joined in. But Amelia focused on the men who stood side by side, Sommerset having risen to give his seat to Lady Garmoyle. Neither man looked pleased with the added company. She could only imagine what the environment was like at Sunnydale.

"Lady Amelia, have you not managed to catch a gentleman's eye yet?"

At Lady Garmoyle's question, she forced herself to look away from the men, but not before noticing a tightness in Sommerset's jaw. "This past season was my first, and though I did have a couple of offers, I'm taking my time. It is an important choice to choose the man one will spend their life with." She forced herself not to glance at Sommerset, keeping her focus solely on Lady Garmoyle.

"Oh my, you turned away two suitors?"

Her mother answered for her. "She turned down offers from two gentlemen. Her father and I agreed with her decisions. They weren't right for her. She is still young, and hopefully, next season she will find her husband. I was in my third season before I made my choice. I would not have it any other way for my daughters."

Lady Garmoyle frowned. "I cannot imagine allowing young women to choose their own husbands. My father chose mine, and I'm sure I would have been content with my husband if he had lived longer." The woman lifted a finger to the corner of her eye. "Unfortunately, he died in a carriage accident shortly after we married."

"And that is why we welcomed her as our guest this winter." Lady Enderly gave Lady Garmoyle a sympathetic look. "Poor dear."

But as Amelia dared a glance at the men standing quietly in

the corner, there was no indication of sympathy from either of them. In fact, their stoic expressions mirrored each other, in concert for the first time since coming to call.

Harewood cleared his throat. "I'm afraid we must take our leave. We have many more calls to make today." He bowed to her mother. "Lady Wakefield, it has been a pleasure to visit you and your daughter again."

Taking his cue from Harewood, Sommerset moved forward. "I hope our paths will cross once again during my stay. Thank you for your hospitality, ladies."

With that, the two men strode from the room. Though everyone watched them depart, she noticed a predatory gleam in Lady Garmoyle's gaze. Did Sommerset know he had an admirer? She'd have to ask him at his next sitting. As the conversation turned to the masquerade, Amelia found herself wishing she could have left with the men. Then again, it was a small price to pay to assure Sommerset sat still during their last session. Hopefully, there would be no further requirements from him now that he knew what she could accomplish if he did his part.

At that thought, she imagined him leaning against a fireplace like the one in the room. He'd have to have that twinkle in his eye and his lips barely lifting in amusement.

"What will you go as, Lady Amelia?"

Lady Rose's question forced her back into the conversation. "I'm not sure. I've always thought it would be enjoyable to dress as a muse."

"Enjoyable? To dress as one of many with no particular name?" Lady Garmoyle looked down her nose at the suggestion. "I just learned of this masquerade, but I can think of a number of other people to dress as."

The woman's personality reminded her of her second art tutor. The tall, very thin man often looked down his large nose and pronounced her attempts plebeian at best. Yet whenever she asked why, he refused to tell her what she needed to do to improve. She soon figured out, he didn't want her to improve so he could keep his position, which he didn't. "What would your costume be?"

Lady Garmoyle raised her chin. "I would be Mother Nature, or Lady MacBeth."

"Lady MacBeth? Why would you wish to disguise yourself as a woman who convinced her husband to murder the rightful king?"

The woman shook her head as if pitying her. "I have no care about what the lady did. The fact is she was a sympathetic heroine. That's what young women should portray at a masquerade."

Lady Macbeth was sympathetic? For the first time, she was thankful that Joanna had made her act in her Shakespeare plays. At least she knew Lady MacBeth was not sympathetic.

"I'd like to be dressed as a butterfly." Lady Rose smiled clearly happy with her choice. "That way I can flit about without staying too long with one group."

Seeing Lady Garmoyle about to squish the pretty insect idea, Amelia clapped her hands together. "What a lovely idea, and you would make such a lovely butterfly."

Lady Garmoyle gave her a pitying look. "Now what would you know of butterfly costumes?"

Her mother was quick to respond. "Amelia is an artist. She even exhibited at the London Academy of Artists just this past season. If anyone knows what would make a pretty butterfly, it is she."

Lady Garmoyle had the sense not to comment and simply inclined her head.

For once, Amelia was pleased by having had the opportunity to exhibit, if not for the honor than to be able to keep the opinionated lady from further judgements. "Granted, I did not exhibit any paintings of butterflies, but I have completed a few."

"Oh, would you advise me then on my costume?" Lady Rose looked at her with such hope in her eyes that she couldn't decline.

"Of course. I would be happy to be of assistance."

Lady Rose turned to her mother. "I do believe I'm going to enjoy this masquerade ball."

As the conversation turned to the weather as it always did this year, she contemplated Sommerset's reasoning for having her present when he called. He barely paid her attention, which was well done of him, but she could not discern what had been so important that he used the favor of her presence to bargain for his obedience while in the sitting the day before. Even at the thought, she yearned to leave for her studio. With one sketch of him, she could now possibly do others, deciding on the perfect pose for her oils when they arrived.

As the women rose to leave, she promised Lady Rose that she would attempt a drawing so the younger woman could pursue her costume creation. Lady Rose had an innocence and pleasantness about her that made her enjoyable company and her youthfulness gave her an eagerness in life. Though only a few years older, Amelia envied that. Her muse was a harsh taskmaster and demanded serious study. Even more so now that she had a very real deadline for marriage. Unless…

"I suppose I will have to determine my costume now and set to work on it immediately. I had not expected to be busy on such a project immediately upon arriving." Lady Garmoyle gave a heavy sigh as if she were being imposed upon.

Lady Rose's face fell, and Amelia couldn't hold her tongue. Did the woman not see how she dampened everyone's spirits, or did she not care? "I think your idea of Lady MacBeth is quite unique. You would make a very majestic queen."

Immediately, Lady Garmoyle's demeanor changed. "Do you think so? Yes, I imagine I would. I believe that is what I will be. As a queen, I would be the highest-ranking person at the ball."

Amelia's mother looked askance at the woman, but didn't bother to correct her assumption that dressing like a fictional queen would give her additional societal privileges.

Lady Rose smiled widely, her excitement once again showing. "That's splendid. We really should finish our calls so that we can get started."

As the women exited the room, Lady Amelia held in her laugh until the front door closed and she was safely back in the drawing room. But the minute her mother rolled her eyes, she gave her laughter free rein.

Her mother joined her before she raised her brows. "Lady MacBeth?"

She dropped into the chair that Lady Macbeth had just vacated and gave a haughty frown to mimic Lady Garmoyle. "I do believe I shall be a queen so everyone may bow to me."

Laughter followed her statement as her mother shook her head. When she gained control of herself, she wagged a finger at her. "Amelia, you do that so very well."

She continued her haughty demeanor. "But of course. I am, after all, a well-trained actor. Just ask the lovely Joanna. In fact, I know everything about everything and so no one could possibly know as much as I about a butterfly costume. How plebeian." She tried to continue her mimic, but she burst into laughter again.

"We really mustn't." Her mother wiped tears from the corners of her eyes.

She shrugged one shoulder. "It can be our secret. What harm if no one knows?" She sobered. It was her same reasoning for having Sommerset privately pose for her.

Her mother contemplated her statement. "Perhaps, but it's best we refrain or it would be far too easy to do so in public. That young woman, widow or not, will soon push Lucinda's patience. Lady Rose is such a sweet young lady. I cannot see how these two are such friends."

"I think their family makes friends of those opposite of themselves. Look at Lord Harewood and Lord Sommerset. One is not only dark in looks, but also quite stiff and arrogant. While his good friend is light and more approachable as well as having a warm temperament." She simply couldn't imagine Harewood teasing a woman or traveling through the rain for her.

"Lord Harewood? Did you not find him pleasant today?"

She silently groaned. She should have never made her observation out loud. "I found him as I always do. Nothing more, nothing less."

Her mother lifted her embroidery loop, a clear indication she would be getting back to her work. "And what of Lord Sommerset. This is the second call he has bestowed upon you. I would say that reveals an interest."

She waved her mother's comment aside. "Hardly. The first time, as I informed you, was to request my expertise. This time he was simply fulfilling his duty to be dragged about Bedford as the newest guest and introduced to all. I pity him, actually."

Her mother looked at her at that. "Pity him? The man is clearly going to cause a stir. I haven't figured out what it is, but there is something in his appearance that is quite likeable. Were you ever able to create a sketch from your memory of him?"

She hated lying to her mother, but too much was at stake. "I did start one. Now, that I've seen him again, I may go back and see if I can add to it. Of course, that will have to wait." She rose. "First, I must finish my letter to Joanna before any more of our neighbors come to call."

Her mother pulled the needle out from where she had left it to rest. "Once word gets out that there is not only a new bachelor in Bedford, but also a lady widow as well, I have a feeling we won't be seeing many callers." Her mother paused before giving her a wicked grin. "At least not until after the Noells' masquerade ball."

Her mother made a good point. All the more reason to work on her artwork. After today, she would resume her afternoons in her studio. First, she'd sketch out a butterfly costume and send it over to Sunnydale Manor. She hadn't planned to attend the masquerade in anything but a mask, but with Sommerset present, it could be fun to design a costume for herself. It would have to be simple, so as not to take any time away from their sessions. But it also must be unexpected. As she walked back to the desk, an idea came to her, and she grinned. Oh yes, that would do nicely. Nicely indeed.

CHAPTER NINE

ANDREW BUTTONED THE last button on his borrowed trousers when a step outside his door made him tense.

"Sommerset." As his name was uttered, his bedroom door opened and Harewood stepped in. "What the blazes are you wearing?"

"Shut the door, will you?" He stepped away from the view of the upstairs hall to avoid anyone seeing him.

For once, Harewood didn't ask three more questions before doing as he was asked. "There, it's closed. Now answer me why you look like you should be working in the stables?"

"I do?" He stepped back in front of the looking glass and examined the loose-fitting shirt, wide black trousers, and brown boots. He grinned. "I do." Or rather his body did, but his hair was far too neat. Running his hand through it didn't help, so he mussed it as best he could. Did it look scraggly enough? He tilted his head, not shaving definitely helped make him look like a ruffian.

"The devil take it, Sommerset. Answer me."

He faced Harewood. "I'm in disguise."

Harewood's brows shot up. "Obviously. Is that your costume for the Noells' masquerade? You do know many men of our age do not dress in costume."

"No, it is not my costume, but unlike you, I do plan to completely disguise myself for the masquerade." The look on Harewood's face almost had him laughing, but he knew well enough that Harewood despised being laughed at for a lack of knowledge.

"If I follow your meaning correctly, you are in disguise but not for the masquerade. Pray tell, why the disguise?"

As much as he wanted to string Harewood along and goad him on not figuring it out, he refrained. After all, it had been Lady Amelia who had been the one to think of it, not him. He would have blithely continued visiting her as an earl. She really was quite astute. "I am going to Thornwood Park for another sitting. Lady Amelia suggested I do so in disguise to avoid any rumors."

Harewood made himself comfortable in the winged back chair near the window. "And being visited by a lowly stableman would be better? Don't you think that would hurt her reputation more?"

He shook his head. "No. A stableman may simply be coming for instructions or be sent for some other reason which I have no doubt she will think of once she sees me."

Harewood tapped his fingers on the arm of the chair. "I thought you'd given up this foolishness. You haven't been to Thornwood Park since we called there four days ago. Why today?"

His stomach tightened at the reminder of his absence. Did she think he'd forfeited their bargain? He'd explain once he made it to her studio. "No, I pledged to fulfill this bargain and I keep my word." He took one last look at himself, pleased with the transformation. The clothing felt a bit rough on his skin compared to his own, but overall, it was comfortable. Now, he just needed to leave Sunnydale Manor without anyone noticing him.

"You do know there will be other available ladies at the masquerade. You may find one that would enable you to marry much faster."

Turning, he pinned Harewood with the stare he gave a servant who dared to disobey him. "You mean like Lady Frederica?"

"How many times must I explain. I had no knowledge that Lady Garmoyle was the former Lady Frederica. Even if I did, would you have not come here because of her?"

That was a good question, but the answer was obvious, at least to him. "No. I still would have come. I would not break my troth. You, better than anyone, know that."

Harewood sighed. "Yes, I know."

"It sounds like you are having second thoughts about your choice in a wife for me."

Harewood rose. "Damn right I am. She wasn't supposed to require you to pose for some amateurish painting. She was supposed to turn you down."

He strode toward his friend and clapped him on his shoulder. "You can't be right all the time."

Harewood shrugged him off with a grumble.

"I would be much obliged if you predicted something else for me, such as my ability to win the lady's heart."

That caught his friend's attention. "You plan to make her fall in love with you?"

He nodded. "I'm not sure if 'make' is the correct word, but yes. I am hoping she will have strong feelings for me by the time this painting is complete."

"To what end?"

"To insure a happy marriage, what else?" He grinned.

Though Harewood continued to stare at him in confusion, he strode toward the door. "Now, if you'd make sure no one is in the corridor between here and the servant stairs, I will be on my way."

"You're the one dressed like you're about to muck out the stalls. I should be giving *you* orders. Better lose that attitude, man." Harewood strode forward and opened the door then looked one way and the other before motioning him forward. "Or I'll have you fired."

Bowing his head, he barely kept from grinning. "Yes, sir." Without lifting his head, he brushed by Harewood and headed for the back stairs. His focus now was on getting out of the house unseen by servants and his hosts alike. At least today, he needn't worry about Lady Frederica, or rather Garmoyle. The ladies of the house had gone to the village to make final purchases for their costumes.

Making the ground floor without incident, he stepped outside with barely enough time to duck behind a bush as two footmen rounded the corner, heading into the house. His heart pounding with the excitement of his mission, he sprinted from the house to the stables. Getting Leonardo out could be tricky, but luck was on his side. The stablemaster directed the grooms in bringing out the horses for some exercise. Since they were occupied at one end, he saddled Leonardo and threw two horse blankets over the saddle. He waited until the stablemaster went into the harness room before walking Leonardo out into the cold sunshine.

Wrapping the blankets around himself, he mounted Leonardo and trotted him out until he neared the forest not far from the westside of Sunnydale Manor. They slipped in between the trees, walking over the brown leaves that littered the forest floor, the sun shining between the bare branches. Unfortunately, it meant anyone behind at the Enderlys could see him. As soon as he broke through to the other side, he raced across the field down toward the forest that lay on the east side of Thornwood. The slight hill would hide him from anyone riding at Sunnydale.

Entering the woods, he dismounted and tied Leonardo to a tree before throwing one of the blankets over him. Though the sun shone in a sky absent of any clouds, the temperature was far colder than the last time he visited Bedford. As he made his way through the trees to the last major obstacle of his journey, he hoped the chill kept the gardeners inside. He stopped at the edge of the wood and studied the landscape. Not a soul was in sight. Did that mean Lady Amelia wouldn't be in her Grecian studio either? He scanned the building. With the sun shining, he couldn't determine if there was any light inside, the windows reflecting the landscape back at him.

He'd come this far, so there was no reason to turn back and every reason to continue. Taking a deep breath, he raced across the open field before reaching the tall shrubs not far from the studio. Scanning the area one more time, he stealthily sidled up to the door and knocked. He waited, his breath causing small puffs in the air as his heart raced. Just as he was about to knock again, the door opened and Lady Amelia stood there in an apron, mouth open in surprise, with a smudge of lavender pastel on her nose.

Jubilation filled him at his success, and he quickly stepped inside and closed the door, barely keeping from reaching for her. "I'm here." He grinned as he removed the blanket with a flourish and hung it on the hook next to him. When he turned back, he found her mouth closed, her arms crossed, and her brows lowered. "Are you not pleased to see me?"

She turned on her heel. "You were supposed to be here two days ago. To say you are tardy would be an understatement."

He strode around a table to position himself in front of her. "True, but my delay was not of my doing." He held out his arms. "If I had my way, I would have been here by dawn the next day and every day between then and now."

She remained stiff and unyielding. "You obviously think this endeavor is a frivolous whim and seek only to indulge me." She uncrossed her arms and lifted one palm up toward a half-finished canvas. "It is far from that. If you cannot give this the consideration needed, then how can I be assured you would fulfill your responsibilities as a husband?"

Her accusation found its mark, and he sobered instantly. "Lady Amelia, I admire your talent and do not take my obligation to you lightly, either as your subject d'art or as your betrothed and future husband."

The challenge in her eyes as she raised her right eyebrow induced him to explain far more than he'd planned. "I could not have come any earlier without causing danger to your reputation. And as you stipulated that we pretend no familiar relationship, I was forced to remain at Sunnydale until it was safe to sneak away."

"Are you saying that you were unable to simply tell the Enderlys that you wished to go for a ride or into the village or to visit a blacksmith?"

He wanted to smirk at how alike they thought as he had used each one of those excuses to get away as well as two others. "I did indeed attempt each one of those, but with so many people staying at Sunnydale, someone always insisted in accompanying me."

"Always?" The doubt in her voice was reflected in the tilt of her head.

He would have to tell her. "Yes, always. Unfortunately, the person who has been the hardest to avoid is the one person I had hoped to never meet again."

She leaned her hip on the stool next to her. "And who might that be?"

"Lady Frederica, I mean Garmoyle." He ran his hand through his hair as he turned away from her, not wanting to see her reaction until he explained his true feelings about the situation. "Lady Garmoyle, before her marriage and widowhood, once had aimed to marry me by whatever means possible. She maneuvered me into a situation in her family's garden that would make it impossible for me to avoid it."

"You are being rather vague."

At the lack of censure in Amelia's tone, he finally faced her. Her gaze though steady, only appeared curious. That in itself made the story far easier to tell. "She arranged for us to be alone and attempted to kiss me. I was shocked and stepped back. I admit in my naivete, I did not handle it well. She then accused me of playing with her heart and told me she would tell her father that I had taken liberties with her person."

"And thereby you would be forced to marry her, her goal from the start."

"Yes." He remained silent as she thought over what he said.

"But you are not married to her, so how did you avoid such a miserable existence." Her lips quirked up as if she tried to hold back a smile.

That alone released the tension in his abdomen. "Harewood."

Her eyes widened. "Was he spying on you, or did he know something about the lady she'd prefer not be known?"

His relief turned to caution at the devious path her thoughts had taken. "As it happened, Harewood had overheard her telling a friend that she expected a request for her hand from me that very night. Since Harewood was well aware that I had minimal interest in Lady Frederica, he did not trust her motives when she suggested we take a stroll in the gardens." He grimaced. "Harewood has an uncanny ability to foresee outcomes of circumstances before they happen. He decided to take Lady Frederica's mother for a stroll and follow us, unbeknownst to us, and they witnessed the entire event. Just as Lady Frederica declared she'd tell her father, Harewood stepped onto the path with the lady's shocked mother, surprising us both. Her mother declared that she would do no such thing."

"Oh, I do so wish I could have seen that." Amelia's eyes sparkled with amusement. "Whatever did she do?"

He stepped closer to her as if by some magnetic force. "She transformed in a way I cannot forget. One moment she was hurt and in tears and the next she furiously hissed with vengeance." He shivered, despite the warmth of the room, a common occurrence whenever he thought of that moment. "It was as if she embodied the devil himself, as if she were the snake in William Blake's Temptation and the Fall of Eve illustration in *Paradise Lost*. She promised repercussions against the both of us through a string of curses I've only heard in the vilest of back alleyways."

All amusement vanished as Amelia frowned. "You must take her warning to heart. 'Heaven has no rage like love to hatred turned, nor Hell a fury like a woman scorned.' I remember not who wrote that, but my sister Joanna could tell you. It is something my Aunt Mabry often said about rejected women. She had been the recipient of such revenge in her youth."

Having his concerns about Lady Garmoyle validated beyond Harewood, both relieved and troubled him. "I do not believe she actually had feelings for me. It happened upon my third time in her presence. But I do not wish to endanger your reputation, so it has been my sole purpose to keep her from discovering our meeting."

Lady Amelia looked down at her hands and wiped them on her apron. "I doubt very much that she would wish to force us into marriage unless she thought it would be a nightmare for you." She looked up at him and a slow smirk formed her full lips. "Perhaps I can pretend an abhorrence of you, so as to mislead her."

He appreciated the thought, but he didn't want Amelia involved with someone like Lady Garmoyle. His instinct said that to voice his feelings on the matter would put her off, so he simply ignored the comment. "Whatever the lady's reasons for coming to Sunnydale Manor, I think we should complete your artwork as soon as it is safe to do so."

"Yes. We have a lot to do." She turned to a half-finished canvas and set it on the floor against the wall and lifted a blank one to put in its place.

He scanned the room for the best place to pose. Artists preferred light coming in from the side as he'd noticed. Dressed as a mere groom, he should have brought a bridle with him. His gaze landed on the horse blanket, and as she set up her paints, he walked over and pulled it from its hook and laid it over the one chair in the room that had no arms. The only other furniture was a settee, which would be odd, a winged back chair, stools, and tables. Pleased with his decision, he lifted his foot and set it on the blanket on the chair. Now he just needed to decide on his boon for remaining silent and still.

CHAPTER TEN

AMELIA POURED WATER into a tall ceramic vase and set her new brush in it, the story of Lady Garmoyle still swimming in her head. Her judgement of the lady had gone from poor to complete dislike. How sad that a woman would resort to such tactics. It wasn't as if the lady wasn't pretty. She simply had an uncalled-for arrogance about her that she could hide if she held her tongue. Had she really been that anxious to be wed?

As an artist, she could not imagine being in a hurry to marry. Turning around, her breath caught and she swallowed hard. Sommerset's loose shirt hung open, revealing a good expanse of his naked chest as he leaned his elbow on his knee upon the chair. His broad shoulders seemed wider in the servant shirt and the shadow about his chin made him appear harsher like a champion gladiator. While the stance was absurd, she couldn't seem to take her gaze from him though she'd never capture his image if she didn't move.

"Will this do? Or…" He raised himself up and set his hand on his knee instead. "Or would this be better?"

She forced herself to take in the complete image of him. He really was quite stunning. Already, her fingers tingled to begin her work. "You may want to consider—"

He twisted so she only had his back, leaving his hand on his knee and he looked over the opposite shoulder. "I could stand like this?"

Not sure if he simply teased again or honestly thought he was helping, she grinned. "Now you're almost in the *Discobolus* pose."

His eyes lit with recognition. "Ah, by Myron. Let me see." Without preamble, he dropped his foot, emptied the crumbs from her plate of seed cakes on the table and lifted it high in the air like a discus as he bent as if to send it off. "I believe that's like this?"

Actually, it was exactly like that. "Yes, that's it. But I don't believe that will be comfortable and I doubt I could capture the entire image in a few minutes."

His head, which had been turned toward the plate behind him that he held aloft, swiveled to look at her. "Do you doubt my strength?"

Oh, now he definitely teased. She tsked. "Such ego. How could I know your strength without some example?"

He stood straight again, scanning the room. "Is there something you wish me to lift to give proof of my prowess?" His gaze landed back on her. "You perhaps?"

Even as her cheeks heated, she countered. "Are you saying I am the heaviest object in the room?"

"Not at all." He placed his hand over the open V in his shirt. "You are absolutely correct. Lifting you would prove nothing. Perhaps if I revealed my strength so that you might examine it."

Before she could anticipate it, he grabbed hold of the back of his shirt and pulled it from his trousers and over his head, then whipped it over his right shoulder to hang down his back. "Do you wish to examine?" He posed like Michelangelo's David, the shirt his slingshot as he held it over his shoulder, his other hand curled around an imaginary shot.

Her mouth went dry, and her heart started to race. *Magnifique.* The adjective her European art tutor had used with barely a handful of masterpieces filled her head. She couldn't have resisted his invitation if she wanted to, and she definitely didn't want to. She stepped closer, studying his biceps in his right arm, not a little impressed that such strength was revealed. As she moved around to the front of his torso, she clasped her hands together to keep from touching the ridges of his stomach and the mounds that formed his chest. She'd always thought the David was the epitome of the male form for a man in his twenties, but Andrew Crauford, Lord of Sommerset far surpassed that touchstone.

She continued her journey around him, quietly swallowing upon viewing his naked back, his shoulders far larger than she'd thought with muscles she hadn't anticipated. If she couldn't paint a masterpiece of him, then there was no hope for her. The thought brought a thrill of exhilaration rifling through her. It almost left her breathless.

He looked over his shoulder at her. "Do I pass inspection for the discus thrower? Or do you prefer a different stance?"

Recalling her purpose, she stepped around to face him. "I believe you could meet the challenge of the pose. However, I'm not confident in my ability to do it justice quite yet. Let's begin with your foot on the chair."

He returned to his original pose, with one hand on his knee. He was in profile, so she wanted to make the most of his arms. "Put both hands on your knee."

He did as instructed. "Like this?"

She stepped back. No, it wasn't right. "Twist toward the window a little." Even as he did so, it was clear it wouldn't work. "No, no, that won't do." She stepped closer. "Look in the direction of your knee, but not at it. Yes, that's good. Now straighten your back as if you were in the military."

"A profession not allowed to me."

"No, of course not. You're an earl." The position still wasn't right. She wanted arrogance, strength, and just a bit of danger. She placed her hand under his chin to nudge his head up an inch, but froze, or rather combusted if the heat she felt in her fingers was any indication. Quickly, she dropped her hand. "Just lift your head a little. Yes."

Anxious to put space between them, she walked back to her easel and moved it so she could face him. Quickly, she took her paintbrush from the water and dipped it in the brown madder paint.

"You're not using pastels today?"

She started with his torso since it called her more than anything at the moment. "No, I'm not." Adding more paint to her brush she continued with her strokes.

"Do you prefer pastels for sketching and watercolor for your final product? I thought most painters use oils, or are those mainly for men?"

At his question, she stopped. "There is no determination of medium based on the gender of the painter. Watercolor simply allows for far more variations of color. Though to be clear, my plan is for the final painting to be in oils." She dipped her brush in color once again and continued.

His brows rose and he looked at her just as she started on his profile. "How many paintings do you plan? I can hardly be worthy of so much effort."

She let out a breath of frustration. "I do not know yet. What I do know is you must not move or speak or how can I paint you? You'll come out with two heads and half a body."

He gave her a sheepish look. "I apologize. I am not an expert at posing for a painting. I much prefer to be on the other side."

Since he hadn't turned his head back, she gave in to her curiosity. "By the other side, you mean as the painter?"

He chuckled. "Hardly. I believe I established the fact that I cannot paint. No, I prefer to be the viewer."

"Ah, I see." She lifted her brush, but he continued to look at her. "Please face forward."

"Oh, yes." He finally turned his head. Quickly, she painted his profile, his hair coming down longer than it actually was. Why did she keep doing that?

"Have you thought about what—" A knock at the door interrupted him and he whipped his head around as he brought his foot down.

Her heart skipped a beat as she dropped her brush and took a step toward the door, but it opened and Mariel walked in.

"I was about to go out riding and I thought I'd bring you—oh." Mariel halted as she stared at Sommerset then quickly averted her gaze. "I didn't know you had begun your sittings."

Relieved it was Mariel and no other, she strode forward and took the box from her. "Yes, we just started, but it wasn't planned." She opened the box, pretending that having her sister find a half-naked man in her studio was the most normal of things. "Oh, you brought me something to eat. You are such a dear."

"Yes, well, I needed some fresh air and you've been out here since this morning. When the cook said she planned to make rout cakes, I offered to bring you some before I took Zephyrus for a gallop." She looked at Lord Sommerset, who had donned his shirt again. "But I only brought enough for one person."

He strode forward. "That was very thoughtful. I'm not hungry. She just has me standing about here while she does the difficult work." He smiled kindly.

But Amelia could tell her sister was rattled. She clasped her hand. "Thank you. I'm so relieved it was you."

Mariel glanced at Sommerset again and back at her. "If you truly want to keep your pact, I suggest a plan for the next person who knocks at the door. If it had been Mother or Father, banns would be posted this Sunday whether you had accomplished your painting or not."

The serious tone of her sister's voice brought back her initial concern upon hearing the knock. "You are right. I will keep the door locked from now on."

"That would be wise." Mariel pointed to the easel. "Have you begun painting already?"

Looking over her shoulder, she quickly judged if it was appropriate for her sister to see. Then again, her sister had been married, so of course she'd seen a bare-chested man. "I have, but just in watercolor. You're welcome to view it."

Mariel moved before the painting, and she anxiously awaited her thoughts. Mariel was always kind, but also always truthful.

She moved closer to her sister, whose cheeks had become flushed.

"It is an excellent likeness so far." Mariel quickly stepped away. "I'll leave you to your creation. I just came for the excuse to enjoy the sun. Though it's terribly cold, it is pleasant to finally see so much light." She briskly walked toward the door.

Confused, Amelia opened her mouth to question her, but Mariel stepped through to the outside, her hand on the knob. "Be sure to lock this." And with that her sister closed the door and was gone.

Now that was odd. Mariel didn't even look at Sommerset nor wish him a good day. Her sister always had perfect manners.

"You appear concerned." Sommerset's comment invited her to share her thoughts.

"I am." She locked the door then meandered her way back to the unfinished watercolor. Studying it, she could see no major errors. Yes, there was much more to do, but it was passable and there was certainly no reason for her sister to get flustered. "I'm confused why my sister would be embarrassed." She moved her gaze from the painting to him. "Not only has she been married and widowed, but before that she was betrothed to a man she loved with all her heart." She pointed to the painting. "I'm confused why this would cause her to blush."

"I see. So your confusion is with your sister's reaction to the painting and perhaps my state of undress?"

"Yes." She shook her head. "My Aunt Mabry had no such qualms at viewing the classic statues of Greece, nor did I for that matter. The human form is simply an aesthetic."

Sommerset leaned his hip on the stool next to him as his lips quirked in what surely was amusement. "If I may, I have a theory on your sister's reaction."

Convinced he was about to tease her, she crossed her arms.

"And that is?"

"First, I would like to suggest that though she and her first love—"

"That would be Marcus Stratton, second son to the Viscount of Blackmore."

He cocked his head then continued. "As I was saying, though your sister was betrothed to Mr. Stratton, if he was indeed worthy of her, I doubt she viewed him without his shirt. In fact, my impression of your sister is that she is quite proper and would not have allowed anything beyond a few chaste kisses."

A little uncomfortable with the fact that she had obviously gone beyond what was proper in his eyes and society's, she unfolded her arms and shrugged her right shoulder. "Yes, I imagine you are correct. But then she married the Earl of Beaumont, so she should be knowledgeable of the male form."

He stared at her uncomprehendingly. "The male form? You speak of it as if it is a piece of artwork."

"It is. The human form, though complex, is a wonderful piece of art. Though Joanna would say it is a marvelous feat of science."

"Ah, I see." He stood and walked away, his back to her, his hastily donned shirt falling to mid-thigh and covering up his own well-made form. Finally, he turned back. "The Earl of Beaumont? Was he not rather along in his years?"

She grimaced. "Older than my father."

He crossed one arm and rested his other elbow on it, his chin upon his fist. "Why did she choose to marry him?"

She looked away, not liking where the conversation had led. "I think we should return to the painting." Stepping closer to the easel, she felt a certain comfort in its presence.

"Amelia."

At his familiar use of her name, she sucked in her breath. "Yes?"

"Why did your oldest sister marry a man old enough to be her father?"

As much as she didn't want to discuss it, they had gone far

beyond the usual bounds of society anyway, so he might as well know. "She married him to save our family. My father had an unscrupulous solicitor, and we were on the verge of being destitute." She shivered at the memory of the dinner when her father told them. "It had not been long after Mariel had news of Mr. Stratton's demise at the hands of Napoleon's army, and she had become a shadow of herself. I even feared she'd follow Belinda to the grave."

She clasped her hands together and stared at them, the feeling of possibly losing another sister still lingered in her heart. "She offered to marry to assure our family's continued happiness. Though my parents argued against it, and my sister Joanna assured her she could bring us back to comfort within a few years, Mariel found the perfect husband. Lord Beaumont was old, desperate for an heir, and very wealthy. My father, Joanna, and our new solicitor drew up the marriage contract and the two married within the month."

"And so your family kept your comfort at the discomfort of your sister. Old Beaumont died with no heir, so I imagine that added more wealth to your coffers."

At his harsh tone, she snapped her head up, but he was turned away, his thoughts hidden. She'd never heard him speak so. Hesitantly, she answered his implied question. "It did, but the wonderful piece is that we got our Mariel back. I think marrying and running a household for Lord Beaumont gave her life purpose again after Mr. Stratton died. When she returned home, she seemed at peace."

"Hmm, I imagine."

Something in his tone made her want to comfort him but also clearly indicated she shouldn't pry. Too curious to let it go, she had to ask. "Do you find what Mariel did to save our family wrong?" She didn't like that thought and stood ready to defend her sister.

He faced her, his magnificent shoulders slumping. "No, I understand what she did. It was very noble of her. I know of many women who have sacrificed their…happiness, for their family. I only thought of her and how uncomfortable it must have been to marry someone of such an advanced age and so desperate for an heir."

Something in his tone told her that he spoke of things she knew little about, but as long as he thought Mariel noble, she was satisfied. She strode back to the easel. They had spent far too long on Mariel. Picking up her brush, she made a slight correction in the color of Sommerset's hair. Or should she think of him as Andrew now?

"What are you doing? Don't you need me to pose?" He strode forward. "May I see?"

Surprised by his turnabout in mood, she stepped back. "Of course. You are the subject."

He stood right next to her to view the watercolor. "That I am, your bowl of fruit, as you described it."

Heat filled her cheeks. "I did rescind that particular description. If asked now, I would most likely say you were my goat."

"Goat?" He looked at her, his whisky-colored eyes wide with surprise.

This close, she could see the flecks of gold and dark brown that made them so fascinating. She really needed to capture those in the final painting. "Yes, goat. You are constantly moving and bleating."

As his brows rose, she kicked herself for being so rude, but then he laughed. It was a laugh filled with enjoyment and life. It reminded her of when she was a child and innocent of her silly dreams. Warmth filled her at the memory of that feeling.

"You are correct. I suppose it's in my nature. I'm not used to staying still nor of being quiet." His eyes glowed with mirth and acceptance of who he was.

Oh, to feel like that. Would being his wife make it easier or harder? "At least I have been able to capture a bit of you so far."

He turned his head to view the painting once again. "The torso is like looking in the mirror."

Heat rose in her chest at the compliment. "You stare at yourself in the mirror often then?"

He grinned. "No, but I think I may have to now that you will be painting my likeness, so that I may compare appropriately."

She rolled her eyes. "There won't be anything to compare unless you go back to the chair and stand as you were before. Understand?" Though she smiled, she really did want to get more of the watercolor done before he had to leave.

He gave a deep bow. "Yes, my lady. As your groom, I will do whatever you say."

She doubted that very much, but wasn't beyond testing his offer. "Then, my dear man, please remove your shirt and stand with one foot upon yonder chair."

He gave her a cheeky grin just before he pulled his shirt over his head. "As you wish." Wiggling his brows at her, he strode back to the chair. When he reached it, he turned his back to her and placed his foot as she requested. "Like this, me lady?"

His attempt at a street seller's language was pitiful. She moved her index finger in a circle. "No, turn so you're facing the door."

"Like this?" He turned his face in profile, but his back still faced her.

She had no doubt he teased her purposefully. Stepping around her canvas, she wound her way past the stool and table. She never claimed to be a neat artist, which made navigating her studio a bit of a challenge. By the time she reached him, he'd lifted one arm up while his other hand rested on his hip. "Now you're either teasing me or you don't have much intellect in that handsome head of yours."

He immediately whipped around to face her. "You think I'm handsome?"

She wasn't fooled for a minute by the widening of his eyes and raising of his brows since his lips kept quirking upward. "If you are looking for compliments from me, you'll be waiting a long time. I appreciate your exterior aesthetic for my painting.

That is all. Unlike Shakespeare, I do not believe that 'apparel oft proclaims the man'."

He swooped his arms upward. "But I barely wear any clothes."

She bit down on her lip to keep from smiling. "Be that as it may, you do remember what your stance was before my sister arrived, and before I lose the light, I would hope as a gentleman that you would return to it."

"How can I deny such a simple request?" He dropped his arms and repositioned himself to almost the same position.

His torso though, was at the wrong angle. "You just need to turn yourself a little." Reaching out, she placed her hands on his back to adjust him. The shock of his warm, smooth skin was complicated by the hard strength beneath it. Her breath caught as he moved according to the pressure of her hands.

A pleasant heat filled her, making her want to touch him again. She stood back to view him, but quickly stepped forward again. "Here, bend your arm a bit more." She touched his biceps and inner elbow, thrilled at the feel of the muscle moving beneath her fingers.

Once more the heat of pleasantness filled her. It had to be a new understanding of the human body! She stepped back, and though tempted to touch him again, she needed to get back to her easel while the feeling was with her. "Good. Now hold that pose." She bumped into the stool in her hurry to return to her canvas. Grabbing up her paintbrush, she dipped it into the burnt umber she used to outline and shade and began to paint.

"Do you maneuver all your models in such a way?"

She dipped her brush again, the understanding flowing through her as she brushed on color, adding layers to hint at what was beneath the skin.

"How many men have you had model for you?"

His question seeped through her focus, causing her to look up, only to find he'd twisted to face her again. She frowned, not happy, but at the thought of touching him again to move him back, her pique vanished. "You are the first man to model for me." She set down her brush and moved toward him, this time pushing the stool out of the way to have better egress when she returned to the canvas.

"You mean the only man."

At his tone, she snapped her gaze to his. There it was. That predatory gleam like the lion she imagined him to be. Deep within the kind and teasing demeanor lay the true man. His look sent a tingling through her down to her toes, which in itself was unusual. It was usually her fingers that tingled and then only when she was anxious to create. "Yes, of course. You are the only man to model for me." She gave him a crooked grin. "However, modeling means remaining still and quiet."

He moved one hand from his knee and cupped her cheek. "And what do I receive in return for being a proper model?"

At his touch, her breath caught. That the feeling of warmth occurred either way was mystifying. "What would you request?"

His gaze settled on her lips and she barely kept from licking them. She sincerely hoped he would not want a kiss. That was hardly what these sittings were about. They needed to focus on the painting. The pressure of time weighed heavily on her, and her instinct now confirmed that she could paint her masterpiece with him as her subject, but he must remain her bowl of fruit.

His gaze finally raised to meet hers. "I would like to know what your costume will be for the Noells' masquerade ball."

She blinked at the surprise request. "Why would you wish to know that? Is not the idea of a masquerade to hide one's identity?"

His grin was slow and mischievous. "Not necessarily. Many simply enjoy dressing as something other than they are. I, myself, was thinking this groom's outfit might be just the thing."

She squinched up her nose. "I don't think that would do at all." She looked askance at him. "Unless you were hoping to entice one Lady Garmoyle with your willingness to obey her every request."

His whole body stiffened. "I can find something else."

"I suggest you do. She plans to be Lady MacBeth, so avoid any queens walking about the ballroom to be overly cautious."

"I will. However, since we shall all be disguised, it seems the perfect opportunity for us to be in each other's company since no one will know who we are. But if I know what costume you are wearing, I can find you." His countenance made it clear he was rather pleased with his deduction, but there was bound to be unmaskings and many wouldn't even bother with a mask.

"And if I tell you my costume, you will stop moving and talking?"

"You have my word." He laid his hand over his heart to exaggerate his seriousness about something hardly serious and yet more so than it first appeared.

She gave a heavy sigh as if he asked for a great boon. "If you must know, I plan to go to the masquerade as a shepherdess."

"Like the one of true love in Catel's painting?"

Horsefeathers, she'd forgotten about that painting. It had too close a connection to him. She'd have to devise something else. "Now will you please take your pose?"

"Only for you will I stop bleating."

Relieved by his promise and his ability to take her jest about him being a goat in stride, though to be truthful, he did seem to get into everything like that particular animal, she studied his position. "You just need to move your face to the left." She touched his chin to nudge it a bit more in profile. Unable to resist, she swept her fingers through his hair just over his ear to see it clearly.

His shoulder came up and his hand imprisoned hers. "That tickles." He let go of her hand and brushed his hair back. "Will that do?"

She grinned. Between the warmth filling her and discovering he had a weak spot, she could have purred with happiness. "That's just right. Now face the door again." She laid her hand on the back of his neck as he swiveled his head. The strength even there sent an excited spark through her.

Quickly, she returned to her canvas. Her heart beat hard with foreseen success. For the first time, she knew, with no doubts at all, that she could accomplish her goal. She picked up her brush and viewed the man that would make her dream come true before setting paint to the canvas once again. Her masterpiece was in the making. Now all she needed to do is follow her instincts.

CHAPTER ELEVEN

ANDREW STOOD NEXT to a potted plant and studied the dancers currently performing the Quadrille. He'd been at the masquerade for over an hour and he still had not spotted his quarry. Though there were at least seven shepherdesses in attendance, one of which he was quite sure was Lady Beaumont, not one of them was Amelia.

The little minx lied to him. He should be irritated, but he couldn't help but admire her ingenuity in turning the tables on him. The problem now was to find her and extract a fair payment for her perfidy.

He adjusted his "belly," a large, feathered pillow his valet had tied around him before he'd donned the brown robes and cincture of a Franciscan friar. The large cowl helped to hide his own hair while the headband with very short bangs made of horsehair made it appear his own coloring to be dark. He had Lambert to thank for the entire costume, having borrowed the robes from a friend and created the headband himself. As a valet, the man surpassed all expectations. Now if he could just figure out what costume his lovely bride-to-be would wear.

He studied a blonde Roman Empress. There were only three empresses but the one dancing was the only one with the correct color hair. Yet even as he watched her skip down the center of the room, he shook his head. It wasn't his future wife. The Empress moved too stiffly. Amelia was light of foot and her svelte form graceful. He let his gaze wander, keeping his sights on blonde women, which unfortunately, were in the majority. While he'd recognize Amelia's lighter shade in daylight, in the candlelight, it was hard to distinguish hues.

Having eliminated all blonde empresses, shepherdesses, goddesses, Circassians, sultanas, and angels, he began studying every other female with light hair. The six queens in attendance all sported dark hair, and one in particular of diminutive size and wearing a plaid sash, he kept his distance from. Unless of course Lady MacBeth was willing to confess her sins to a Franciscan friar. That could be interesting, but best not to tempt fate. Since over a hundred women attended the extravagant affair, it could take him all night to find Amelia. The longer he searched, the higher her payment would be. He had hoped to steal a kiss, but now he may extract more.

The music stopped, and he scanned the last round of dancers. Harewood strode off the floor directly in front of him. Dressed as a Musketeer, his friend had eschewed a mask and donned a musketeer hat, making it obvious who he was. That his chosen costume was one of the recently disbanded French guard would invite much speculation come the morrow, probably exactly what Harewood hoped for.

"Have you not found her yet? I noticed a gaggle of shepherdesses by the punch before the last dance."

Andrew clasped his hands together and lowered his head. "Women do not form gaggles. That's geese."

"Humph. By the sounds that issued forth when I strode by, I believe my descriptive word more apt. Now do stop looking down. You look guilty."

"I am guilty." He lifted his head and wiggled his brows. "I have nefarious intentions."

"It's barely improper to steal a kiss from one's own betrothed. Everyone does so." Harewood readjusted his large hat, the feather bouncing wildly as he moved it. "If your art bird wished to paint something of interest, there are plenty of characters to be found here." He motioned toward the room with his hand, though the blue silk cloak he wore caught in his wide glove cuff, and he became entangled in it. "Dratted uniform. No wonder France lost to us."

He swallowed his laugh, knowing Harewood would not see the humor in his predicament. "Have you made your bow to the queen yet?"

Harewood shook his arm until the cloak finally fell away. "Which one?"

"Lady Macbeth."

"Hardly. The more I learn of that woman, the more I believe you are indebted to me for saving you from a life with her. Do you know she instructed my mother on how to thread her needle and lectured my father on the sins of drinking alone? Since when is that a sin? If it is, I'm going to hell alongside Prinny, though for quite different reasons."

Unable to refrain, he lifted his hand and made the sign of the cross in front of Harewood.

"Oh, will you stop that."

He chuckled. "I thought only of your soul."

"The devil you did. You thought only to irritate me and to have fun doing it. Is that what you do when you sit for your portrait?"

"Yes. I talk a lot and move about too."

Harewood stared at him, eyes wide. "I thought you were courting her. Does she find that charming?"

"Not in the least." He grinned. "But it does get her attention, though I don't think she sees me as anything more than, well, a bowl of fruit."

"If you're still a bowl of fruit to her, you may need more lessons in seduction."

He'd had far too many lessons in seduction, many right alongside Harewood, so for him to pretend a greater experience annoyed him. "I have no need of that. At our last meeting, I was shirtless and she touched my bare skin multiple times."

"That sounds promising. Did she swoon? Blush? Need to take some air?"

Even as he thought back, the disappointed, disgruntled feeling he had when she'd gone back to her easel to paint, filled him. "No, she returned to her painting. As I said, she sees me as no more than a bowl of fruit."

"Would that be strawberries and grapes, or pineapples and pears?"

He looked down at himself. "I'm thinking a large melon."

Harewood laughed, a rather unusual sound, considering his normal cynical view. It must have to do with having the ability to assemble current happenings then conclude an outcome, and always be right. Or rather, almost always. "Perhaps she simply has no interest in bulky shouldered, tanned men who look like laborers." He twirled his fake mustache. "She most likely has more refined tastes and finds those of us with a slender build and pale skin much more aristocratic."

It was true that despite the two of them competing in similar sports and other activities while at Oxford, he often helped his men in outdoor labor, preferring to understand the family estate from all angles. Therefore, he did sport darker skin than Harewood, but he'd never found that or his broad build to be a hindrance in the bedroom. "I don't believe that's it. I think she simply sees the human form as another *objet d'art.*"

"Then, my dear friar, what are you going to do about that?"

It was a fair question, and one he'd pondered since he'd left his last sitting. "I find myself now in a rather enviable position as I must seduce her with both words and touch." He gave Harewood a smug smile. "That is, of course, if I can find her." He winced at the fact he'd been unsuccessful so far.

"I told you where the shepherdesses are. Why are you still talking to me?" His friend turned toward the room to scan the crowd.

"Because that is not her costume."

Harewood frowned as he turned back to face him. "What do you mean? You told me she said she'd be a shepherdess."

"She lied."

Once again, Amelia's actions had shocked Harewood as he stood there, mouth agape.

Andrew had to admit, he enjoyed seeing his friend speechless. That alone was worth having her by his side for the rest of his life.

"She…she…lied…to you?"

He nodded. Was it odd to be proud of her for lying? Most likely, but he didn't care. She'd paid him back for being an uncooperative model and that pleased him. He always envisioned himself with a biddable proper wife, but something changed since his father's death. His instinct told him Amelia was exactly what he needed in a lifelong mate. Life would never be boring with her by his side.

"Are you sure you still want to marry this woman? I will support you if you decide to break the agreement you made with her."

That Harewood was completely serious bothered him. "Yes, I still plan to marry her. I just need to find her so I can press my suit."

"You do know that usually you court the woman *before* the betrothal, right?"

He put his hands together as if praying. "Sometimes, you just need to have faith, my son."

Giving a loud snort, Harewood turned on his heel and moved off, obviously tired of his company. It was just as well as he still had yet to find Amelia and talking with Harewood too long would give his own identity away.

He needed to be more strategic in his search. What would she wear to a masquerade? Dressing as an artist would be far too obvious, and with so many neighbors knowing her penchant for painting, he doubted she would risk being discovered. He hadn't seen any female artists, though he was sure there was a Michelangelo and a Rubin enjoying the ball.

Someone bumped into him from behind, and he turned, hoping she'd found him accidentally.

"Oh, pardon me, good friar. I did not see ye there blending in with the potted tree." The feminine voice attempting a lower-class accent to match her street seller costume wasn't the woman he sought, but he played his part and folded his hands. "Blessings upon you, fair lass and prayers for better eyesight."

The young woman giggled before joining a group of revelers nearby. He scanned the crowd, but Amelia was not among them. He moved his gaze to the next group and then the next. He spotted Harewood's sister Rose in a pretty butterfly costume, but none of the ladies with her fit Amelia's shape and size. Amelia was more a sprite with a narrow waist, small bust, and her pixie like nose.

"Well, dash it all. Who'd have thought she could end up in such a hobble." The street seller's voice carried, which fit her language. Could Amelia have decided to dress as someone of a lower class? He shook his head. He couldn't imagine that. It was more likely she'd dress prettily, perhaps as a bird or a butterfly like Harewood's sister.

The street seller lady laughed loudly, catching his attention once more. He should probably move to another area so he could further his investigation. Taking a few steps toward the center of the room, a comment Amelia had made floated through his mind. *I believe it was more that we were an oddity, like a monkey paraded about at court.* While there were no monkeys at the ball… He stopped and glanced back at the street seller. Amelia's humility had caught his attention from the beginning. Maybe he was looking for the wrong costume and in the wrong place.

If, as he now suspected, Amelia dressed in something that would attract little attention, he needed to relocate his search to the fringes of the room where a lady's maid or governess costume would more likely be found, if the owner wished to portray their part more authentically. He strolled along the perimeter of the large area, though he was sure he appeared to waddle with his fake belly. He'd already determined that looking at eye color beneath the shadow of a mask was quite difficult, so he would have to find Amelia by instinct alone. He had navigated halfway around the room when he caught the scent of violets.

Of course! Following his nose brought him to a group of three women. Though all three were blonde, he immediately recognized her. The way she held herself and her wide smile revealed her identity.

He grinned at the cleverness of her costume. She'd piled four hats upon her head, each looking about to fall, but obviously pinned or sewn together. Attached to her wrist was a pin cushion with various hat pins, and she had two felt birds and three flowers affixed to her left shoulder. Her white mask had been embellished with flowers, ribbons, and a pair of tiny scissors, effectively covering most of her face with only her nose and mouth visible. She'd dressed as a milliner, and a very pretty milliner she was too. As usual, she wore a spring-colored dress, pale green, that was set off by the multitude of pastel hats on her head and the décor on her shoulder and mask.

Triumph filled him as she glanced his way. "Oh dear, I do believe a friar has come to lead us in prayer." She gave him an amused smirk. "Father, please allow us to wait until the morrow in church."

The other ladies chuckled and turned toward him.

He lowered his voice to disguise it. "I would not dream of interrupting your frivolity. However, if any of you wish to confess, I am at your disposal." He let his gaze rest on each lady.

The woman closest to him, laid a hand on her chest. "Oh no, I am not ready to confess. I have yet to sin tonight!"

The other patted his wide sleeved arm. "And I fear, good sir, I'm not likely to sin with you, so as with my friend, I must keep searching." The woman laughed and with that, the two ladies hooked arms and disappeared into the crowd.

He stepped closer to Amelia. "And what of you, miss? Do you have anything to confess?"

"Me? Now why would you assume that of me?"

Purposefully, he let his gaze roam from the top of her hats to the hem of her dress and back to meet her gaze. "I cannot imagine such beauty can be resisted by every man present here." He opened his palms to indicate the entire assemblage.

She laughed quietly. "Then dear friar, I fear your judgement is poor. Perhaps it is due to being cloistered with your brothers. It can be difficult to understand the ways of the world when so isolated. Many a man respects a woman's virtue and would not presume otherwise, even if she be no more than a modest milliner."

Her reply pleased him. "Then since I have been cloistered for so long, would you walk outside with me and enlighten me on how life is beyond my monastery walls?"

She stiffened. "It would not say well of me if I were to go off with a stranger."

That she didn't recognize him was clear, but that she hesitated because of it had his heart beating hard with pride. She held to their bargain as strongly as he did.

Suddenly, her gaze moved past him.

He looked over his shoulder to see Harewood winding his way through the crowd toward them. With no mask on, his identity was obvious, and Amelia might easily guess who was beneath the monk robes. Confound it.

"I think some fresh air on the terrace for a short while would be most welcome." Her sudden capitulation surprised him.

Did it have anything to do with Harewood or did she suddenly become curious about the friar before her? Not about to question his good fortune, he faced her again and held out his arm to lead her away toward the open garden doors. The chill air greeted them before they stepped out, perhaps the reason most people milled about away from the exit. He was pleased he wore the warm monk robes, though his bare feet, in the uncomfortable sandals, already began to grow cold.

"I fear I will have a very short while to update you on today's mores." Despite her supposed fear, there was laughter in her voice. "I do believe winter has joined us early this year."

So used to avoiding being alone with a woman, he paused just outside the doors before remembering that being with her was what he wanted. He continued just to the right, not far from the warmth of the ballroom, unwilling for her to grow too chilled, yet out of sight of Harewood or anyone else for that matter.

He disengaged his arm to step in front of her. He took her gloved hand in his. "My dear miss, I fear I must leave the cloister, for your beauty has overtaken me and I now renounce my vows."

Once again, she laughed at him. "Dear monk, I am hardly worth renouncing your vows for. I am no more than a simple milliner. Why you know nothing about me beyond my work." She patted the hats on top of her head with her free hand.

"But I can guess." He held up his hand so she wouldn't interrupt then closed his eyes. "I believe that you are a kind person who does for others." He opened his eyes to judge her reaction. She kept her smile, but it was not relaxed. "I also believe that you are very knowledgeable about your work. You seek perfection, but don't feel your work is worthy."

Her smile disappeared as she stared at him.

He grasped her hand to his chest, or as close as the pillow would allow. "I believe you are afraid that without your work, there is no point in life. I believe you are afraid that in anything else in life, you will be mediocre at best, but I know that cannot be."

Behind the elaborate mask, her eyes glistened in the lantern lights of the terrace, and his heart ached at the confirmation in her tear-filled eyes. With his free hand, he cupped her cheek. "You are worthy beyond your own understanding." Unable to resist, he leaned forward and kissed her.

At the feel of her soft lips yielding to his, a possessiveness like none he'd experienced before took hold. He snaked his hand behind her neck and deepened the kiss, coaxing her to let him in so that he might taste the wonder of her. As her mouth opened to him, he delved in to taste her heady flavor, a mixture of tang from the punch and pure Amelia.

A need built in his abdomen that raked up his back, demanding he pull her into his arms, but he kept it at bay, not wanting to scare her away.

As her tongue met his, he barely stifled a groan at the sweet sensation. Her tentative movements assured him she'd never opened to another man and his body's demands to claim her grew stronger. He had to stop before he lost all his senses. Forcing himself to withdraw from her warmth, he started to pull back, but she thrust her tongue into his mouth even as her free hand clutched his shoulder.

His whole body leapt with joy, including his manhood, which was well covered by the robes and pillow. Unfortunately, he couldn't stifle a groan as she explored his mouth with her tongue. At the sound, she pulled away, startled.

He let her go and her gaze roamed his face before she shivered. He opened his mouth to offer to take her in, but received a slap across his face.

"You assume too much, sir!"

Stunned, he stared at her, true fury alive in her eyes. Then with no other word, she marched back into the ballroom and disappeared from sight.

He pressed his hand to his stinging cheek. Yes, he deserved that, though to be fair, a kiss was an appropriate recompense for having lied to him. She had reacted to him with far more passion than he'd expected. He leaned his back against the wall of the home, the cool air helping to get his body under control. However, it did nothing for his stinging cheek.

His euphoria vanished in an instant. For her to have slapped him meant she didn't recognize him, which had been the point of his costume. Was he to then conclude that she thought herself kissing a stranger? If so, then how staunchly did she keep to their bargain, and more importantly, would she fulfill her part of the agreement after the painting was accomplished?

For the first time since agreeing to Amelia's proposal, he was assailed with misgivings. No longer confident, he moved toward the open doors to the ballroom. He needed to keep vigilant and see if she engaged with any other gentlemen at the ball. The last thing he needed was a wife who could not keep her word.

❦

CHAPTER TWELVE

AMELIA STARED OUT the window of her studio, the blank canvas long forgotten. There was nothing of any import to look at. The leaves were gone, the gardens put to bed for the winter, the birds flown south, and nothing moved under the overcast sky. It was the stillness that captivated her, that urged her to paint it, but she'd tried before. There was no possibility that a painting could capture the ultimate lack of movement in a living, breathing scene. It was a small mystic moment that soothed her soul more than anything else had been able to so since the masquerade five nights prior.

She refused to allow the memory to disturb her short peace. Tears and crumbling sketches had brought her no relief from the physical awakening Andrew had brought forth in her. Nor the anger that burned inside her that he could kiss a strange woman with no thought of her. His very presence upset her, yet he was necessary to creating her masterpiece. It had to be accomplished or she'd be like her mother, never knowing where her talent could lead her. And it definitely led her to Andrew. He was the key to her *tour de force*. Every fiber of her psyche told her he was the subject that would release her best work. He just couldn't touch her…or another.

With her heart racing again, she tried to refocus on the stillness outside, but it was of little use. Her mind had wandered to her dilemma once again. With a sigh, she finally rose and took a sip of her cold morning tea. Even her marmalade toast remained half-eaten. She stared at the blank canvas across the room. No image formed in her mind except that of a masked Andrew pulling her closer as his lips descended upon hers. "This will never do."

Setting down her teacup, she opened the little drawer in the small desk beneath the tea tray and pulled out Belinda's miniature. She ran her finger over the glass, still amazed at how perfect the likeness was. But it was more than simply what Belinda looked like. Somehow, she'd captured who Belinda was. "I could use your special kind of peace now, Bea. Could you send some?"

A knock at the door had her staring hard at the miniature of Belinda, but when the doorknob jiggled, she knew it had to be Mariel. "I'm coming."

After laying the miniature back in the drawer, she wound her way through the furniture and opened the door, her heart leaping. "Joanna!"

Her sister grinned. "I knew you would be happy I arrived. I come bearing gifts."

Though she didn't feel she could confide in Joanna, her sister always proved an excellent distraction. She gave her a hug, then ushered her in from the cold, taking the packages and setting them down on her sketching table. "Are these the oil paints?"

Joanna hung her cloak on the hook revealing a royal blue walking dress that brought out the blue in her hazel eyes and complimented her dark tresses. "They are. I purchased every color I could find." She winked. "I even dragged James to a few other shops for more."

"I didn't think your booksellers sold oil paints."

"How little you know." Joanna moved into the room and looked at the two easels with blank canvases. "Where is all your work?" She lifted *The Education of the Feminine Species* from the table nearby. "Has my book helped?"

Amelia paused in untying the packages. "It has, but it also

hasn't. I'm still working with it." She pointed to a stack of paintings leaning against the south wall. "Those are some of my new ones."

Her sister moved to where she'd pointed and started looking through the canvases. "Does Mr. Hennessey know you've been painting him? I imagine he would be quite surprised to discover that gardening was such a fit subject for artwork."

"I'm sure the poor man would die of embarrassment if he saw those." She resumed pulling the oil paints from the brown paper wrapping. In total, there were over a dozen colors. "Wherever did you find the persimmon and lilac paints?"

"At a little shop at the Burlington arcade. Have you been there?" She continued to pull paintings and view them. "I do believe that you are getting better with every one you paint."

She rolled her eyes at her sister's back. "I thought we established that you have no eye for good or poor paintings."

Joanna looked over her shoulder. "I thought I had no eye for aesthetics?"

She shrugged. "They are too closely related to discuss the difference." She held up her hand as Joanna opened her mouth. "No, we're not going to discuss it."

"But it's fun."

"No." She grinned at her sister's pout then carefully set the paints in a box and carried them to her supply table. She would save them for Andrew's next visit if he still wanted to keep their bargain. She moved to the east window and scanned the grounds. It would not do for him to arrive today while her sister was there. Joanna would ask far too many uncomfortable questions.

"Oh, this is magnificent. Naughty, but truly remarkable. However, did you get one of the grooms to pose for you?"

She snapped her head around to find her sister pulling the blank canvas from an easel and setting the watercolor of Andrew on it. She always let her family view her finished work, so it hadn't occurred to her that the sketches and paintings of Andrew might cause comment. She would have to be sure to disguise them better.

Forcing a laugh, she moved closer. "I didn't. As I said, your book does help."

Joanna studied the painting. "There's something familiar about that profile. I'm sure I've seen this man, but not in the stables."

Seeing no help for it as her sister would hear that Andrew was visiting Bedford, she waved her hand as if it were obvious. "Yes, that's Lord Sommerset's profile. He's visiting Lord Harewood and the Enderlys. He came to call a few weeks ago." She stood next to her sister. "I thought he had a very classic profile, so I sketched it first then tried the paint. Does it look as if it is all one man to you?"

"It does. What a creative idea."

She gave her sister a saucy smile. "You should have seen my costume for the Noells' masquerade." She took her sister's hand and led her to the settee with its back to the east window. "But first you must tell me how wonderful your school is."

Joanna settled in. "It's even better than I dreamed. Lady Astor is such an asset and we just hired two more instructors. Lady Elsbeth has a mind for geology and is now determined to visit Ireland to see the basalt rock columns."

To see her sister so happy with what she'd created at Silver Meadows made some of her own resentment over not inheriting the property fade away. "And what of the duke?"

"James? He's an incredible instructor, though I do think one or two of the women are a little in love with him and two others are intimidated by him. The first I can understand, but the second baffles me."

She laughed. Of course James would be intimidating. As far as she knew, he'd read every book in Christendom and even some outside it. "Joanna, your husband's knowledge can be a tad overwhelming for those of less education. I don't imagine he could be a little less, um, knowledgeable?"

"You jest."

"I do. I'm sure as your students learn more, they will feel more comfortable around him. Have you decided when you will add the focused courses yet?"

Joanna's brows lowered and her lips puckered before she responded. "I'm still putting plans together for that. I do believe that every woman wishes to learn more in a different field."

She patted her sister's hand. "Poor Jo. You'll figure it out."

"I suppose." She squinched up her face, then laughed. "What about you? You said you went to the Noells' masquerade ball. I so wished we could have arrived for that, but the school is just taking all our time and we love it." Her happy smile communicated nothing but joy. "What costume did you wear?"

She proceeded to regale her sister with the antics of the evening and the gossip that ensued the rest of the week. Though she mentioned the friar, she never admitted to going out on the terrace with him. That happening would remain between herself and Andrew, even if he didn't know it was between them.

One of the footmen arrived with a new tea service and sandwiches, and while enjoying the food, they chatted for over an hour. Afterward, Joanna decided to repair to the house to rest.

Once again alone with her thoughts, Amelia moved to her sketching table. However, moments after Joanna left, there was another knock on the door.

"You couldn't have forgotten to tell me something." She opened the door, fully expecting Joanna, only to find Andrew standing there rubbing his hands together, his breath causing small clouds of air to appear.

"I wondered if she'd planned to stay all day." He strode past her and whipped off a dark blue wool cloak. Beneath it he wore brown pantaloons and his shirt, but no cravat, waistcoat, or tailcoat.

Ignoring the heat that filled her chest and face, she closed the door and locked it. Despite having planned to pretend nothing had occurred at the masquerade ball, her anger surfaced so quickly, she had no time to hold it back. "I heard you enjoyed the ball last weekend."

He stood by the fire warming his hands, but at her words, he looked over his shoulder. "So I did. Did you?"

She set her hands to her hips, unable to refrain from voicing her irritation. "I understand you kissed someone."

At that he turned around. "How do you know that?"

She narrowed her eyes at him. "A lady in a Milliner's costume. You can't deny it."

He looked askance at her. "You did say we were not to appear to know each other well. What better way to throw off the scent of the gossips?"

"I can think of at least a dozen." She strode toward him, but two tables stood between them. "Is that the kind of loyalty I could expect in our marriage?"

His face lost all expression as he strode forward as well, stepping around the first table. "I was not aware that it would matter to you."

She wasn't aware of that either because she'd never thought seriously of marriage, except as something to avoid as long as possible. Obviously, it did matter. She lifted her chin. "And if I say it does?"

His gaze turned thoughtful as he studied her. "Then I would be loyal to you."

His capitulation stymied her. She had basically asked him not to have a mistress, which was most common, though not with her family. "Why would you be loyal to me?"

"Because you requested I be." His lips formed a soft smile. "Many a man respects a woman's virtue and would not presume otherwise, even if she be no more than a modest milliner."

As he repeated her own words from the masquerade her heart skipped a beat. "You knew it was me!"

"I did." He grinned. "But how did you see through my disguise? I thought you thought you were kissing another man. To say I was angry would be putting it politely."

An odd relief flowed through her that he'd known it was her

from the start, but he deserved to stew. "Oh, I didn't at first." She sashayed around the table in front of her, bringing them face to face. "By the way you waddled, I thought you Lord Natchet, but then you didn't have nearly enough wrinkles."

"I know naught of Lord Natchet, but not having wrinkles could still make me anyone else."

She rubbed the bottom of her chin as she looked past him at nothing in particular. "This is quite true. However, when I noticed Lord Harewood approaching and you turned in his direction, your cowl revealed your true hair color." She smiled slyly. "An artist never forgets a color."

He laughed, capturing her free hand in his. "I'm truly humbled by your powers of observation. I admit, when I discovered you had lied about your costume, I feared it would take all night to find you. But then..." He lifted her hand to his nose and inhaled, his eyes closing in what could only be considered pure happiness.

Her heart raced, and the heat she'd felt upon touching him the first time filled her.

He opened his eyes and gave her a devilish grin. "Then I smelled you, followed your scent like my best hunting dog."

She pulled her hand from his. "You found me like a dog? How terribly common." She thought his method inspired, but didn't wish him to know.

He shrugged. "As long as I found you, I did not care by which method, especially after you lied to me."

Oh, no, she would not feel guilty for that. "I only lied because you purposefully made it difficult to paint you just so you could request another boon."

He had the wherewithal to look chagrined. "You have found me out."

Feeling far lighter than she had all week, she smiled. "You are forgiven. Now, shall we get started?" She gave him a stern look. "Will you behave today, or must I expect to grant you another favor?"

He put a hand to his chest and gave a short bow. "I promise to remain quiet and still for you." He winked. "After all, I was repaid for your lie with a kiss, so I am content."

Heat suffused her cheeks, and she quickly turned away. She couldn't let her new curiosity in him sway her from her course. Soon, not only would she know what she'd been doing wrong in her paintings regarding male figures, but her fingers burned with the knowledge that she had the right subject to bring her creative talent to its peak. "I'll gather my supplies. Joanna brought me new oils, so I will practice with them today."

"Practice?"

She turned her easel around so she could view the settee. "Yes. Oils are more difficult to use because I must mix colors for those I want but don't have. Also, there will be layers of color, so I will need a bit of linseed oil to thin the paint and make everything blend correctly." She dragged her supplies table over to the easel before crossing the room and stepping behind the yellow and gold striped settee to pull the white curtains closed. Finally, she retrieved the violet silk cloth from the top of her chest which she'd originally planned for a set of pillows for her bed and draped it on the settee.

"It appears you have a particular setting in mind."

So focused on her plan for the painting, his comment startled her. She had planned to have him lean against the wall for the next painting, but that was before she'd had the oils. She was anxious to use them. When they arrived, she envisioned him lying back like Dionysus, the Greek god of wine, vegetation, festivity, fertility, and madness. She paused in pulling a new paintbrush from a drawer. Genius talent and madness were far too closely related and the path she followed now could well bring both. Shaking her head at her own whimsy, she closed the drawer and set the new brush on the clean wooden palette. She scanned all her items to make sure everything was in reach.

She looked up to give Andrew instruction, but found him sitting in the chair next to the table with the tea service. "What are you doing?"

He held up the half-eaten fruit cake. "I'm eating. You wanted me to be quiet and since you obviously have a scene for this painting in your head, I thought I'd wait for directions out of your way."

He was right, of course. She'd ignored him as if he knew what she wanted. "Thank you. When you finish, could you please remove all your clothes?"

The cake dropped back to the plate. "I thought this was practice."

"It is. I'll need to get your skin tone correct and I want to try this image first. I don't have a vision for the final painting yet. I need to see most of you."

He rose and pulled off his shirt. "You said *most* of me. What would you like me to keep covered?"

The telltale heat was back, but she forcefully ignored it. He was simply a model for a painting that she had to do correctly. He wasn't the man who kissed her the other night until she wished her clothes would fall from her body. No more than blancmange was her favorite food, which it was. "I would like you to remove all your clothes then lounge on the settee with the violet silk draped over your, umm, groin area."

Oh, horse feathers. She could feel her entire chest and face turning red. Quickly, she spun back to the canvas, having only caught a glimpse of his amused smile. She kept her back turned and focused on opening her paints and creating her palette of base colors. She didn't see a need for three of the colors at all.

"Is this what you wished for?"

She glanced up and stared, her breath catching in her throat. He sat on the settee, legs crossed at the ankles in front of him, his hands behind his head. The dark skin tone of his torso seemed to glow as it disappeared beneath the deep violet silk. His large, muscled thighs were revealed below in a far lighter shade, tiny golden hairs catching the light. His legs tapered down to where his feet were set one upon the other. She breathed in. He truly looked like a Greek statue, but alive and warm and filled with color and nuances.

She wasn't sure which excited her more, the vision he made for her painting or how she felt looking at him. Her stomach seemed to be filled with tiny fairies buzzing to and fro and a strange ache started deep inside her.

"Amelia?"

At his use of her name, she blinked as if coming from a trance. "Yes. I mean, not quite." Flustered, she moved forward, but this time, she hesitated to touch him. She swallowed hard as she tried to focus. "Could you lean against the side and bring your legs up on the settee more?"

He dropped his arms and readjusted. The violet silk fell away a bit more, revealing the crease below his hip.

She couldn't seem to take her gaze from the area. She tried to think rationally. Joanna's book was very explicit in what was beneath the cover, and she'd seen Michelangelo's David and a copy of the statue of Laocoön and his sons. But to have a living breathing male before her caused her heart to race, making her breaths shallow.

Forcefully, she turned her body away to meet his gaze "That is more what I had in mind." Unable to resist touching him, she moved closer and laid her fingers under his chin. "Tilt your head back a little as if you are being fed grapes."

His head moved, but his gaze remained on her. "Grapes?"

She lifted one shoulder. "I'm imagining Dionysus enjoying himself."

A slow smile lifted his lips before he darted his tongue out and licked them. "I can imagine that too."

Heat filled her and she quickly dropped her hand. "Good. Think of yourself as a god."

A quiet rumble sounded in his chest as if he were holding back a laugh. "Only for you."

At his words, her gaze roamed back to his and there was far more meaning in his eyes, but she didn't want to know. Instead, she touched his thigh, the heat radiating from it as hot as inside her chest.

He jerked slightly, and she pulled back as if she'd touched hot coals. "I didn't mean to make you uncomfortable."

He grasped her hand, his abdomen contracting as he held himself up. "Your touch could never make me uncomfortable." He released her. "Touch anywhere you like."

Mischief had her thinking about touching him beneath the silk, just to see how much he meant it, but she was far too much a coward. So she laid her hand against his thigh again. "Just move your leg a little to the left." As his leg pulled away from her pressure against it, she silently wished there was somewhere else she could touch, but he was exactly how she'd wanted him. "Perfect."

Quickly, before she invented an excuse to touch him further, she turned away and strode back to her easel. When she had her paintbrush in hand, she paused. He really *was* magnificent. "If you get tired, please tell me. Oil takes longer than pastels or watercolor. I may get lost in the painting and forget you need to move."

"You have had other models?" Though he spoke to the ceiling, his tone proved he didn't like the idea.

She dipped her brush into the Naples Yellow and mixed it with the Raw Umber. "Only female models and even those were very few." She started with his torso. "And only on the continent. I doubt the *ton* would appreciate my artistic efforts even with a female model." And the *ton* would surely shun her if they knew what she was about now.

Returning her gaze to him, she studied the planes of his chest. Something about it had her yearning to touch him again. Was this why male models weren't allowed for female artists? Was this longing she felt what led to a woman losing her innocence? Refocusing on the painting, she remained where she was. No matter how she felt, her goal was far different from other women. She just had to keep that in mind.

But as she began his face and mixed the perfect color for his lips, her mind drifted again. She had intimate knowledge of those lips. She knew their texture and taste. Licking her lips, she took that knowledge into account as she painted. This time, she forced herself to keep his hair short and she darkened the color at the memory of Joanna viewing her watercolor. Carefully, she changed the nose and kept him clean shaven, which he wasn't. She'd not seen any men beyond laborers and grooms with such a beard, though many of her class sported beards. As she'd touched his chin, she'd found it rough, and it caused tingles in her belly.

Moving to the violet silk, she quickly mixed her Venetian red and Indigo to her preferred color and painted it easily, but as she moved to his thighs, heat seemed to fill her. Determined, she began the long strokes that would bring his legs to life. She tried to focus on every nuance, but she wished for her fan as she wiped sweat from her brow with the back of her hand. The more strokes she made, the harder it was not to touch him.

He remained true to his word, not asking any more questions, nor moving in the slightest. He just lay there allowing her to ogle him all she wished. At that thought, she dropped her brush onto her palette. At the noise, he turned his head. "Are you finished?"

She rubbed the back of her waist with her fist and glanced at the clock. An hour and a half had passed, and he hadn't moved. Guilt filled her. Was that why his muscles seemed to stand out more. "I'm so sorry. Please be comfortable."

He sat up, the silk almost falling from his lap, but getting caught on something. He slapped his hand down to hold it in place. "I never realized how strenuous posing for a portrait could be."

"Have you not had your portrait painted?" At his age, it was common to have sat for at least two by now.

"There is one done of me when I was but four. However, my parents swore they wouldn't have another one done until I had 'settled.' At least that was the word they used."

She chuckled. "No doubt you were as talkative and active

back then as you have been for me…until today."

"I was, but more so. Did I not do well for you today?"

She had to give credit where it was due. "You were perfect today. Thank you. In fact, you are welcome to dress if you like. I believe I can finish the rest now that I have your figure."

"Really?"

She studied the canvas already noting what she'd add and the changes she'd make so it wasn't obvious it was him. "Yes, I have enough now." She looked back at him to tell him what to expect with the final painting and her words died on her lips.

He had risen, leaving the silk behind, and walked to where he'd left his clothes. His entire backside was there for her to enjoy and enjoy she did. His buttocks were far more enticing than any marble statue and her fingers itched for a completely different reason. For the first time, she wished she could sculpt. Now she was torn on what side of him would be best for her final painting…and which side she most wished to touch.

CHAPTER THIRTEEN

ANDREW PULLED ON his pantaloons first, hoping the fall would help to hide his slowly receding erection. When he'd initially agreed to pose nude for Amelia, he hadn't thought it would be an erotic experience, but lying there, knowing she was studying every part of him had been a battle for control, one he had finally lost.

He hadn't realized how dispassionate an artist could be. The night he kissed her, he'd tapped into her passion, and if he wasn't mistaken, her curiosity, one that was anxious to be satisfied. Yet today, except for a couple of blushes, she hadn't seemed to be as affected by his unclothed state as he was. Was that due to her lack of knowledge? Could it be that a female virgin, a person with no knowledge of the pleasures of the flesh, couldn't be enticed due to having never experienced pure bliss?

Sitting in the straight-backed chair, he pulled on his boots. As a young man, ignorance hadn't hindered his own randiness, but boys were raised with a different focus and with far more freedom to explore carnal relations. Perhaps Amelia just needed to learn what she was missing. He had no doubt that a fire could be lit inside her. Now to determine how to best light it.

He grabbed his shirt from the table and rose, throwing it over his head, but not bothering to button it. Glancing at Amelia, he found her focus solely on the painting of him. That she could so quickly become engrossed in something other than himself caused an odd sort of jealousy to creep into his mood. It made no sense since the painting was of him, but he couldn't shake it. Stepping between the furniture, he came up behind her to view her work, taking in her unique scent of violets. He frowned. It was him, but not him. The man had dark hair on his head and chest, a different nose, and a sharper chin. "Who is that?"

"Oh." She started as if she hadn't heard his heeled boots as he'd moved behind her. She didn't turn to look at him, but instead stared at the man on the settee in her painting. "It's you, but modified to look like someone else." She finally looked back at him. "When my sister was in here, she found the watercolor and recognized you. I told her I used your profile, but the body was from a sketchbook she'd given me." She looked back at the painting. "I didn't want to risk anyone thinking you might be coming here."

Though he didn't want her to lose her reputation either, a part of him resented that they needed to hide their relationship so thoroughly. It was her blasted bargain that he agreed to that forced the secrecy. He still understood why, but he found that now he wished to tell the world that she was his and be done with all the subterfuge. "If I'm your model and to be presented with the final product, I expect it will actually be of me." He hadn't meant to sound so stern, but at her wide eyes as she snapped her head around to look at him, she'd obviously noticed.

"Are you expecting to instruct me on what to paint?"

At her bristling tone, it was obvious she didn't like that idea at all. "I would not be so bold. I have a good eye for art, but no talent in the creation of it."

That appeased her, her blue eyes seeming to darken as she set down her paintbrush and turned her body to face him. "I couldn't imagine being happy not being able to paint, no matter how poorly."

He'd never told anyone how it felt, but looking into her sympathetic gaze, he was sure she would understand. "Nor could I. I did make more than one attempt. More than a dozen if I'm to be truthful. All were harder to look upon than not painting at all. It is frustrating beyond the telling to see a vision in your mind and not be able to create it."

"Perhaps that was your difficulty. I can see the whole painting, but I must have pieces of it in front of me. When I try to sketch from memory, everything goes wrong. Terribly wrong. But when I have something in front of me..." her lips formed a small smirk. "Like a bowl of fruit, then I can capture every nuance and shadow."

He appreciated her reference, and it did help take the sting from his failure. "I tried a bowl of fruit, a dog, a fire, a sunset, a curtain, a chair—"

"A chair?" Her brows rose, but her smile still played about the corners of her lips.

"Well, it was a rather ornate chair." Grinning now, he appreciated her humor. He liked that she found amusement in the smallest of things. "Alas, even the chair failed me. That is why I turned to collecting great art. I feel I can appreciate what goes into its creation more than some others."

"Just some? I'd say you can appreciate it at a level very few achieve. Your eye is excellent."

Pride filled him that she thought so highly of him. "What about you? You obviously have talent." He motioned toward the oil on her easel. "What drives you to paint?"

Her brows lowered. "At first, while small, it was a way to distinguish myself from my sisters. As the youngest, they all wished to baby me."

"And you didn't welcome that?"

"Absolutely not." She set her hands on her hips and lifted her chin. "I wanted to be their age, though I was so much younger. My mother encouraged me as she used to paint, so I was indulged, but I never felt I truly had talent until my Aunt Mabry."

He remembered her mentioning her relative before. "She's the one with whom you traveled to Europe."

"Yes. Joanna used to read to her, which actually helped her to sleep. She was supposed to travel with Aunt Mabry to Europe, but the Christmas before they were due to leave, I did a painting of Aunt Mabry's dog."

He couldn't help smirking. "Her dog?"

She wagged her finger at him. "She loved that dog. Bushel was his name. Or maybe Peck. I can't remember. The point was, she loved that dog and when she opened my gift she was stunned. At first, I was afraid I had created such a horrendous likeness that she was appalled, but it wasn't that at all."

An unreasonable pride swelled in his chest. "She was stunned by how well it was done."

"Yes." She smiled at the memory, a true smile with no amusement in it, and it was breathtaking. "She said I had talent, and determined at that very moment that I must accompany her to Europe."

"How did the Duchess feel about that?"

"Duchess? Oh, Joanna. She was relieved. She and Aunt Mabry had very opposite views on everything." She leaned in closer. "To be honest, Joanna would rather have her nose buried in a book about the great colosseum than actually visit it."

"Blasphemy." He grasped his chest as if appalled and widened his eyes.

She chuckled. "My feeling as well."

He dropped his hands, a new understanding about her growing. "You say it makes you happy. So will you always paint?"

A sadness filled her eyes and she looked away. "I had thought so, but it cannot be."

Confused, he placed his fingers under her chin and turned her face toward his. "Why?"

Still, she didn't look at him, but her right shoulder lifted before dropping. "It's of no consequence."

"Amelia, look at me." He had to know what had changed for her.

She finally lifted her gaze to meet his. Resignation seemed to radiate from her eyes. "Aunt Mabry had promised that when she passed, I would inherit Silver Meadows, her estate. She said there were only two roads for a woman of my standing. I could either be wealthy in my own right and pursue my painting to my heart's content or follow my mother's path and marry and give up my art to be a lady of a household."

Knowing that she had agreed to marry him if he posed for her, his stomach clenched at what that meant, but he needed her to tell him. "But you didn't inherit Silver Meadows, did you?"

This time, she turned away from him and lifted her paintbrush. "No. Aunt Mabry left it to Joanna. She felt Joanna had become so unmarriageable that she needed it more. So I may never know what I'm capable of as an artist."

She dipped her paintbrush into the black, mixing it with some of the linseed oil then stroked the color into his hair on the painting, which in his opinion did not make it better.

He felt dismissed, as if she didn't wish to talk to him, but he recognized her action for what it was, self-preservation. Dwelling on the past was painful, so she turned to what gave her joy to assuage her hurt. He wanted her to know that he could be a source of comfort as well. If he could somehow help her be at peace with her decision to marry him, then—suddenly the pieces fell into place. She wanted one more chance to paint before taking on the duties of a wife. But he had to be sure.

Laying a hand on the bare skin between her neck and shoulder, he leaned in. "Why did you want me as the subject of your artwork?"

He felt more than heard the intake of her breath as she reacted to his touch, but she continued to add to the painting.

"If you must know, I think that you could be what I need to create a masterpiece."

Stunned, he didn't move. Him? In a masterpiece? He studied her profile, looking for any hint of a smile, some sign that she jested, but there was none. "Many great artists don't reach the pinnacle of their talent until they are older."

"I know."

When she didn't elaborate, understanding dawned. She didn't look to him for comfort. He was her source of hope. The realization struck him to the core. The responsibility of that place in her life was immense, and yet he was honored with her profound trust that his presence could bring forth her greatest work.

Not knowing what to say, he stroked his hand down her back to the top of her pale green dress and kissed the base of her neck.

"What are you doing?" Though she tried to sound authoritative, her words came out in a breathy release.

He lifted his head to whisper in her ear. "I'm touching you."

"Oh."

When she didn't continue, he resumed by kissing the outside of her ear, then below it toward the violet scent emanating from her. He couldn't resist kissing her neck where a satin ribbon, the color of her dress, encircled her throat. He followed it to the back of her nape where wisps of her soft hair tickled his nose.

Her head lowered as if she wished for more, but he wanted to be sure. Once again, he whispered in her ear. "Do you like my touch?"

"I do."

The words were almost too soft to hear, but they were clear. Kissing the nape of her neck yet again, he moved his hand over the bow tied at the top of her dress, and pulled one end.

Her intake of breath was the only reaction, so he fingered the remaining knot, leaving the ribbons hanging and her bare skin visible. Desire shot through him at the unusual occurrence. Where were her stays and shift?

He stroked one hand down her back, pushing aside the material. As the dress fell away, he let his kisses follow. The softness of her skin and the warmth of her body were far too enticing to stop. When he reached her narrow waist, he could no longer resist, and pulled his shirt over his head once again. He straightened and wrapped one arm around her waist, pulling her back tight against his chest.

She melted into him, and her head fell back against his cheek.

He breathed deeply into her hair. On his exhale, he spoke. "You're perfect."

Her body stiffened. "Far from perfect, you mean."

Nuzzling her neck, he wholeheartedly disagreed, but arguing with her about something so obvious wasn't what he wished to do at the moment. "I want to touch you everywhere."

Above his arm, he felt her heart beating quickly. Her own excitement fueled his forwardness. "Would you like that?"

"I don't know."

Her honesty helped him remember she was yet untouched. "Why do you not wear a shift beneath your dress?" It was quite scandalous and not something he'd thought she'd do, though he was pleased at the outcome.

Her right shoulder came up. "I spilled watercolor on my last clean one and had my maid wash it. I was not planning to see anyone today."

He smiled. "Then I am twice as glad I was able to sneak away." Still holding her close, he used his free hand to lower her sleeve, causing her front neckline to hang loosely from her. From his view over her shoulder, her pert breast was clearly visible, though in the shadow of the dress.

He moved his hand from her arm to her collarbone, tracing it with his fingers.

She turned her head and her lips found his own neck, causing a shiver to race through him. "You smell of leather and pine."

She was too observant by half. "And you smell of violets and your skin is softer than rose petals." He let his hand lower as he spoke until he cupped her fine breast. It filled his palm perfectly.

Her hand came up over her dress, imprisoning his beneath it. "You shouldn't."

She was right, he shouldn't. "I know. But I want to feel you more than I want to breathe."

She tilted her head to catch his gaze. "And will you hold your breath until you can?" The teasing light in her eyes made it clear she thought he exaggerated. Little did she understand her allure to him.

"I will, if I need to." He didn't mask the need in his gaze, letting her see exactly how much he wanted her.

Her smile faltered. "Far be it for me to withhold life-sustaining air from you." That she still managed a coherent thought meant he had not stoked her desire enough yet. Something he needed to remedy.

She dropped her hand to the side, giving him free access to her.

If she couldn't feel his heart pounding against her back before, she had to now, for he was finding her capitulation far more intoxicating than he'd expected. Free now to move his hand, he brushed his finger over her bare nipple.

"Oh, my."

Her whispered exclamation was all he needed to continue his quest. Once again, he brushed her nipple with his thumb, its taught peak hard and round. Unable to resist, he rolled it between his thumb and forefinger.

She moaned, her head falling back against his shoulder.

How he wanted to taste her. His erection jerked in his pantaloons at the thought, pressing into her lower back, and her head came up.

Before she could ask any questions, he pulled his hand from her dress, turned her in his arms and kissed her.

He stifled a groan at her sweet taste. But when she lifted her arms around his neck and explored his mouth with her tongue, he growled deep in his throat. Instead of scaring her, it seemed to excite her, and she pressed her body against his.

He forced himself to allow her to learn, holding himself back even as she took it upon herself to suck on his tongue. Despite his best intentions, one hand slipped beneath her dress to cup her bare arse cheek, the round softness of it fueling his desire.

They had to stop.

He didn't want to.

Her hands rifled through his hair, holding his head captive, before she nibbled at his lips then placed kisses along his jaw, against his neck, and on his chest. If she moved to his own nipples, he'd be lost. Gently, he cupped her chin and tipped her head to gaze into eyes the color of bluebells. And how long had it been since they'd seen bluebells? The odd thought recalled him to his purpose. "I must leave now."

Myriad emotions passed over her face, from disappointment to irritation to resignation. Yet, she gave him a crooked smile. "Afraid of me?"

He grinned. "Very afraid. You could easily lead me astray."

She gave a soft chuckle. "Just call me Delilah."

"No. You are and will always be Amelia, beautiful, talented, kind, and provocatively passionate."

Heat rose in her cheeks. She lowered her head, but then looked up at him through her lashes and pushed him away. "Begone." She waved her hand toward the door, her head rising in haughtiness. "I'm done with you, footman." When she brought her hand down, her dress slipped, and she snatched it to her.

He laughed. "Would you like me to serve as maid before I go?"

"Please." She turned her back to him, and he forced himself to tie her dress once more. When he finished, he stepped back quickly, fixing his own attire.

"Will you return tomorrow?" She stood with her hands clasped, giving him an enigmatic look.

She never asked when he would come again. "Doubtful, but soon, I hope. Most likely not before the Enderlys' Christmastide Ball. I understand they open the seasonal festivities here in Bedford. Sunnydale Manor has been cleaned from the ground floor to the attic."

"That's still four days away."

At her disappointed tone, his hope rose. Could she perhaps be feeling something for him now? "I know, but I doubt I'll be able to slip out. Lady Garmoyle is my biggest concern and both Harewood and I are unsure of what she might do. She always finds a reason to be with one of us. Luckily, Lady Enderly asked for her assistance in choosing decorations and they went into the village today."

"Of course. I understand. It's just that I hoped…"

She turned away, moving to the window farthest from him and looking outside.

"You hoped what?"

Her shoulder came up in her usual shrug. "I just wished to start the next painting." She turned to face him, a smile on her face, but not one that reached her eyes. "I'm sure you have many people to make happy while visiting. I won't expect you until after the ball."

She'd withdrawn from him and it bothered him, but there was little he could do about it now. Glancing behind her, he could see the day was waning and he hadn't brought Leonardo, not wanting him to stand in the frigid cold for the entire day.

How had she gone from passionate to teasing to polite within minutes? Not seeing any way to reverse her mood, he wound his way back to the door and pulled the borrowed cloak from its hook.

"Don't forget at the Enderlys', we must appear to have no more than a passing acquaintance."

Her distant tone and reminder chaffed at him, but he nodded in acknowledgement. "Until then." Moving to the door, he reached for the handle.

"Andrew?"

At her use of his given name, he halted, and turned toward her. "Yes."

She smiled. "Thank you. For everything today."

The mischief was back in her gaze and his own quick reaction surprised even him. He smirked. "It was my pleasure." Wiggling his brows, he turned and left, an odd relief and hope causing him to walk much faster.

The woman's mercurial moods were difficult to follow. Was that because she was an artist, or because she was beginning to mean more to him than he expected? It was a question he wrangled with all the way back to Sunnydale Manor.

CHAPTER FOURTEEN

MARIEL HANDED HER a cup of eggnog. "You must be thirsty after four dances in a row."

Amelia accepted it gratefully and sat in the chair next to her sister, which was located against the far wall. Mariel looked particularly beautiful in a bronze dress that made her chestnut hair almost shimmer and gave a healthy glow to her face. "Why don't you dance?"

Her sister grimaced. "I'm far too old and in no mood to entertain suitors. I've already been married. I have no plans to do so again. Lord Beaumont provided well for me after he died."

Amelia rolled her eyes. "Only because Joanna negotiated the marriage contract." She paused before patting her sister's hand. "Was it awfully dull, being his wife?" She never talked with Mariel about her marriage because Mariel didn't broach the subject, but now Amelia found she had hundreds of questions.

"Oh, no, not dull at all. It was a very large household to run, plus the London house, and he liked to rent a place in Bath. I do believe I spent most of my time planning the next move."

That wasn't exactly what she meant. "But what about conversing with old Beaumont or having dinner alone together?"

Mariel's whole demeanor changed, her back suddenly ramrod straight. "It was like most other marriages, I'm sure. I listened politely and agreed with all he said. We rarely ate alone as there was always someone to be entertained, mostly his peers. When we weren't entertaining, he often went to Brooks's and was home after I retired." She smiled kindly. "I suppose that would sound dull to you."

She shook her head, though in fact it did sound rather dull. "I think I'd rather that than the conversations in Joanna's home. All that reading and debating." She rolled her eyes. "Now that would be dull."

"Shh." Mariel scanned the area. "Don't let Father hear you say that." The gleam in her eyes made it clear she jested.

"Now that you mention father, where are our parents?" She studied the room, not willing to acknowledge she knew exactly where Andrew was, but not her parents. He had danced two dances so far. One with Rose Enderly and another with a young woman who had blonde hair and rosy cheeks, based on how many times she blushed in his presence. Why would he want to dance with her? She didn't like it.

"There they are." Mariel motioned with her head. "See, next to the entrance of the room. My guess is Father will make an excuse soon to go to the Enderlys' library."

She found her father right where Mariel said he was. "Oh yes. Notice how he takes another step closer to the archway?"

Mariel laughed. "Mother noticed, too. Don't think she patted his arm because of something he said. That's definitely a warning to stay in the company longer."

Her sister was right. Her parents had developed a silent communication over the years. Would she and Andrew have something similar? It was too difficult to imagine. When she was a child, she imagined it quite well, but as a grown woman with the promise of personal wealth and no need to marry, she'd stopped thinking of it. Then when that wealth was taken away, she'd focused only on one goal, her masterpiece.

She couldn't have explained if asked, but her instinct told her she was about to achieve her goal. And then—

"How is the painting progressing?" Mariel's voice had lowered, which brought her out of her musings.

"I'm very pleased with it." She thought about trying to explain how she felt, but decided against it. Mariel couldn't understand. Neither could Joanna or even her mother. The only one who might understand was Andrew. A wave of quiet happiness flooded her. Yes, he might well understand.

"Lady Amelia, I did not see you over here with your comely sister." Andrew stepped up and nodded to each of them. "Lady Beaumont, you are looking lovely this evening."

Her sister stiffened, but as usual was polite. "Thank you, Lord Sommerset. Are you enjoying your stay here at Sunnydale?"

"I am. It had been years since I was here last, and I didn't realize how much I missed Lord and Lady Enderly until I returned."

Movement behind Andrew caused her to look past him. Lady Garmoyle was headed their way. "Not to interrupt, but I do believe Lady Garmoyle is making her way over here. You may want to find Lord Harewood." That would also, hopefully, eliminate the chances of having to talk to the woman.

He didn't turn, but he definitely stiffened. Did Mariel notice?

"Actually, Lady Amelia, I was hoping I could have this next dance."

She stared at him in shock. They were to pretend only a minor acquaintance. Simply him coming over to talk to her could cause comment in their village, but a dance was out of the question.

"I believe that an excellent idea."

Mariel's comment had her whipping her gaze to her sister. "You do?"

Her sister nodded, her stern gaze brooking no argument.

Of course, to refuse would cause much more gossip. She didn't like being manipulated when they had an agreement. She returned her attention to him and politely smiled. "Of course. It would be an honor." She rose, not unaware that Lady Garmoyle had paused and was engaged in conversation by another guest.

Andrew held out his arm, and she set her hand on it as they walked to the center of the room where other dancers had lined up to dance the Quadrille. At least it wasn't a waltz. He walked her to her place, then stood opposite her in line with the other men.

As the dance began, she curtsied, he bowed, and they began the pattern. She had to wait until they came side-by-side before she could express her displeasure. "This is not what we agreed to."

He leaned his head in, keeping his voice low. "One dance will not set tongues wagging. To not dance with an eligible Mabry would cause far more curiosity."

They separated, turning to others. She smiled politely as was expected. If that was his reasoning, he'd best dance with more eligible women. Though that also unsettled her. When they came together again, she looked at him to express that exact thought, when he caught her gaze with his own and a new vision burst upon her.

The acropolis. He needed to be standing on the acropolis, not a god, but a hero, a champion. Her fingers moved of their own accord. She could see it!

"Am I right?" He raised his brows.

With the vision before her, she simply nodded, no longer caring what they conversed about.

He looked forward again. "Try not to step on Lord Ravenshire's toes."

His warning forced her to focus on what she did as he left her side again. She kept her smile on Lord Ravenshire but itched to tell Andrew that she knew what the painting would look like. Why did she have to see it in the middle of the night, in the middle of a dance?

Finally, they came together again. As he placed her hand on his arm she squeezed, but kept looking forward as required. "I saw it. The painting."

"You did? Now?" His voice sounded as breathless as she felt.

"Yes." She smiled widely, caring not if people thought she was in love or some silly notion like that. She just had to share this with him. "You will be standing, powerful, triumphant." As she said the words, she saw a lion standing with him. "With an animal."

He leaned in. "A dog?"

She breathed out. "A lion."

She felt his arm beneath her hand jerk before he spoke. "Yes, next to me."

It wasn't the words, but how he said them, that told her he saw the vision too. She looked at him. "I want to start now."

They broke apart again, but she didn't feel that they were apart. She could feel his presence even when not looking at him. It was a strange sensation, but a pleasant one.

Finally, the dance ended, and she curtsied.

As he led her back to her sister, she cocked her head to look at him. "Is tomorrow possible?"

He met her gaze with a smile. "I hope so."

When they reached Mariel, they found her frowning. She immediately sat next to her sister. "What is it?"

Mariel shook her head. "I fear our sister is going to make a scene."

"What?" She looked in the direction her sister faced and grinned. The music had started up again and Joanna's skirts were moving as she obviously tapped her toe beneath them. That was a sure sign she'd be dancing soon. "It's hardly a scandal for a married couple to dance."

Mariel continued to frown. "No, but it's not appropriate when so many young couples are present and the dance floor is limited."

She glanced at Andrew, who grimaced.

When had Mariel become such an old woman? She was barely twenty-six. Amelia turned to say just that when she caught sight of Lady Garmoyle approaching. "If you really want someone to frown about, take a look." She nodded toward the woman making straight for them.

Andrew immediately bowed to her. "Lady Amelia, it was a pleasure. Lady Beaumont." With that he turned and disappeared into the crowd.

She wished she could do the same, but it was no longer possible as the lady in question bore down upon them.

"There you are." The unwelcome woman stopped, slightly out of breath.

"Good evening, Lady Garmoyle. It is a pleasure to see you again." She smiled sweetly, not sure if the woman had been looking for her or Mariel.

"Hmph, you could have seen me earlier, but you have been dancing most every dance."

"I do love to dance."

At the woman's scowl, Mariel broke in. "Were you looking for us for a reason?"

The woman's face changed from irritated to friendly in an instant, causing the hair on the back of Amelia's neck to rise. "Yes, I was. Dear Lady Enderly tasked me with asking Lady Amelia to take a few moments, if she would, to look at a painting in the library. Lady Enderly says it has become scratched, and she was wondering if it could be repaired."

That was odd. Lady Enderly had not mentioned it to her. "I'm sure I would be happy to take a look, though I have little experience with art repair."

Lady Garmoyle smiled. "Wonderful."

Mariel, always her champion, couldn't let her comment go. "Amelia is far too modest. She is truly talented and if anyone can repair the painting, I'm sure it is her. I have a beautiful painting she created for me of my horse. Do you enjoy art?"

Lady Garmoyle fidgeted with her skirts. "Not particularly. I only offered to take care of this task because Lady Enderly worried she'd forget with so much to do in preparation for the ball. I do want to please my hostess."

Feeling the necessity of adding to the conversation, she lied.

"How nice of you."

"Yes, well, I do wish to be helpful. Shall we?"

Surprised, she lifted her brows. "Now? In the middle of the ball?"

"If you would? I'd like to let Lady Enderly know the outcome tonight."

She glanced at her sister then lifted her shoulder. "Very well." Rising, she was just in time to hear a waltz called and glanced across the room. Joanna eagerly spoke to her husband, if her gesturing hands meant anything. When he gave a short nod, the two turned toward the room.

Grinning, she looked at Mariel. "Be prepared to be scandalized."

"What?" Lady Garmoyle's eyes rounded. "Why?"

She waved the lady off. "Nothing. It was a private conversation I had with my sister."

"Very well." Lady Garmoyle began moving through the crowd, looking to see if she followed every few steps.

The Enderlys were circumspect in their invitation list, so there were enough guests to make the event a success, but not so many that it was difficult to move about or sit for the midnight meal. In no time, they had reached the large opening of the ballroom.

"You know where the library is, correct? I only ask because your mother is such a good friend to Lucinda."

She blinked at what she was sure was a slight sneer, but Lady Garmoyle smiled at her as if it was wonderful that the two women were friends. "Are you not coming to the library?"

"I would very much like to, but I have two more tasks I need to complete." The lady's smile widened. "As soon as I finish those, I can then enjoy the evening."

Understanding how much went into the evening and how Lady Enderly must be pleased by Lady Garmoyle's help, she nodded. "Don't let me keep you then. I will take a look and find you later."

The woman waved her hand. "Don't worry. I'll find you." Then she turned on her heel and scurried back into the ballroom.

There was something about lady Garmoyle that reminded her of a mouse, but she couldn't quite figure out what it was. Not wanting to miss another dance, she started down the corridor toward the library. All the doors had been thrown open and each room decorated for the season. Candles burned brightly, inviting guests to mill about, but the library doors were closed.

She smirked. Lord Enderly did not open his library to female activity very often. No doubt that was why the room's double doors were not open and welcoming like the rest of the house.

Turning the knob of one, she strode in. "Oh, I didn't realize you were in here."

———

He should ask another lady to dance, but after Amelia's revelation regarding the painting, Andrew didn't wish to converse with anyone else. She said he'd be standing and looking powerful. With a lion? The image in his mind had him straightening his shoulders. He could see himself standing next to a fountain with water coming from a statue of a lion. Or did she mean a live animal? Maybe standing in a garden with a lion lying before him?

He fervently wished to discuss her vision for the final painting, but he needed to avoid her for the rest of the evening. He didn't want to. His body tensed and he examined why. It wasn't that she had been dancing with other men. He felt no jealousy at all. He was well aware that her interest in men was not strong. Then why did he wish to monopolize her time?

The answer was so obvious he almost missed it, and when he caught it, he smiled.

He loved her.

The irony was not lost on him. He'd set out to have her fall in love with him and instead, she'd captured his heart. That had to be what the warm feeling in his chest was. He'd like to ask Harewood for his opinion, but the man had never loved anything beyond his first puppy. He scanned the room, curious about which couples were in love and which were simply married.

At that moment, the Duke and Duchess of Northwick swept by in each other's arms, twirling in time to the waltz, completely oblivious to everyone else. *That.* That was two people in love, but he could hardly ask Amelia's sister about such a private matter. As the couple continued to circle the dance floor, he became aware of discussions growing quieter. Most everyone in the room watched the duke and duchess. Did the guests understand why they stared? His instinct told him not many did.

He took the opportunity to meander his way around to where Lady Wakefield, Lady Enderly, and Harewood stood, also watching. Lady Wakefield had her hands clasped to her chest, her eyes shimmering with unshed tears. He was no expert, but he could tell they were tears of happiness. He reached into his waistcoat and pulled out a handkerchief. "My lady?" He held it out to her.

She moved her gaze to his. "Oh, thank you." Dabbing her eyes, she returned to watching her daughter until the dance ended. Finally, she turned back and handed him his handkerchief. "I know it's silly, but we never expected Joanna to wed. To see her so happy and in love just fills my heart." She blinked rapidly as if to stop her eyes from welling up. "Now to see if my Amelia can find her happiness too."

Lady Enderly looked pointedly at Harewood.

He stiffened. "Do not look at me, Mother. We've discussed this."

Andrew frowned at Harewood. "Discussed what?"

Lady Enderly didn't wait. "It has been a dream of mine to have my son marry one of the Mabry sisters."

Surprised, he stared at his friend. Why hadn't Harewood told him that? Was that why he suggested Lady Amelia, so he wouldn't be pushed into marriage?

Harewood's face grew taught with tension, a small tick beneath his ear, proving he wasn't happy. "We all know that. However, Lady Amelia is not…"

At Harewood's hesitation, he found himself ready to defend her. "She's not what?"

Lady Wakefield laid her hand on his arm. "She's not Belinda."

Belinda? Harewood had loved Amelia's late sister? When? How? And how come he'd never said anything?

Harewood's gaze raised to scan the ballroom. "It was a long time ago. I was barely out of leading strings. Just a child."

Lady Wakefield smiled sadly. "A child with very good instincts."

So that was why. It was before he'd met Harewood, and not one to share his feelings, he'd never mentioned it. Was it hard for him to be around the family?

"Well, I do so want to have grandchildren before I'm bedridden." Lady Enderly gave a heartfelt sigh.

Harewood returned his gaze to his mother. "I'm sure Rose will be happy to provide you with some."

Andrew glanced toward the dance floor, where Lady Rose participated in the Quadrille. When he turned back to the group, he found Lady Enderly studying him speculatively.

"Lord Sommerset, you have known Rose all her life."

"No." Harewood's emphatic statement had them all staring at him.

Lady Enderly appeared exasperated with her son. "Why did you say that?"

"Lord Sommerset is not interested in Rose's hand in marriage. I do not want to ever have to decide between my good friend and my sister."

That Harewood would be torn in loyalties between himself and Lady Rose was a revelation, and he was humbled.

Before Lady Enderly could react to such a forward statement, a footman approached Harewood, handing him a note. Harewood opened it. "It appears my father would like my opinion to settle a debate going on in the library." He gave a short bow. "If you will excuse me."

"Tell your father if he wants to debate to wait until after

dinner." Lady Enderly waited for an acknowledging nod, before she turned back to them. "I do so wish that he could find a woman to marry. But I fear no one will want him."

Lady Wakefield patted Lady Enderly's arm. "If Joanna can find someone, there is definitely hope for your son. He is intelligent, handsome, and the heir to your estate. Just be patient." Lady Wakefield turned to him. "Will you be staying in Bedford for Christmas?"

"I'm afraid I must leave before then. My brother will be home from Oxford and my mother is expecting me. I invited Lord Harewood to join me."

Lady Enderly raised her eyebrow. "Do you have a sister? Any neighboring young ladies that might find him of interest?"

He laughed. He hadn't realized exactly how desperate Harewood's mother was to have him wed. "I do not have a sister, but yes, there are a number of young ladies in the area. I will caution that he has already met a few of them."

Lady Enderly waved her hand as if that was of no import. "Then it's time he became reacquainted. I will suggest he spend the rest of the festive season with your family. I have no doubt that my husband will—"

"I'm sorry to interrupt." Lady Garmoyle appeared suddenly.

How had he not noticed her approach?

"What is it, dear?" Lady Enderly immediately focused on Lady Garmoyle.

Lady Garmoyle wrung her hands and looked at each of them worriedly before finally returning her attention to their hostess. "I think perhaps you'd best see." She looked at them again. "All of you."

Immediately, a fission of worry slid up his spine. As they followed the woman out, he scanned the ballroom for Amelia. She wasn't dancing, and he didn't see her. Hoping she'd gone to the ladies' retiring room, he followed, trying to figure out what was afoot and how to intervene. If Lady Garmoyle was involved, it could be life changing for any of them.

They stopped at the library doors where the lady turned to look at them. "This is rather shocking, so prepare yourselves." Then with a flourish, she opened the two doors upon which, they viewed Harewood and Lady Amelia talking.

At first, he didn't understand why there was a problem and then he did, his heart hammering inside his chest. No!

Lady Enderly broke the stunned silence. "Felton! What are you doing in here alone with Lady Amelia?"

The two, who had stopped their conversation to look at them, both frowned.

He glanced at Lady Garmoyle's smug expression and knew. Whipping his gaze to Amelia, he found amusement shining in her eyes. How could she find this funny? Did she not realize she'd be forced to marry Harewood? He wouldn't allow it.

Lady Amelia nodded to Harewood, who held out his palm to her in deference. Finally, she addressed them. "Why would you think, two intelligent, unmarried people would be alone in the library?" Her gaze lit on Lady Garmoyle and turned calculating.

Lady Garmoyle straightened. "Because you are." She gestured to the rest of them. "We are all witness." The woman's gaze shifted to Harewood, and she no longer hid her gleeful triumph. She didn't even know she'd harmed them both in the process.

Amelia's eyes sparkled with humor. "My dear, lady. We are hardly alone. Right, Father?"

"That is correct." The creak of leather came from one of the wingback chairs next to the fireplace as Lord Wakefield rose and faced them all.

Andrew had never been so relieved that Amelia's father enjoyed books more than people. Profound relief swept through him, and he took a deep breath to restore his equilibrium. The urge to ask for Amelia's hand in marriage in front of everyone right then was too strong to deny, and he opened his mouth to do so, but a niggling doubt had him staying silent. What if she refused him? If she was fully invested in their bargain, she may well do so, and they were so close to completing it.

Wakefield walked over to where his daughter stood and pointed at Lady Garmoyle. "This woman, if the conversation of my daughter and Lord Harewood is to be believed, arranged this to trap Lord Harewood into marriage with my daughter in revenge for the lord having foiled her attempt to trap another man in marriage to her."

He could keep silent any longer. He stepped forth. "This is true. I was the man she attempted to trap into marriage, but I was fortunate enough to have Lord Harewood walking in the garden with her mother at the time. Despite having found a husband, she is bent upon revenge."

Lady Enderly turned to look at Lady Garmoyle. "Is this true?"

The woman refused to admit the truth. "I'm completely flummoxed that they could think so ill of me. Yes, I was in the garden with Lord Sommerset a couple years ago, but I only went out there because I knew my mother and Lord Harewood were there too."

Anger burned its way up his spine that she could look so wounded when she knew she lied. He glanced to Amelia, thankful that she was nothing like Lady Garmoyle, and found her smiling.

She linked her arm around her father's. "Then why did you enter this room with all these people in attendance," Amelia gestured to all of them, "as if we had been caught unchaperoned?"

The lady lifted both her hands in supplication. "I only did so because I knew you had come in here and when I noticed Lord Harewood slip in, too, I thought that he was interested in you. Lady Enderly had always hoped that would be the case. So I thought if she were to see that Lord Harewood already had affections for you, she would be pleased."

Andrew couldn't stay silent any longer. "And how did you know that Lady Amelia was in here?"

Before the woman could answer, Amelia spoke. "She told me

that Lady Enderly wanted me to look at a painting in here that was in need of repair. She insisted I do so immediately."

Lady Enderly frowned. "There is no painting in here in need of repair."

He addressed Harewood next. "And you said you needed to come in here to settle a debate your father was having." He looked about. "I don't see your father."

Harewood lifted his chin. "My father was not in here when I arrived."

The plan became clear to Andrew. "And I will guess that if we find the footman who gave you the note and ask him who it came from, he will point to Lady Garmoyle."

Clearly caught now, the woman started to cry to Lady Enderly. "I admit I did arrange this assignation. I only hoped to please you."

Lady Wakefield, silent until now, stepped around Lady Enderly to confront Lady Garmoyle. "You would trap my daughter into a marriage she didn't want to satisfy your own thirst for revenge? My daughter? An artistic genius who needs time to produce her best work with which to grace mankind? Do you understand how petty and small your motivation is, and how large the ramifications your scheming could have had?" The woman's voice had risen to such a fury that they all stared.

Andrew could feel Lady Wakefield's need to strike out at Lady Garmoyle and was both pleased and concerned. He strode to her and stepped between the two women. "My lady, I fear that one of such small mind cannot appreciate your anger."

Lady Wakefield finally looked at him and took a deep breath. "You are correct. Thank you, Lord Sommerset. I will simply let it be known among the *ton* that this personage is not welcome among those of us with higher breeding."

Lady Garmoyle gasped as Lady Wakefield gave her the cut direct and gracefully walked to where her husband stood with her daughter. "I believe it is time we returned to Thornwood."

"Louisa." Lady Enderly stepped forward as the three headed

for the door, her worry over her lifelong friendship clear for all to see.

He doubted that their friendship was over. Lady Wakefield was simply in a pique. "She will reflect and come to understand that it was not your fault."

At his words, Lady Enderly turned to look at him, but her gaze went past him where Lady Garmoyle stood. "You are no longer welcome here or anywhere my family resides. You are a viper." With that, she turned to him, her usual calm friendliness back in place. "If you would be so good as to escort me back to the ballroom?"

He held out his arm. "It would give me the utmost pleasure."

"Come along, Felton. I don't want you left alone with anyone this night."

Harewood gave her a formal bow and followed them out of the room.

As they moved toward the entry of the ballroom, a footman was sent for the butler and soon Lady Enderly had given directions for the removal of Lady Garmoyle by morning. His pleasure that he would no longer need to worry about the woman bent on revenge was cut short upon re-entering the ball. There were still hours to go and the one woman he wished to be with had left, but to keep up appearances, he must attend to a few more ladies.

Tomorrow. He promised himself that tomorrow would be the end to the subterfuge. He would convince Amelia they could no longer wait. It was time to finish the final painting and be formally betrothed. Already, he could imagine the pleasure on his mother's face when he told her he'd be getting married and that there would be a winter wedding.

CHAPTER FIFTEEN

AMELIA STARED AT the dark clouds and overcast skies. She'd come out to her studio early, anxious to plan the perfect painting. She could feel it in her soul, but then the footman had brought out her breakfast with a request from her mother to come back to the house due to the weather. She'd sent back a note saying she couldn't. She just hoped her mother understood that she needed to paint today.

She scanned the fields that bordered the forest between Sunnydale and Thornwood, knowing in her head that Andrew probably wouldn't come today, but in her heart still hoping he would. It had been pelting hail since breakfast and three hours later the ground looked like an ice sculpture.

She finally turned away from the window and went back to her sketch. It lay on top of old sketches she'd done of the acropolis years ago. She'd decided on the exact angle and where Andrew would be. The Parthenon would rise above him on his left and a clear blue sky would fill the upper right. He needed to be painted in the sun, despite the weather. Could she do a general sketch of him in the center?

She picked up her brown pastel that was almost gone. She should use another color, but it just felt right and allowed her strokes to flow. Pulling another sketch she'd done of Andrew, she drew the rough outline of him looking forward. Shuffling through her sketches, she found the one of him without his shirt, but he faced the wrong way, his torso twisted. Frustrated, she dropped the pastel on the table. She was wasting her time.

Rising from her stool, she stalked to the fireplace, adding another log to the fire. She definitely didn't want to go back to the house while hail continued to come down. Glancing out the window again, she frowned. It looked like it had turned to rain. That was a hopeful sight as it might melt the coating of ice on the ground, but she was still in no hurry to go out in it.

What could she use to sketch Andrew's body when she'd not seen it in the position she wanted? This was her downfall as an artist and one of the reasons she could never be a master. She always had to have her object or person in front of her, or at least a sketch or painting of her subject. Now, she was right back to her old frustration of not being able to paint the male body as—

Her gaze fell upon her chest. "Of course." Striding over to it, she unlocked it and grabbed Joanna's book on *The Illustrated Pleasures of Seduction*. Bringing it to the table, she unclasped the lock and opened it.

It opened not to the page she needed, but to a different page where a man sat upon a straight-backed chair and the woman straddled him. She'd viewed the image before, but this time as she stared at it, she could see Andrew sitting there. His mouth on her breast as the man's was in the sketch. Her belly tensed as something tightened between her thighs. The woman's back was arched, her head back while the man gripped her buttocks.

Not comfortable with how her body reacted, she flipped the pages, but another sketch caught her eye. The man stood behind the woman, his arse tense, his thigh muscles clearly outlined as a line indicated he pressed the woman against a wall. The three-quarter view, revealed one of his hands grasped her breast while the other wrapped around her abdomen, her leg lifting slightly.

She slammed the book closed, her heart suddenly racing and her breathing shallow. Had she caught a fever coming out in the bitter cold? She felt her cheek with her palm. It was warm, but not hot. Was it the book? She stared at the book that she'd deemed so helpful. She rifled through her sketches on the table until she pulled out the one she'd done of Michelangelo's *David*. Looking at it, her body did not react. Because there was no woman?

Ever since Andrew's last visit, her skin seemed over-sensitized from his caresses, so much so that she'd changed her dress for the ball last night three times. If he affected her in this way, then it might interfere with her painting…or did it help? Pulling out the oil that was him, yet not him, she studied it. She wasn't fond of it because it didn't look like Andrew, but she couldn't help noticing how perfectly she'd captured his body, his expression, and his position. She'd completed it after he'd left, after he'd touched her so intimately. Was that the key to unlocking him in a painting? Feeling him and being touched by him?

She shook her head at such fanciful notions. Purposefully, she sat on her stool and opened the book from the beginning, flipping over the dedication page to the images of the nude man and nude woman on each facing page. She paused, waiting to see if her body heated. When it didn't, she let out a breath. "Good."

Though she hadn't seen Andrew in this particular position, from what she'd seen, he was more muscular, broader, and a lot more attractive. Still, the sketch could help her place him in the setting and set the perspective correctly. Picking up the pastel, she began to sketch again. As she worked, she could almost see Andrew standing there and the form began to look more like him than the book image. Happy with what she had so far, she was ready for the lion. Standing, she stretched her back then returned to her chest. She had a few sketches of lions she could use to determine the perfect position.

Lifting out a stack of animal sketches, she brought them back to her table when a knock sounded. Her heart skipped a beat, and she ran to the door. It couldn't be him, but hope rose hard.

Throwing open the door, she gazed upon a very wet Andrew. "Oh, no. Hurry, come in and warm yourself by the fire."

He stepped inside and whipped off the dark blue cloak, sending cold droplets everywhere, before hanging it on a hook. The water immediately began to pool beneath it. "I must have slipped and fallen at least a dozen times. It's like a frozen lake that's been flooded with water out there. I'm soaked through."

She stilled. His white shirt was plastered to his chest and his wheat-colored pantaloons accentuated each nuance of his thighs. As the implications of his condition finally registered, her heart clenched. He could take a chill! "Take your clothes off."

He looked at her and grinned. "As you wish, my lady."

She ignored his grin, her worry crawling up her back like a monkey she'd seen at the Tower of London who'd crawled up a visitor. "You're going to become ill if you don't take them off right now and go stand by the fire." She turned away from him to search for something he could dry himself with. She'd brought the purple silk back to the house, but she'd worn a shawl under her own cloak two days ago. Quickly, she strode to the armchair in the far corner and pulled the soft shawl from its back.

Turning toward the fireplace, she opened her mouth and froze. Andrew stood before the fire naked, bent over, shaking out his hair, water hissing as it hit the hot grate. Then he lifted his head and laid his hands on the mantel. The view of his wet backside had her crumpling the shawl in her hands. Heat as hot as any fire filled her, but she couldn't look away. He was magnificent in a predatory animal way. The realization was validation for her vision of his painting.

Finally, moving forward, she held out the shawl. "This might help with drying off."

As he looked over his shoulder, his whole body shivered once. "Thank you. I didn't realize how cold I was until I came inside here." He took the shawl and began wiping his arms when he suddenly sneezed.

"Oh, no." Her chest tightened with fear. The sound of his sneeze echoed the one which had initially separated she and Belinda when Belinda had taken ill. Her heart pounded. She didn't want him to die. Spinning around, she strode back to the entrance and pulled her warm, dry cloak from the hook. It had a few droplets from Andrew's, but otherwise it was dry. She returned to him to find him drying the calf of one leg, by resting his foot upon the straight back chair. Though she could see part of him beneath his thigh, she resolutely raised her gaze. The man could be dying. It was not time to ogle him. "Here." She held out the cloak, turning her face away to give him privacy.

"What is this?"

"It's a dry wool cloak to put about you and help you warm. I don't fancy marrying a corpse."

His soft chuckle was his only response before the cloak lifted from her hand.

"I'm covered. You can look. What do you think? Does it suit me?"

She turned her head, her tension leaving for a moment as she laughed. "You look like a wolf in sheep's clothing."

He wiggled his brows. "Perhaps I am."

Relief filled her that he hadn't sneezed again or coughed yet. "Now sit while I heat the tea again. You need something warm inside you, so you don't take a chill or worse."

"What could be worse? Dying in your arms would be a happy way to leave this earth."

She spun on him. "Don't! Just don't." She swallowed hard, her fear gaining ground inside her.

He was halfway to sitting, but at her outburst, he rose again and stepped forward, clasping her shoulders. "What is it? Tell me." His brown eyes searched hers, concern etched in his brow.

Angry, and not knowing why, she tersely complied. "Belinda came home chilled, then sneezed. She was immediately separated from the rest of us. She had contracted scarlet fever."

His hand cupped her chin. "I promise you; I will not die of this blasted cold."

She grabbed his hand and yanked it down. "You can't promise that. Mother promised that Belinda would recover. Joanna promised to get her better, but she died anyway." She expected him to argue with her, prepared to make her point.

He dropped his hands. "You're right. I'd best get warm as quickly as possible. I don't want to miss being married to you."

At his words, her heart filled and relief flooded her. "Thank you." He truly wanted to be married to her, the painter, the least perfect daughter. She didn't understand it, but it filled her with anticipation to be his wife. Quickly, she poured the remaining tea from the silver setting into the hearth teapot and set it over the fire. Then she added more coal to make the single room warmer.

"Come here."

Though it sounded like a command, his statement was softly spoken. She brushed her hands against her painting apron and stood before him.

He pulled one of her hands and guided her onto his lap. "This warms me. Having you with me."

She smirked. "More like *on* you."

His brown eyes seemed to darken at her words. "Yes. I want you on me. I also want you under me and next to me."

His words brought the sketches in the book to life, and she clasped her hands, staring at them as her cheeks heated. She didn't know how to respond.

"Will you kiss me again?" His voice seemed lower, more like when he'd dressed as the friar. "That will warm me more than wool or tea or the fire."

She turned her head to face him. Licking her lips, she stared at his. She'd liked how it felt to kiss him. She also liked touching him, and to be fair, she liked how he had touched her. If they were married, she'd be his, but he'd also be hers. Wrapping her arms around his neck, she kept her gaze on his lips. They were like hers but different, not as full or as soft. Lowering her head, she tentatively touched his. They were just as she remembered. She increased the pressure of the kiss and his lips opened.

Unable to resist, she slipped her tongue between them and tasted him. It felt like coming home. The texture and taste familiar yet a little different, a touch of cognac on her tongue. He allowed her the pleasure of exploring and she grasped his hair in one hand, tilting her mouth more, wanting to get closer somehow.

His tongue thrust forward into her mouth and his arms grasped her harder. The titillating pleasure she'd felt with her kiss transformed to spiking excitement, as if a kitten changed into a lion. Her toes curled and heat swept through her, her limbs weakening. It wasn't enough.

Suddenly, he broke the kiss and held her away from him. "We can't."

"We can't?" Still reeling from the feelings he'd brought out in her, she shook her head, acknowledging he was right. "No, we can't."

His breaths were as shallow as hers. "Not yet."

Something bumped against her arse and she jumped up. "What's that?" She stared at his lap, the cloak now having a bump in it.

He chuckled. "That is me, or rather what you do to me."

Drawings in *The Illustrated Pleasures of Seduction* came to mind. Most had the man and woman hip to hip, but she remembered one that showed that man's part not small like Michelangelo's *David,* but stiff and long and straight. Her gaze flew back to his lap, then she spun on her heel and grasped the table with the silver tea service. Flustered, she grabbed a teacup and lifted the kettle from the fireplace hob. "You need to warm up." She poured the tea into the cup. Adding sugar and milk, though she didn't know how he took his tea, she stirred it.

"I believe I'm quite warm."

She lifted the cup to give it to him and stilled. He'd risen, no longer wearing the cloak, but had her shawl wrapped around his hips.

"I believe we have a painting to be completed, correct?"

She stared at his body, his wide shoulders tapering down to his hips, his mounded chest fading into the ripples of his abdomen, his muscular thighs beneath her shawl tapering to equally muscular calves and then back up. "Beautiful." The word slipped from her lips without thought. She blinked. "I mean you will make a beautiful painting." She finally met his gaze, a soft smile having formed on his lips.

"Only because you can paint it. I'd say we are a good pair."

She swallowed. What he meant was a good pair now in her studio and soon in life. The prospect of marrying him no longer seemed frightening. Maybe because she knew this painting would be what she hoped or maybe because she could imagine living with him, having breakfast with him, even sharing a bed with him. The images calmed her.

"Have you decided how you want me to sit for this one?"

His return to their purpose had her handing him the cup. "Yes, but I insist you drink some of this before we start. I can show you the sketch I was working on."

He took the teacup with no argument, and obediently sipped.

She rolled her eyes at his action and moved over to her sketching table.

"What kind of book is this?" He reached past her as they came to the table and lifted *The Pleasures of Seduction*, setting his teacup on the stool.

Horsefeathers, she'd forgotten it was on the table. She held out her hand. "It's a book of sketches that I've used to figure out the male body. I've had trouble with it in the past, having never had a willing male model before."

The book had closed as he lifted it, but now he opened it. His eyes widened and his brows rose. Then a slow, seductive smile formed on his face as his gaze left the pages to meet hers. "Are these the types of images you were hoping to paint?"

She couldn't see what page he opened to until he tipped the book so she could see a woman on all fours and a man behind her. The heat that rushed to her face was almost unbearable and she looked away. "I only use the front figure."

He tilted the book back to turn the page and then the next,

obviously enjoying each image.

Mortified, she stood absolutely still. But soon it was clear he teased her, each facial expression becoming more exaggerated than the last as he viewed another page. Shaking her head, she turned away and pulled the sketch from the table. "If you want to see my plan for your painting, you'll have to put that book down." She strolled toward her easel where a blank canvas awaited her.

"Perhaps I could take it back with me and study it further." His silent approach on bare feet startled her, as well as his breath brushing the back of her neck.

"No. It's not my book." She raised her hand to forestall him though he remained behind her. "And no, I will not tell you whose book it is." She held the sketch against her chest. "Now, do you wish to see how you will need to stand for this painting?"

"I do." His tone had changed from teasing to serious, so she spared a look over her shoulder. He had stepped back to allow her to present her idea.

Her excitement over her vision returned and she set the small sketch in front of the canvas. Her heart thudded in her chest with anticipation as she stepped aside to allow him to view it.

He walked forward. "This is the Parthenon." He pointed to the columns in the upper left corner.

"Yes." Impatiently, she kept silent as he studied it.

"The composition is well designed. What will be here?" He pointed to the blank space in the lower right.

"That will be the lion I mentioned at the Enderlys' ball last night. He'll be standing next to you, your hand resting on his back."

He moved his gaze from the sketch to her, his eyes almost glowing. "I'll look like an ancient Greek hero."

She smiled, pleased that he could see what she sought to convey.

"It's brilliant."

His praised filled her heart. "Then you agree this is it?"

He nodded, but stopped. "You *will* paint me to look like me."

"Oh, yes. This is the painting that you can decide if you would like to own."

"You mean that we would like to own."

At the reminder that this would be her final painting before marriage had her stomach tightening. "Of course." She took a deep breath in an effort to accept that hard fact. "This way we can have something to remember my painting as the go years by."

"Amelia, why do you say that?" He stepped closer, making it a little hard to ignore the expanse of his bare chest.

She shrugged her shoulder. "I know I won't be able to paint once we are married, but as long as I have my one masterpiece, I will be satisfied." She gave him a weak smile. "I just hope this painting results in the vision I have in my head."

He frowned and took her hand. "Why do you think you cannot paint once we are married? I fully expected you to continue painting."

She blinked, trying to comprehend what he said. "But I'll have a household to run, parties to plan, children to scold, and wifely duties to attend to. How can I paint?"

"I admit that all you mention is indeed part of marrying me, especially those wifely duties." He wiggled his brows.

She rolled her eyes, but couldn't help smiling, especially when her body seemed to be excited about those.

"But if we must have fewer visitors so you may have time to paint, I'm happy to make that concession. Painting is part of who you are and I—like who you are. I want my children to not only respect their mother but also be proud that she has such talent."

Her eyes welled up and she couldn't speak, her throat having closed. She'd never considered she could be married and paint. Her mother hadn't. Yet here was the Golden Adonis offering her the dream she'd always had along with himself as well. She wiped her eyes with the back of her hand and took a deep breath. "I never thought…I mean I never expected…" She gave up and threw herself into his arms. "Thank you."

✦

CHAPTER SIXTEEN

ANDREW HELD AMELIA to him, his own heart full that such a small gesture could mean so much to her. He liked making her happy. He wanted to make her happy for the rest of her life. He knew, deep in his soul, that he loved her. Maybe, this small act would allow her to open her heart to him. Her reaction earlier to his wet condition gave him hope that she already cared a little. He breathed deeply, and the scent of violets filled his senses as the woman in his arms warmed his heart.

Eventually, she pulled back, and he loosened his hold though he didn't let her go. "I will always strive to make you happy."

She didn't meet his gaze, but a light flush filled her cheeks. "I would also like to make you happy." A slow smirk formed on her face and as she looked into his eyes, her own twinkled. "But first I must paint to make us both happy."

"Yes, of course. I must pose as a Greek hero." He lifted his chin and looked off to the corner as if he were Theseus triumphant over the Minotaur.

"Um, yes, but for me to paint, you do need to release me."

He frowned as if confused, then pulled her closer and gave her a thorough kiss. When he was sure she wasn't thinking about painting him so much as kissing him, he let her go. Her slight stumble pleased his male ego. "Now, where do you want me?"

She took a minute to refocus her gaze then moved past him.

"Over there. I will consider the edge of the window frame the final column of the Parthenon. For a lion…" She looked about before dragging the straight-backed chair over. "Come here. Face the easel and rest your hand on the back of the chair." She grinned. "We'll consider this the back of the lion."

He strode to where she stood and did as she asked.

She walked back to the easel, her pale blue skirts beneath her painting apron, swishing against the stool. Turning the easel around so she could paint and face him, she stepped to the side of it and stared at him, her brows lowered. Finally, she shook her head. "That's not right." Scanning her studio, she stopped at her sketch table. "This might help though." She dragged her stool from her table over to him and pushed the chair out of the way.

She stepped back a few feet. "Lay your hand on the stool. Good." She walked back to her easel once more. Her brows knit then she shook her head. "No, it's not right."

Again she came toward him. He waited, curious what she would do next. He didn't have long to wait.

Her hands came up to the front of his shoulders, their softness against his skin hard to ignore. She added pressure to his right shoulder, and he gave into it. When she didn't immediately pull her hands away, he looked at her to find her studying his chest. Blast, if she kept that up, things would get uncomfortable fast. He took an extra deep breath, forcing his chest to rise.

She jumped back, her cheeks turning rosy with her blush, but she remained focused on her task. "That's better. I want you facing me but with a very slight angle as if you have just halted."

Again she returned to her easel, but didn't even look at him before taking up her paintbrush and adding a few strokes to the canvas. Then she finally took another glance. Once again, she halted, her nose squinching up as she studied him.

He held back a chuckle. She reminded him of a five-year-old who had just been told she must eat boiled turnips.

"Oh, of course." She gestured toward him with her brush. "Please take off the shawl. That is why nothing seems right."

Despite knowing she wished to paint him nude, he didn't think she'd actually do so, especially after seeing how she'd done the sketch from the questionable book she used. "Are you sure?"

"Yes. Sometimes sacrifices must be made for art." She dipped her brush into a color on her palette and returned her attention to the painting.

Sacrifices? He hoped she did not mean that it was a chore to have to look at him while unclothed. He didn't plan to make love to her any other way. Untying the knot he'd made at his waist, he dropped the shawl on the table. Despite how cold it was outside, the warmth of the room made it comfortable.

Returning his arms to her preferred position, he waited for her to turn back, hoping her face wouldn't scrunch up again. He'd never thought about how he looked to women without his clothes since he'd never heard any complaints. But now, he was more than curious how his bride-to-be would react to his nude body. After what seemed like an hour, but was most likely only minutes, her gaze returned to him.

He remained completely still as her focus went straight to his pelvis. If her parted lips and faster breaths were any indication, she was not afraid or horrified by what she saw. He had to ask. "Did that help?"

Her gaze snapped to his. "Uh, yes. Yes, it does help." Then as if remembering she was supposed to be painting him, she scanned his whole body. "Maybe turn your head just slightly to the right."

He turned his head, but didn't like the position because it made it harder to see her.

"No, not that far. Face me more."

That was better. It was easier to see her, but her brows were lowered again.

"No, no." She set down her brush and moved forward. When she reached him, she laid her hands on either side of his face and moved his head.

Unfortunately, her skirts brushed against him, causing his body to react.

Her hands then lowered to his waist. "And twist just a bit, no, that's far enough."

He felt himself growing hard. He doubted that was what she wished to paint. Since she had only seen unaroused men in statue form, he doubted she'd thought of how her touch affected him, that was, if she even knew that it affected him. He grasped her hands as they moved over his stomach. "Perhaps you should just tell me what you want."

"But it's easier if I put you in position."

He closed his eyes for a moment, trying to control his body's reaction, but even though he didn't see her, he felt her hands, inhaled her scent, and heard her voice. He opened his eyes and stared into her curious blue gaze. There would be no hiding his attraction to her. Hoping it wouldn't scare her away, he stopped fighting it. "Amelia, when you touch me, you arouse me."

Her confusion remained for a moment before she looked down between their bodies and her eyes widened. She took a step back and he let her go. "I didn't know, I mean, I didn't think, I…does it hurt?"

As she stared at him, he grew harder, making it difficult to answer without laughing. "No, it doesn't hurt. It is simply my body's way of getting ready to make love to you."

Her gaze finally snapped up and her cheeks, neck, and chest turned a rosy red. She clasped her hands over her chest. "I'm sorry. I didn't realize."

It was obvious she didn't know how to proceed. "May I suggest that you return to the easel and try to capture as much of your vision as possible? There is a chance that my body will return to normal if you are out of reach."

She took a couple more steps back and bumped into her sketching table. "Yes, yes, of course." She turned and hid behind her easel, no paintbrush or palette in her hand.

He gave her a few moments to regain her composure, but he'd need more time than that. If this wasn't so important to her, he'd get dressed and end their time together. She was so very tempting, but he would not take her until they were officially wed.

When minutes went by and she still hadn't moved, worry started to gnaw at his confidence. "I think you'll need your paintbrush to continue."

One hand reached out and grabbed the palette with the paintbrush from the nearby table and pulled it behind the painting. Though he couldn't see her, her skirts were visible, and they moved, proving she'd started to paint again.

Letting out a breath, he focused on his position. Finding that too easy to do, he thought about his estate, the books, his tenants, his mother, anything but the woman painting him. He did well, his body relaxing again until she spoke.

"Stop frowning. You're supposed to be triumphant."

At her voice, he moved his gaze to find her hand with the paintbrush on her hip and her gaze on his face. "What are you thinking that you scowl so?"

His last thought had been about how his tenants were making it through the winter, which brought to mind his temporary financial difficulties, not something he wished to discuss quite yet. He'd save that for after they were betrothed, so he could explain in detail what his situation was. "I'm thinking about too much, obviously." He cast about for something that would make him frown. "Last night, when I thought you would be forced into marriage with Harewood, is definitely worth frowning about."

She lifted the paintbrush and waved it back and forth. "That was never a possibility. First, I was suspicious of Lady Garmoyle saying Lady Enderly wanted me to examine a damaged painting when my expertise is in painting or authenticating. The woman always consults me when it comes to art. So I checked the library as soon as I entered to see if anyone was there, and I found my father. He often sneaks away when attending a ball there."

Pleased that she had good instincts, he wanted to know more. "So what were you and Harewood discussing when we all walked in?"

She grinned. "We were deducing that Lady Garmoyle had planned for us to be trapped into marriage in order for her revenge to be complete against Harewood. My only question was if it was luck or planned that I be involved in an effort to hurt you too."

He shook his head. "No, she never knew I visited you."

"Never? Does that mean she has left?"

"Yes. I did not leave Sunnydale until after her carriage was out of sight. We had to wait for the hail to cease before she was willing to travel. Though I will say no one was pleased about her delay except Lady Rose. She did not understand that Lady Garmoyle's friendship was only a ruse to reside close enough to exact revenge upon Harewood and myself."

Amelia shook her head even as she moved back behind the painting. "Poor Lady Rose. She is such a sweet woman, but I fear her mother has not taught her nearly enough. I wish Joanna could convince Lady Enderly to send Lady Rose to her school."

Surprised by Amelia's comment, he had to ask, though he knew she wouldn't want him to move now that she was back to painting. "Your sister runs a school?"

She poked her head out from behind the easel. "That's a secret. Please do not tell anyone. She wants to see if it can be successful first."

"I promise not to say a word." Though why a ladies' finishing school would be a secret, he wasn't sure. As his mind wandered to other things, he was able to be still and quiet for almost an hour, but eventually his thoughts returned to Amelia. Questions like, would one of their children have her talent came to mind. He hoped so. Would she like living at Lyonsmere? It had a similar Greek inspired temple on the grounds, but much closer to the house. Would she like him to turn that into her studio? Or would she prefer a room in the house? He'd prefer she was closer, so he could interrupt when he wished. Would she enjoy being his wife and those wifely duties?

From her responses to his touch at their last rendezvous, she might. Her skin was so soft and her breasts the perfect size. Not only was her scent enchanting, but the taste of her had him craving her far beyond what was acceptable in their current relationship. He wanted her to be his. Now.

At the sound of her clearing her throat, he moved his head to look at her.

She pointed with her paintbrush, an amused smile tilting her lips upward. "You're growing again."

Blast, he'd forgotten. "I can't help it. I was thinking of you."

"I'm not sure if that's good." She set her brush on her palette and put it on the table, her hand reaching behind her to rub her back.

He relaxed his stance. "It's very good. It means I find you tempting."

She let her gaze flow over his body, making him harder. "I find you tempting as well. I'm glad that I don't have a body part that makes it so obvious." Her amused smile was back in place.

Was she laughing at the state of men? Her ignorance was a reminder that he would be her only lover and that just caused him to want her more. "Since we are resting at the moment, you are welcome to touch me if you wish."

Her smile faltered, but she didn't shake her head. Instead, she moved closer. "Anywhere?"

Damnation, his balls tightened at the insinuation in her voice. He swallowed hard to clear his throat. "I told you once before you can touch me anywhere you like."

The mischief in her gaze had him wondering if he should rescind his invitation, but he couldn't back down now. He wanted her to be comfortable with him.

She sashayed toward him like a much more experienced woman than what he knew her to be. Her tongue came out and she licked her lips. "And can I touch you how you touched me last we painted?"

His groin reacted even as his heart pounded in his chest. The woman was a natural vixen. "Is that what you want to do?" His voice came out raspy, and he cleared his throat.

She scanned his body again as if deciding where to touch first. "Yes, that's what I want to do." She spoke to his chest, not his face.

He swallowed hard as he thought back on how he'd touched her. At least his hands had never travelled up her skirts. He stilled as he remembered they actually had, but only to cup her perfect buttocks. Would she remember? "Then you are welcome to do so."

At his answer, she lifted her gaze to him, and a sly smile formed on her lips. The look alone sent his blood racing. Blast, how did he get himself into such a situation, standing naked in a room alone with his intended, allowing her to touch him as she wished?

Her hands lifted and settled on his shoulders. Like any true artist, she explored his shoulders with each hand, pressing, smoothing, lightly touching as if she were blind and learning what he looked like. She ran her fingertips across his collar bone, just as he had done to her before her hands found his chest muscles. As her finger tips brushed his nipples, he sucked in his breath. It was as if she remembered every movement he made.

He steeled himself for what came next, but it didn't help as she rolled his nipples. There was something far too erotic with standing still and letting her do as she pleased. But as her fingers trailed downward over his abdomen, he caught her wrists. "I did not take such liberties of you."

She looked away a moment. He could almost imagine her thoughts, thinking of a way around the parameters he'd set, which were essentially none until now. She returned her gaze to him. "If I allow you to reciprocate, may I continue?"

His erection jerked, and he barely stifled a groan. He played with fire and if he wasn't careful, they'd both go up in flames. But even as he wrestled with his morals, his body refused to listen to reason. "Agreed." He released her hands to see if she would indeed go farther.

She held them before her, not moving, except her gaze, which ran down his chest to his pelvis. Finally, coming to some kind of decision, she placed her hands on his abdomen, smoothing them over the ripples of his stomach. Her touch was not light, nor was it hard. It was as if she stroked a lion, wanting to caress but not wanting to be turned upon.

As her hands moved lower, he held his breath, still not believing she would actually handle him, still hoping her maiden shyness would rear up, but his hopes were dashed as one hand grasped him. He let out his breath in a quiet whoosh and closed his eyes. Her touch was curious as her hand moved from his base to his tip in innocence. When she gave his head the same inspection she'd given his shoulders, he gritted his teeth. The pleasure-pain of holding back was strong.

Just when he thought he'd have to stop her, she stepped away.

"I do not think you are a typical man."

At her words, he snapped his eyes open, his curiosity as aroused as his body. Despite that, he could only manage one word. "Why?"

She turned away and strode back toward her easel, though he hadn't missed her flushed appearance. Pleased that she had been affected by touching him, he grabbed the shawl and wrapped it about his hips, but he was far too sensitized and pulled it off.

Glancing her way, he found her painting. His heart still raced from their intimate encounter, and she was painting? Needing to cool off, he contemplated going outside, but after her reaction to him being wet, he simply strode to where his cloak hung and stood against it. It was the only item of clothing that still held the cold and damp, since the others were quickly drying by the fire, where he'd left them.

He imagined the icy puddles he'd fallen in on the way to Thornwood. Then he thought of his mother and her frail grasp of her new life. Finally, he thought of Lady Garmoyle as she grinned in what she thought was her most triumphant moment. Each vision helped him relax as long as he didn't look at Amelia. When he had himself somewhat under control, he strode to the fire where he pulled on his pantaloons and quickly buttoned the placket.

Turning back to see what his betrothed did, he found her still painting, as if inspired. That hadn't been what he'd expected from allowing her to touch him. Doubt crept in that perhaps her flush was not because she felt sexual excitement when she'd touched him, but artistic excitement. Scowling at the possibility, he stealthily slipped behind her to see what she worked on. Any hurt ego evaporated as he stared at the painting.

She'd replicated him on canvas, not just a perfect copy, but with his personality somehow coming through. He shook his head. That was impossible, but the more he stared, the more convinced he became. She had his full naked body exactly as he was, including the small birthmarks on his left forearm and thigh. She even painted the scar on his shin from when he'd fallen down the garden steps at the age of five. And unlike the classic statues of ancient Greece and Rome, she'd painted him in full arousal.

He wrapped his arms around her waist, and she started as if she'd forgotten he was in the room. "That's me." It was probably the weakest thing he could have said.

"I know." She looked back at him with a beaming smile. "It's you, not just your appearance, but who you are. I captured you. At least, I think I did."

His chest tightened. She'd captured him more than she knew. "You did. It's not just like looking in a mirror, it's like knowing that's me, the person."

She nodded, her gaze softening. "You bring out the best of my skill."

As he looked into her eyes, he felt it. A mystic moment, far beyond the skill of any man or woman. Gently, he turned her to face him and cupped her cheek with one hand. "You are mystic."

Her eyes widened briefly before her smile of agreement lit her face, and he kissed her.

He let his love lead the kiss, gently inviting her to melt into him, to be of one heart.

As she did, the paintbrush fell to the floor and her arms wrapped around his neck. She pressed herself against him, her breasts in her fine cotton dress heating his bare chest even as her mouth melded to his.

Somehow, she had become the center of his life. Now, he wanted to be the center of hers. Holding her close as he teased her tongue, he stepped back, bringing her with him until his calves hit the settee. His hand found the ties at the back of her calamine blue dress and loosened them. She wore her stays and shift beneath, but he didn't let it deter him. Bringing her pleasure beyond anything she'd ever known was his goal and he'd not be thwarted.

CHAPTER SEVENTEEN

AMELIA DIDN'T KNOW if the feelings flowing through her were triumph or desire. Andrew was more than she'd expected and what he made her feel both excited her and scared her, but she was beyond caring now. She'd achieved success and now she wanted to celebrate…with him, the man who had made her dream come true.

At the loosening of her garment, she grew anxious to remove it and broke their kiss. His eyes seemed to shimmer with gold, his gaze filled with desire. Her heart hitched at his intensity and her body warmed, her skin too sensitive now to bear the weight of her dress any longer. "Off." It was the only word she could form as she lifted her arms in the air.

As if intuitively understanding, he pulled her dress over her head and removed her stays, leaving her in her shift as he laid the garments carefully over the wingback chair nearby. When he turned back to her, his gaze swept over her and his pantaloons revealed a bulge.

The feelings inside her were chaotic, bumping into each other like marbles in a glass bowl. Caring, desire, fear, triumph, excitement, happiness, all collided against each other. Yet as she searched her heart, the pillow that laid them all to rest was trust. She trusted Andrew. He would keep her safe.

He moved forward, reminding her of the lion she had yet to

add to the painting, but she wasn't afraid. His gaze met hers and a secret smile played about his lips. "I can bring you pure bliss if you will allow it."

His request melted any concerns lingering in the back of her mind, and her nipples tightened as if they knew they were meant for him. Now, she wanted him to feel her, all of her this time. The realization was strange, but true. He was her muse and would soon be her husband. That thought didn't strike fear into her anymore. Now...now she found herself anxious to have him for always. As if all worries had been lifted from her, she smiled shyly. "I would like that very much."

He stepped up to her, taking her hand and guiding her to the settee. As they sat, he whispered in her ear. "I will make you feel wonder and ecstasy."

His breath against her ear sent excited shivers down her spine. "Yes." She let her head fall back, giving herself to him.

His kisses started then, on her neck, her collarbone. Her shift loosened and his kisses moved lower.

Heat built between her thighs as she anticipated his next kiss. Then his mouth found her breast and she grabbed his hair, arching into him. "*Yes.*" He lowered her back on the settee, his mouth only leaving her to pay attention to her other breast. She couldn't breathe deeply, and she didn't care. She felt like Ruebens' painting of Leda and the Swan, honored to be worshipped and pleasured by a god.

She moved her hands from his hair to his back, his muscles moving beneath her fingers as she stroked the strength of him. When his teeth nibbled at her sensitive peak, she moaned, pressing her pelvis against the bulge in his pantaloons. A fire raged inside her and only he could quench it. "Andrew."

His mouth left her and he looked into her eyes. "Yes. What can I do?"

She didn't know. "I just want...I need." She searched her mind, not sure how to explain the deep urge in the core of her. Then a word from *The Illustrated Pleasures of Seduction* flashed through her mind. "Satisfaction."

His nostrils flared and his body stiffened as if made of marble. "And you shall have it."

A shrill pang of desire zigzagged from her core to her chest at his words, but she had little time to worry as his mouth returned to her breast and his hand burrowed beneath her shift.

Instinctively, she moved her leg off the settee, giving him the access he needed. Images from the book flashed through her mind. Knowing he would penetrate her had her heart jumping.

"You don't need to search for it. Just let it happen." His breath against her taught peak built the tension between her legs, yet she lowered her hips, trusting him.

His hand soothed as he moved up her leg and through the curls at the apex of her thighs.

She stopped breathing at the anticipation of his next touch.

He raised his head. "Breathe, Amelia. Breathe."

She forced a breath inward even as he moved himself above her. As his mouth descended onto hers, his fingers touched her.

Hot need spiked where he touched, and she sucked on his tongue in response as he played about her, sending spikes of pleasure shooting through her, spiraling her higher toward an unknown feeling.

Just when she thought she'd leave her very plane of existence, his fingers delved inside her and she burst with joy. She cried out in pleasure, his mouth taking he sound, even as she bucked against his fingers, her world exploding into tiny pieces. The happiness coursed through her, shattering her thoughts, and taking her into bliss.

At some point, she must have closed her eyes because as her world righted itself, she opened them to see him smiling down at her. There was an emotion in his eyes she'd never seen before on him, but in the back of her mind she was sure she'd seen it before, somewhere.

"Are you happy?"

His question made her think. She wanted to stretch like a cat, walk about without clothes, run her hands over all of him. "Yes, I'm happy." Another thought interrupted her contentment. "Am I ruined?"

His lips twitched. "Perhaps your innocence, but no, you are not ruined. I will not take you until we are wed. I value you too much."

The sentiment filled her heart even as his word "take" sent a thrill to her core. Now that she knew how it would feel, she found herself anxious for the wedding. How odd, that she, who had no time to think of marriage, suddenly wanted it with the same eagerness as painting her masterpiece. She touched his face. "I'll look forward to that."

His smile turned to a grimace and his body stiffened against her.

"What is it?"

"It is nothing." He pulled himself off her.

She missed having him against her, but she sat up, concerned, pulling her shift up onto her shoulders and tying it. "No, it's something." She stepped up behind him and wrapped her arms about his waist, pressing her face to his bare back. "Tell me." His chuckle reverberated against her cheek, and she lifted her head.

He unclasped her arms and faced her, taking her hands in his. "That satisfaction I gave you, I did not participate in, and so it is..." he looked away. "I cannot explain it right now."

Not satisfied? There was something in her sister's book about a man who does not find his release. It obviously made Andrew uncomfortable, so she'd look it up when he wasn't present. Instead of asking more, she squeezed his hands. "Are you able to help me with my dress?"

He nodded, letting go of her hands to fetch it for her.

Her gaze fell to his backside, the memory of what it looked like bare causing the tingles she'd felt earlier to resurface. She had to admit, she enjoyed looking at him. To be honest, she also enjoyed touching him.

He brought her clothing. After tying her stays, he lifted her dress. "Arms up."

Dutifully, she raised her arms and her day dress fell into place. It was a little wrinkled, but that always happened when she worked in her studio.

"Turn around."

She did as he commanded, and he tied up the back. When he finished, she turned to face him again, but he was already lifting his own shirt over his head. A sense of disappointment swept through her. She was beginning to prefer him naked. Would he undress for her more once they married? She found herself wishing she'd added that to her counterproposal.

Smiling to herself, she moved to the painting where she could view him sans clothes. Once again, she felt as if his image was alive. "This truly is amazing." She lifted her hands and looked at them. "I have no idea how I accomplished this. Or even how I knew you would make this happen."

Fully dressed now, he came to stand next to her. "You were able to do it because you have a gift." He smirked. "And you had such a willing model."

She chuckled. "I would have said challenging model, but be that as it may, the combination melded into something beyond us, I think."

She stood silent next to her artwork and looked up at him. The sense of pride on his face filled her with pleasure right down to her toes. Finally, he spoke. "Do you have enough to finish it?"

"I do." She pointed to her table of sketches where her sister's book also lay, closed now. "I have sketched the Parthenon and lions from the Tower of London. I imagine I can have it finished in a couple of days. You inspired me. I've never done a human figure in just an hour."

He stepped away. "Then I shall view the final piece when I return."

"Return?" Her heart leapt. "Are you leaving?"

"I must return to Lyonsmere Hall to spend Christmas with my mother and brother. Lord Harewood plans to join me. I also need to take care of some business at home. But I will return in the new year."

In her enjoyment of his company, she'd completely forgotten about his family. Of course he would return to them for the last of the season. That was only a fortnight away, yet her disappointment was real. She would miss him. "The painting will be complete by then. You can decide if you wish it to grace the halls of Lyonsmere."

His eyebrows rose. "I doubt very much that the halls would be the place for it, but perhaps my bedroom…or yours."

She smiled. "Oh, definitely mine."

Her answer appeared to please him as his face had taken on the triumphant look of his painting. "I must leave you now, but I promise I will call upon you as soon as I return to Sunnydale."

She stiffened, but then relaxed. There was no longer a need to hide their alliance. "I think I will miss having you to myself here." She gestured to the room.

He stepped up to her. "Soon, you will have me all the time. I have a feeling you will be telling me to go away."

She laughed, finding it hard to imagine such a scenario. "I suppose."

He pulled her into his arms. "Now give me a kiss to remember me by and keep me warm on my travels."

Happily, she looped her arms around his neck, pressed her body close and lifted her face to his. As his lips descended, she opened to him and tangled her tongue with his. In an instant, the fairies in her stomach started to dance and her heart started to race. She moved one hand down and cupped his buttock and squeezed.

He broke the kiss, his breathing rapid. "You're a vixen."

She shrugged one shoulder. "You said you wanted to remember it."

His laughter filled the room. "So I did and so I will." He dropped his arms and moved to the door.

She couldn't seem to make her legs move, so she watched as

he donned his coat. Then as he stepped toward the exit, she flew across the room to stop in front of him. "Do take care and don't grow ill on me."

"I promise to do everything in my power to return to you whole and hardy." He wiggled his brow. "I have much motivation to do so."

She rolled her eyes, but heat rushed to her cheeks, nonetheless. "Now go, so you may return as soon as is feasible."

He leaned down and brushed a kiss across her lips before opening the door to the frigid, but thankfully, dry air.

She stood in the doorway, watching him dash across the gardens and finally into the forest that bordered their land. Stepping back inside, she shivered. Quickly, she moved to the fireplace and added more coal, before returning to her painting. A sigh of satisfaction wafted through her.

It had been a very *satisfying* day.

—

Andrew ran his hand through his hair as he sat at his desk listening to his steward. "I don't understand. If you told them they needn't pay their rents this season, why are they struggling?"

Mr. Foster looked away. "I think they're afraid you'll ask them for the rents in the spring and they won't have it."

"Of all the half-witted ideas!" He slammed his hands down on his desk as he stood. "The harvest was poor, the weather freezing, and when I offer them hope, they ignore it?"

The man finally met his gaze and straightened his shoulders as if he feared what he was about to say would have him dismissed. "I can't say I know what they are thinking, but..." he hesitated, clearly wrestling with how much he wanted to reveal.

Andrew took a deep breath and slowly sank back into his chair. "Do tell, Foster. I'm not going to dismiss you simply because you give me more bad tidings."

"Right, sir. Well, the way of it is, your current tenants were your father's."

When the man simply stared at him as if that was some sort

of revelation, he found himself tamping down his irritation. "Yes, I'm well aware of that. What bearing does that have on this issue?"

"They are used to how your father handled things such as this."

Again the man seemed to think his statement enlightening in some way. "And…" He purposefully didn't ask a specific question, his knowledge of his steward telling him that may lead them off into another subject all together.

Foster's brow rose and he cocked his head. "Your father did not accept any excuse for not paying rents. *Any.*"

His body tensed at what Foster implied. His father had been a gregarious person, always smiling, always happy, always appearing as if he had not a care in the world, at least until he grew sick. The man had never even raised his voice except in laughter or with a bawdy joke.

Leaning back in his chair, he pinned Foster with his gaze. "I suggest you explain what that means specifically."

The man seemed to lose his bravado, his shoulders falling and his whole frame seeming to sink in on itself.

"Hell and damnation, Foster, sit down before you fall down."

The man sat in the wingback chair before the desk, his small frame melding with the thick green cushions.

"My father did not involve me in his dealings with our tenants until the last two years of his life. He wanted them to know me, and he explained how things should be run. So if there is something I should know about, it's best you tell me now instead of years down the road. Do I have a half-sister among my tenants?" That was something he could too easily see occurring while his father was alive.

Foster's eyes rounded. "Oh, no, my lord. I mean, I know of no such happening, sir."

He sat back in his own chair to give the impression that he was relaxed when he was anything but. He was stymied, irritated, frustrated, and out of patience. "Then please do enlighten me on why my tenants being my father's would keep them from using the money they would have paid me to feed their families."

"I don't know the truth of it, but I think it may be that they don't trust in your generosity since your father refused to accept *any* excuse."

There was that emphasis again. "Can you give me an example?"

Foster nodded vigorously before taking his time deciding on one. Finally, he spoke. "Do you know Mr. Rupert?"

He nodded, not wanting to hinder the information from being revealed. Mr. Rupert had one of the largest tracts of land from which they received rent.

"Do you remember when scarlet fever came through three years ago?"

He gritted his teeth, wondering if the man had any idea how frustrating he was. He nodded again. He remembered well because his father had taken them all to Bath that year to avoid the scourge.

"Poor Mr. Rupert. That year, everyone in his family were down with the fever. And when it was all done, it had ravaged those poor souls. He lost three sons and his wife to that curse. May they rest in peace." Mr. Foster made the sign of the cross. "Only two sons and his daughter were left alive, and she too weak to leave her bed. It was harvest time and though he tried, Mr. Rupert and his two sons, as weak as they were, could only get in half the harvest. So he asked your father for more time to pay the rent."

Andrew's stomach tightened, stealing himself against what was to come. Surely his father agreed.

"Lord Sommerset refused. Said if they didn't pay the full rent by the end of the month as required, they would have to leave. And I was the one that had to give them the notice because Lord Sommerset, he put it all in writing."

He didn't want to believe his father could be so callous. "But the Ruperts are still here."

Mr. Foster looked upward as if speaking to the heavens. "It was a truly moving event." He paused as if thanking the lord then resumed his tale. "Your other tenants, hearing of Mr. Rupert's misfortune, sent one son each until Mr. Rupert had a dozen hearty men helping with the harvest and he paid his rent. Now how word got about, heaven only knows." From the self-satisfied smile on the man's face, he obviously had much to do with it.

Andrew tried to reconcile the new information with what he knew of his father and at first it just wouldn't fit the man he'd known. But as he thought back, small snippets of his father's treatment of those who served him had him wondering. It was something he'd look into further, but right now he had a quandary on his hands. How was he to get his tenants to use his gift of their rent money to support their families?

"Mr. Foster, it seems that we must then put our joint intellectual capacity together to find a way to convince *my* tenants that I will not expect rent from them until next season." It was obvious even his own steward didn't trust his generosity. Searching for a logical reason for being generous, he landed on one. "The fact is, if they starve to death this winter, they are of little use to me in the coming year. Correct?"

The man's eyes widened. "You are, sir."

He sat forward again and set his elbows on the desk. "Then what should we do?"

"I could tell them again?" Mr. Foster clearly did not think that would work.

"No, that has been tried. If I had time, I would visit each and every one of them, but now that the new year festivities are over, I must leave in a few days."

The man's face, which had brightened, fell. "Again, sir? Will you be gone long?"

It was an odd question coming from his steward. The man knew well what he was about, but obviously this year had strained his confidence. "Not too long. Maybe a fortnight." He'd have to come home to make sure all was ready for his new bride.

Even at the thought of Amelia, some of his worries dissipated.

He'd taken a risk not asking for the rents based on his ability to woo Amelia. It hadn't occurred to him that he'd feel so deeply for her, but he was pleased he did. He was also fairly sure she felt the same way about him. That meant she'd be happy to have her dowry help *their* people.

He stared at the ink well on his desk. What good was it to sacrifice his rents if his people didn't use that money to feed themselves? Now, he was less frustrated with them and more angry with his father. What more would he uncover about the man before a year had gone by since his passing?

"Sir, might I suggest an announcement of some sort. Perhaps, your footmen could deliver it?"

He looked at Mr. Foster. "An announcement?" It seemed too authoritative to him, something his father might do. His gaze wandered back to the ink well. That was it! "A letter."

"A letter, sir?"

He grinned. "Yes, a letter. I will write a letter to each family, and you will deliver them and read them if they need you to. Then they will have something in writing from me personally that assures them they need not pay rent for 1816."

Mr. Foster rose. "Sir, that's quite generous of you. I promise to deliver every letter."

Something in Mr. Foster's wording made it apparent the man hadn't believed in his kindness either. That had him questioning his own actions as a lord. As soon as he was married and the weather turned, he and Amelia would visit each family to introduce her to them and let them see their new lord and lady were of a different ilk. "Thank you, Mr. Foster. I will have the letters ready for you tomorrow."

"Thank you, sir." Mr. Foster turned and strode toward the door, but just as he reached it, it opened to reveal Harewood. Mr. Foster slipped by, a new jaunt in his step. No doubt, the Lyonsmere tenants would know about the letter and what it contained long before it arrived.

His friend strode in to stop at the chair Mr. Foster had just vacated, only to lean against it. "I trust all is well."

He rose and walked to the sideboard. "It will be." He raised a bottle with good Scotch in it and motioned to Harewood. At his nod, he poured two glasses.

Harewood accepted the glass and took a sip. "You really must give me the name of your purveyor of this. It's exceptionally smooth."

He leaned against his desk. "I'll be happy to."

"And you may want to order a few more bottles right away."

At Harewood's words, he set his drink down. "Why?"

"I'm afraid I have received not-good news that not only affects me but more importantly, you."

Having solved one difficult issue already, he felt up to the task. "Then tell me, and quickly. Talking to my steward is like watching ice melt on a cold day."

"Then I shall try not to be like ice, though I have been compared to such in the past."

He looked askance at Harewood, letting him know clearly that his humor was not appreciated at the moment, even if what he'd said was true.

The man, despite his reassurance to be quick, took time to settle in the chair and take another sip. "That really is quite excellent. So, to my news."

He didn't let his gaze stray from his friend despite the need for another gulp of Scotch.

"The ships we invested in returned but half full."

"Blast it. Why?" He grabbed his drink and took a hearty swallow, happy for the burn that flowed down his throat. It felt a bit like hell, not that he knew what that felt like, but he'd viewed the painting of Dante's *Inferno* by Giovanni Stradano and had a good idea. In fact, he had a feeling he was in circle nine, though why he deserved it, he wasn't sure.

Harewood pulled at his sleeve, a sure sign he was about to hold back. "From what I've learned—"

"Bloody hell, just tell me the truth. I can't address the issue when you withhold information."

Harewood's eyes rounded, but he nodded. "Very well. It appears this frigid weather we've experienced has been happening all over Europe and even in America. What goods are being made or grown are staying in their countries of origin. Trade has ground to a halt."

His mind raced. If the cold weather had affected crops all over Europe and America, as well as at home, there could well be a worldwide famine. It wasn't just himself whose finances hung in the balance, but everyone's. His were just in an unfortunate state.

Throwing back the rest of the Scotch, he pushed away from his desk and walked over to the sideboard. Splashing another dram of Scotch into his glass, he swallowed that too. The heat in his belly was nothing like the need to do something immediately.

"I wouldn't get into your cups just yet. There is more."

He stilled. "More?" He left his glass on the sideboard and walked back behind his desk. Crossing his arms over his chest, he studied Harewood. Something was definitely bothering the man. "What is it?"

"Something I did not foresee."

He smirked. Anything Harewood could not foresee would disturb him greatly. "And what would that be?"

The man's brows lowered, and he shifted uncomfortably in his chair before reaching into his pocket and pulling out a piece of paper. "This."

Even from where he stood, he could tell it was a bill. But everyone had been paid. He'd made sure of that before he'd made any investments. The cheese he'd had for luncheon seemed to suddenly weigh two stone. "And what is that?"

Harewood grimaced. "It is a bill from a local establishment you and I know well in Oxford."

Oxford? They hadn't been there in years. "What does that have to do with me?"

"Christopher gave it to me to give to you before he left for the village. Asked me if I could smooth over the expense for him."

His brother? Fisting his hands, he made no move to take it. "How much?"

"Thirty-three pounds."

"What?" He strode around his desk and grabbed the bill from Harewood. He stared in shock at the items listed. "My brother has a mistress?"

"It appears so."

"But he's only—"

"The same age we were when we began incurring these types of expenses." Harewood raised a brow as if he should have expected this.

"Then how come you didn't foresee this?" He waved the paper. "No, never mind." It wasn't Harewood's fault. He dropped the bill on his desk and moved to the window to stare at the light blanket of snow frozen over the fields before Lyonsmere.

"You need to tell him."

He stiffened. "Tell him what? That our father squandered money on women, paintings, horses, and whatever caught his fancy while working his tenants into an early grave only to die in debt?"

The leather of the wingback chair creaked as Harewood must have risen, his footsteps coming closer. The hand that was settled on his shoulder was that of a very good friend, so he didn't shrug it off, but he wanted to.

"Perhaps telling him everything wouldn't be appropriate right now, but he should know that you were left with significant debts."

He didn't say a word. To admit to anyone besides Harewood that his father wasn't everything he thought was like swallowing fish eggs. He couldn't do it.

"Sommerset, you have to curb the whelp's spending for the next year, or even with the lovely Lady Amelia's dowry, you'll be in this same situation."

He knew the man was right, but that didn't make it any easier to accept.

"You have fulfilled the bargain, have you not?"

He nodded.

Harewood removed his hand. "Then I suggest you have the banns read this Sunday."

"I can't." Now, the thought of telling Amelia that he needed her dowry made him hesitate. This was no longer just about their tenants, but also his brother's mistress, and even the very food for their table. He wasn't unaware of how similar the situation was to what her own family went through and what Lady Mariel had sacrificed for them. He didn't want Amelia to feel like a sacrifice. He wanted her to feel wanted.

"Why can't you have the banns read?"

He ran his hand through his hair and finally faced Harewood. "Because, I haven't asked her father for her hand yet."

"Then might I suggest that you do so, posthaste?" Harewood's raised brows and arrogant tone made it clear there was only one correct answer to his question.

He nodded mutely. The suggestion was sound, the plan appropriate, but his instinct told him, the outcome was entirely unknown.

CHAPTER EIGHTEEN

AMELIA SAT AT the parlor desk watching the snowflakes fall onto the drive up to Thornwood. The first snow of the season was always pretty, but after weeks of ice and rain, not necessarily welcome. It was such a light dusting that running out to enjoy it was not worth the effort. Actually, nothing seemed worth the effort since she'd finished her masterpiece and three other paintings of Andrew. Without him to share them with, her interest in painting more had waned.

"Amelia dear, are you writing to Lady Spencer or daydreaming of summer?"

She turned her head to give her mother a smirk. "Can I not be doing both?"

Joanna, who sat across from her mother reading a book, looked up. "No, you can't, according to—"

"Please." She held up her hand. "Allow me to remain ignorant if I simply accept your assertion."

"As you wish, but Herodotus said the only good is knowledge, and the only evil is ignorance."

She rolled her eyes at her sister. "I doubt very much that my letter to Lady Spencer and my thoughts of summer, if that's what they were, have anything to do with good and evil." She waved her sister off. "Go back to your reading, and I shall promise to only focus on my letter. Agreed?"

"Agreed. I'm finding this book on poison truly fascinating."

Mariel, who worked her embroidery loop, chuckled. "Joanna, the subjects you find of interest will always baffle me."

As Joanna responded, Amelia turned back to her letter. She hadn't written very much, except to ask after her friend's health and her Christmas. She simply refused to discuss the weather, but the only other subject of interest to her was Andrew, and she daren't write about him. But she could write about her painting. Lady Spencer supported her efforts and had already asked for a personal painting.

There was nothing more personal than the one she'd painted of Andrew at the acropolis. She couldn't wait for him to see it. She'd positioned the lion so he crossed over slightly in front, and hid Andrew's private area. An area only she would be seeing from now on. Even at the thought of marrying him, seeing him every day, and touching him in the nights, had her skin tingling.

"Amelia, did you tell Lady Spencer about Lady Garmoyle?"

"Joanna, absolutely not!" Her mother's voice startled her. "We are not spreading gossip."

Joanna's eyes twinkled. "It's not gossip if it's true and everyone at the ball was aware of it."

Her mother looked over her shoulder at her. "Do not tell Lady Spencer about what transpired at Lucinda's ball."

"I wasn't going to. I simply thought to tell her of my painting."

"Have you finished the piece you were working on?" Mariel's voice, though soft, made her tense. Only she knew the truth.

She would have to phrase her response carefully. "I have. And I'm quite happy with it."

Mariel's eyebrows rose before her face softened. "I'm so pleased."

"So that's why you haven't disappeared into your studio the last few days." Joanna set her book aside. "When can we see it?"

Before she could speak, Mariel answered. "Certainly not today." She shivered. "It's far too cold and the ground too slippery."

She gave Mariel a grateful smile. Though she had painted other portraits of Andrew, with clothes on, and half-clothed, she wasn't ready for anyone to see that her best paintings were of him. The only other painting she would rate on par with his was the miniature she'd done of Belinda. She had a feeling her late sister would be pleased by that even if she may have frowned on how it came to pass.

Her mother rose. "It appears we aren't going to have any callers today, so I'm going upstairs to rest."

"Are you well, Mother?" Mariel's caring question brought their attention to the fact that it was rare for their mother to rest in the afternoon.

"I'm fine, just a bit tired. I'm older than you three and can no longer play games until almost dawn."

Joanna grinned as they all recalled the games of the night before. "And you did so with such gracious aplomb."

"Well, there are some advantages to being older, as I'm just a little wiser."

Amelia had to concede that point since her mother had won a majority of the games, which had quite surprised Joanna's husband, the duke, the most well-read of any of them. "I would say much wiser."

"Thank you."

After her mother left, Amelia returned to her letter. *My painting is improving by the day, and I've recently finished a portrait that I'm quite pleased with. I know you may be shocked to read that, but it's true. I still feel my skills to be limited by my inability to accurately paint the visions I see in my head; however, I believe I have reached a new level with objects that are before me.*

She reread what she'd just written. Though she cringed at praising herself, she admitted it was the truth. It wasn't as if her paintings were of any great import to mankind, but they were to her, and her family, and to Lady Spencer. Maybe even to Andrew, who did promise she could continue to paint after they married.

"Oh, it looks like Mother was wrong. We do have a brave soul who decided to call." Joanna rose to walk closer to the window. "I'm not familiar with that crest."

Mariel set aside her loop. "No need to disturb Mother. I'm sure whoever it is won't mind having tea with us. I'll have Channing order us some."

Curious, Amelia set her quill in the inkwell and rose, prepared to meet the mystery guest. She walked to the settee her mother so recently vacated and sat.

When the door to the parlor opened, her heart skipped a beat as Andrew strode in. He appeared more handsome than before and the urge to drag him back to her studio was strong. Dressed in his usual tans and browns, his hair appeared a bit longer, but other than the red in his cheeks from the cold, he hadn't changed in the last few weeks.

Mariel, ever the hostess, greeted him. "It is so good to see you, Lord Sommerset. You remember Lady Amelia."

His eyes sparkled with mischief. "I could not forget such a talented lady."

"My talent only extends as far as my subjects." She smirked, beyond happy to see him.

"Do not listen to her. She is excellent." At Joanna's words, Mariel continued with the introductions. "Do you remember my sister, the Duchess of Northwick?"

He turned to Joanna. "Your Grace. Last I saw you, you and your husband were gliding across the Enderlys' ballroom, putting all others to shame with your skill."

"A very different skill than my sister's. Please sit. I hope you will take tea with us?"

"It would be my pleasure." Andrew settled in the chair Joanna had indicated, which happened to be next to the settee.

Amelia found herself wanting to reach out and touch him, so she clasped her hands together to make sure she did nothing untoward. "I understand you traveled home for the festive season. I trust your mother is well."

He turned toward her. "She is, thank you. She quite enjoyed having both her sons home and treating us as if we were but ten again." He chuckled, the sound warming her to her toes.

The footman appeared at the doorway and Mariel motioned him in. "We had not heard that you had returned to Sunnydale. Have you been in Bedford long?"

Though he faced Mariel to answer, she could feel his awareness of her. How could no one else in the room feel it?

"No, I haven't. In fact, I came directly here from Lyonsmere." He paused as Mariel poured for them all.

Mariel finished and sent the footman away before lifting her teacup. "We are honored to be your first visit."

"Why directly here, Lord Sommerset? I would think you would want to join your hosts?" Joanna eyed him curiously.

He took a sip and set his cup down on the table between them. "Normally, I would. However, Lord Harewood, who joined me for Christmas, promised to give my apologies to his parents as he knew I was anxious to come here."

Joanna's brows raised, but before she could ask a question, he turned to Amelia.

"I have come to ask your father for your hand in marriage."

Her heart leapt with excitement, which was far from what she'd expected to feel. Still, he hadn't seen the completed painting yet.

Joanna jumped up. "Sir, am I to understand that you wish my sister to marry you when you barely know her? Have you even asked to court her?"

Feeling the need to defend him, she held her hand up to her sister. "You mean as Lord Northwick did with you?"

Joanna sat again. "Well, he did."

"Not until after you had already agreed to marry him, correct?"

When Joanna stubbornly refused to answer, she turned back to Andrew and smiled. "Please excuse my sister. She isn't that proper; she just wants to be sure I have a choice in the matter."

His shoulders relaxed. "I understand and am grateful for that. Would you allow me to ask your father for your hand?"

This was it. This was what she'd dreaded from the start, but no longer dreaded. In fact, she was very curious about her future life as Lady Sommerset.

His gaze softened and his tawny eyes filled with warmth. "If you would grant me that boon, I would like to have the banns posted this Sunday."

"In the winter?" Joanna jumped in again. "Surely you can wait until spring."

Mariel finally stepped in. "Joanna, perhaps you could locate Father while Amelia contemplates what *she* would like to do."

Joanna flushed and slowly rose. "Of course. I believe he's in the library." She started toward the open doors then looked back. "Amelia, I—I'll find Father." With that she strode out of the room.

With her sister gone, she turned back to Andrew. "You wish to marry me soon then?"

"I do." He ran his hand through his hair before continuing. "I know it may be sooner than you expected, but this past summer has been difficult, making the winter harder. Our marriage would help greatly."

Confused, she lowered her brows. How would getting married in a few weeks help the weather? "I'm not sure I understand." She glanced toward the doorway to be sure no one was about. "You haven't even seen the painting yet."

His gaze glowed with excitement. "I am anxious to see it and bring it home to Lyonsmere Hall. You have amazing talent."

She found his answer disappointing. Did he not care if the painting had lived up to its beginnings? "So because the painting is now complete, you wish to marry posthaste."

"I do. I cannot wait to bring you home as my wife. The winter will be made easier by your presence. The harvest was minimal as your father probably shared with you. Tenants barely brought in enough to feed themselves. I allowed mine to keep what they would usually pay in rent so they can stay and provide for us next year."

He'd never spoken about his estate before, so the sudden focus confused her. "I think I understand, but I'm confused why getting married in three weeks would matter."

When he looked at Mariel, she felt a shiver of dread crawl up her spine. "Andrew, why do you want to get married right away?"

He took her hand, despite the impropriety of it. "Amelia, I need your dowry to keep everyone in comfort until spring."

"What?" She snatched her hand back, her heart starting to thump hard in her chest. "Why do you need my dowry for that?"

"I have told no one but Lord Harewood. My father left many debts when he died. He was sick for a long time and did not take care of things as he should."

She opened her mouth to protest, but he held up his hand. "Please, I need to tell you. I paid all the debts and still had some to invest, which would rebuild our wealth by springtime. However, this weather has not just plagued us here, but in Europe and America too, and trade has trickled to a halt. Once it resumes, all will be well again, but in the meantime—"

Her chest felt as if a horse sat upon her, but that didn't stop the heat of her anger from getting through. "In the meantime you need my dowry. That's why you wished to marry me. Just for my dowry."

He reached for her hand again, but she moved it away.

"No, that's not why. Amelia, I love you. You are more than I dreamed I could ever have in a wife. You are talented and caring, beautiful and humble, funny and passionate. I want you beside me for the rest of my life."

She shook her head, unwilling to believe anything he said now. "You never said this before, but now because you need my dowry, you love me? How can I trust you? You lied to me."

He sat back in the chair. "I did not lie to you. You never asked about my finances. I haven't even told my mother. I could not bear to see her image of my father ruined. My circumstances are not for public knowledge. I understand that you would never marry a man in a difficult situation, but I am not Lord Blanford."

His affront was genuine, but she didn't care about—Lord Blanford? Why did he bring up—oh. The conversation in the parlor of his London home rushed back. His mother had said, *Lord Blanford squandered his money at the gambling hells and desperately needed a rich dowry if he was to save his estate. His father had cut him off completely.* Lady Hester was to marry him.

In that conversation, she'd stated quite clearly that she would never marry a man who needed her for her dowry, but here he was, in the form of Andrew Crauford, Earl of Sommerset. And he knew! Her fingers curled into fists at her sides as hurt and fury filled her. "That may be, but you kept this information from me purposefully, even knowing how I felt."

He rose to stand behind his chair, gripping the back of it. "Of course I did. You would never have been willing to learn who I was or allow me the privilege of learning about you. I wouldn't marry a woman I could not see as my wife, no matter how large her dowry." He strode back around the chair and sat, leaning toward her. "Amelia, I do love you. I think I fell in love with you the night we stared at the moon, and you talked about mystic moments. I knew I loved you the day you called me a goat. I promise you, our need for your dowry is only temporary."

His gaze burned intensely, so strong that she couldn't look at him. Bile rose in her throat at his betrayal, even as her heart constricted. "If you truly felt that way, then you should have told me." Her stomach tightened so harshly, she felt ill. She'd seen a future with him, a happy future, and he destroyed it. She wanted that future back with the man she'd come to care about, but he'd known she felt and chose not to tell her until now, when he needed her dowry.

Even as images of their time together in her studio flashed through her mind, his laughter, his caring, his touch, pain swept through her. She didn't wish to marry anyone now, ever. She shook her head. "I can't."

"I promise you, nothing is different. I still love you. You can still have a studio at Lyonsmere and paint. Your comfort will be no different than it is now."

She finally met his gaze. "But it *will* be different. I'll always wonder what you are hiding from me because you know I don't like it." Even as she said the words, she knew them to be true. Why did it hurt so much to accept?

"I will be completely honest with you as my wife. Anything you wish to know, I will tell you." Even as he said the words, his Adam's apple moved as he swallowed hard, making it clear there was more he didn't think she'd like to hear.

Her throat closed and she shook her head, unable to say anything. Her heart ached for what she'd imagined with him and her stomach burned with his betrayal.

He finally rose. "I will not apologize for supporting the people under my care. I had hoped you would feel the same way and want to help those who would benefit from you marrying me, but I see that I was wrong."

She didn't watch him as he strode across the room to leave her forever.

"Lord Sommerset." Her sister's voice reminded her that Mariel had been witness to their entire conversation. "What will you do, for your people?"

"I do not know, but I will figure it out. I have to." With those final words he left.

She couldn't help listening to his steps as he strode across the entryway. Each click of his boot heel on the floor like a death knell beating against her heart. She imagined him as he donned his coat and the door opened only to shut behind him, a draft of cold air flowing into the parlor. She shivered, feeling far colder than the air. In fact, numbness started to set in.

The silence in the room became deafening. No doubt her sister thought her a fool for ever making a bargain with a man who could withhold such a compelling truth. Unable to bear the quiet censure any longer, she finally swiveled to face Mariel.

What she found in her sister's gaze was far from condemnation. It was pity and nothing more. She shook her head at Mariel. "I know."

"No, Ames, you don't know."

At the use of her childhood name, she frowned. "I don't?"

"No, you don't. You just let the one man who could make you happy for the rest of your life walk away."

Chapter Nineteen

ANDREW STARED OUT the window of his coach but saw nothing. He felt nothing. His entire future was now erased, leaving an empty one before him. How could she not see? How could she ignore all else?

The coach came to a halt, and he frowned. The door opened.

"Sunnydale Manor, my Lord."

He stared uncomprehendingly at the footman, before remembering he'd told his coachman to stop here. Why did he want to come here? Unfolding himself from the seat, he stepped down and strode up the stone steps, his reason still beyond his reach.

The door opened and the butler ushered him in, taking his coat, hat, and gloves. "I will inform Lord Harewood that you have arrived."

Harewood. Yes, he wished to talk to his friend.

"I did not expect you so soon." Harewood smiled in greeting as he came from the parlor, but quickly lost all pleasantness. "Come to the library. You need a drink."

He followed obediently, still trying to make sense of what he was supposed to do or feel.

"Sit." Harewood pointed to the leather chair where Amelia's father had been that night of the ball.

His friend poured something into a glass and handed it to

him. "I said sit."

Taking a sip, he coughed. "What the blast is that?"

Harewood took the glass back. "Port. I just wanted to make sure you were still conscious."

Not impressed with his friend's humor, he sat just as Harewood handed him another glass. He sniffed it first before tasting. "Whisky?"

"Not as good as yours, but it will warm you from the inside out." Harewood sat in the second wingback chair before the fireplace. "Now tell me what has occurred."

He stared at the amber liquor, trying to make sense of what happened. "She refused."

"To post the banns?"

"No, to marry me."

"She can't." Harewood put his glass down with force and stood. "You had an agreement. I witnessed it and so did her sister. You fulfilled your part of it, now she must fulfill hers. We can force her to the altar."

That was true. Not only did they have an agreement, but he'd also taken liberties with her person. So he could force her, but to what end? "And live with a woman who hates me for the rest of my life? If I wanted that, I could just marry Lady Garmoyle and have my end faster than expected." The whisky warmed him up as Harewood had said, but it also thawed the numbness, and his chest began to hurt.

"Why did she refuse?"

"Because I need her dowry." The pain grew stronger, making his stomach tense.

"You told her that before you married her?" Harewood moved to the fireplace and leaned against the mantle. "I specifically told you not to."

And so he had. "Yes, but I thought…" What had he thought? That she loved him? That she would be happy to help those at her future home? "I misread her. I thought she cared, but I was wrong." As he looked back on their time together, he couldn't fault himself for thinking she cared. Maybe it was simply that he had inspired her, and so she cared for him in that single moment. "Like a bowl of fruit."

"What does a bowl of fruit have to do with telling her you need her dowry?" A small tick beneath Harewood's ear started. A sure sign he was furious.

Why would he be angry? He never expected Amelia to accept him to begin with. "Why did you suggest Lady Amelia as a wife for me?"

Harewood waved him off. "I told you, because she has a substantial dowry."

As if to avoid his own pain, he focused in on Harewood. "No, it was more than that. Did you hope to keep your mother from instigating a marriage between you and Lady Amelia?"

"That would simply be a convenience." He pulled at his cuff. "I just thought you two would suit. She's an artist and you like art."

As if a distraction was exactly what he'd needed, he looked askance at Harewood. "And…"

The man shrugged. "That's all."

"No, there's more. I've known you a long time. What aren't you telling me?"

Harewood lifted his glass and took a hefty swallow. Then he glanced at him and took another swallow.

He waited patiently, determined to know it all.

"I thought she would make you happy."

The words were mumbled in such a soft tone, that he was sure he'd misheard. "Did you say you thought she would make me happy?"

Harewood rose again. "Yes." Then he strode to the sidebar. "Would you like another?"

The pain he'd been ignoring suddenly roared to life, taking his breath away. That even stoic Harewood thought Amelia was for him added to his agony. She was supposed to fall in love with him. He'd never expected he'd fall in love with her. Understanding dawned, and he looked around the wing of the chair at Harewood. "You knew we'd suit. How?"

"I know the Mabrys. Though we avoided them when you visited, that was not possible for me when you were not about. After Belinda died, I would have done anything to avoid them, but my parents and theirs were too close. I saw each sister as they grew. It did not take much deduction or foresight to realize that Lady Amelia would make you the perfect wife."

Tired of craning his neck, he rose, almost sorry he did as his stomach roiled. "If you thought that, then why did you expect her to turn me down?"

Harewood sighed as he swirled his whisky. "Because she wasn't ready to marry yet, but you needed a wife now. I thought the whole notion ill-timed."

He gripped the chair hard, his heart aching, tightening his entire chest. "But she said yes. And you thought all would end happily." He grimaced and held his hand out. "But you were wrong. She doesn't care about me. She doesn't care about anyone. She is simply a well-polished lady who does and says what she's supposed to."

"No, you are wrong about that." Harewood shook his head.

"Am I?" Anger began to build, and it felt so much better than the pain. "Then why is her dowry so important that she would throw away all that I offered her? Why would she deny her own feelings for me which I thought she had? There is no reason."

"I can tell you the reason, but you aren't willing to hear it."

The prevarication just riled him the more. "Come, Harewood. You've seen me angrier than this. Is it that you think I don't want to know, or that you don't want to tell? By Lady Amelia's standards, I should be throwing you over for not telling me all this before."

"Fine." Harewood put his glass down and strode to within feet of him. "Listen carefully."

"I always do."

Harewood shook his head then sighed. "Lady Beaumont."

"Lady Beaumont?" He stared, his fury lost for the moment.

"Yes, Lady Beaumont. She married so the Mabrys could keep the lifestyle they were accustomed to."

He'd forgotten that Amelia had told him about her sister's sacrifice. "But how do you know about that?"

"As I said, our parents are close. Lady Beaumont sacrificed herself for her family's comfort. But that was only after the man she'd originally intended to marry died. I'm quite sure part of her died with him."

"Yes, Lady Amelia told me. Lady Beaumont did what many women do, sacrificed her virginity so her family could live in comfort. It is horrendous, but what does that have to do with Lady Amelia?"

Harewood threw his hands up in disgust and walked away. Turning, he faced him. "Don't you see? Amelia now sees herself as a sacrifice, only this time for your family."

He frowned, not at all convinced by that logic. "That makes no sense."

"Since when do women make sense?"

Something about Harewood's assumption didn't sit right. It was just as well. It was easier to believe Amelia heartless. His hopes for a future of loyalty and happiness had been dashed. Now all he was left with was to figure out how to save his family from poverty. He covered his face with his hands before running them through his hair. Arguing with Harewood wasn't going to solve that dilemma and he had to focus on doing that immediately.

He started for the door.

"Where are you going?"

He halted and looked at Harewood over his shoulder. "Home. I have to try to save it somehow."

"My offer is still—"

"No. I mean, thank you. I promise if I have no other choice but to sell Lyonsmere, I will come to you."

"There's always other women."

He continued out the door, his friend's suggestion causing his stomach to roil with a vengeance. The last thing he needed now was a woman.

—

Andrew added the columns up again. He would have to sell something. He stared at the figure. No, he'd have to sell more than just something. The question was what? The house in London would solve their problems, but how to explain that to his mother? Every authentic painting he owned might get them through the winter, but what then?

He rose from his desk, the need to take a walk urging him beyond his study, but it was frigid outside. Still, he found himself walking to the large window and staring out at the snow-covered ground. After three days of drinking and three days of sleeping, he'd finally woken up to a partially sunny morning ready to take on his responsibilities again.

He rubbed his chest. The ache remained, but he was power-less to make it stop. Would it ever go away? It was hard to imagine not loving Amelia. Maybe when she married. He shook his head, grimacing. Maybe when he married. The thought, as it had for the past sennight, made him physically sick. He just needed to stay focused on saving the Caufield estate without his mother any the wiser. For the hundredth time, a new anger at his father surfaced. It was selfish to blame everything on the former Lord Sommerset, especially because that was the reason he'd met Amelia in the first place. Then again, he'd be better off now if he'd never met her.

Turning back to his desk, he strode across the hardwood floor, his boots sounding a death knell in the room. When had he become so morbid? Sitting once again, he turned the pages of his ledger to review their assets. Unfortunately, there was little he could sell without it affecting his mother. He itched to tell her the truth, but her health, which had improved somewhat after he hired Mrs. Bolton for her, had slowly worsened again. He didn't want to lose her so soon. It was times like this when he missed his father's counsel. Harewood's father still ran their estates, so

Harewood would be of little help.

The Duke of Northwick had offered to share his plans, but that hadn't happened and wouldn't now. He should probably have a meeting with his solicitor to determine what could bring the most funds, what was easiest to sell, and then decide at that point. He looked up at the portrait of his father above the fireplace. "Why do I think you wouldn't have changed your life even if you'd known what would happen?"

The portrait wasn't even well done, so selling it would be of no use, but he definitely needed to move it. That might—

The door to his study opened and his mother strode in full of nervous energy. Nonchalantly, he closed the ledger and folded his hands on top of it. "Good afternoon, Mother."

She waved off his greeting. "Really, Andrew. There is nothing good about it." She sat in one of the chairs before his desk to catch her breath.

He rose and took the chair next to her. "What is it that has you so flustered?"

She set her fingers against her temple. Her hand seemed smaller, bonier. "It's Cook." She said the word as if it was the most distasteful word in their language. "She served carrots at dinner last night. You wouldn't know because you were abed. But Mrs. Bolton was appalled at their quality. You must talk to her."

"To Mrs. Bolton?"

"No. You must talk to Cook and tell her that if we are served such mediocre vegetables again that you will dismiss her. Mrs. Bolton says that the only way to get the servants to do as you wish is to threaten to dismiss them." She gave an emphatic nod.

He stiffened, his instinct fully alert. "I'm not sure that would be the best way to approach the subject. After all, Cook has been with us for over ten years now and we have never had any problems with her." Though he knew a few of the staff were a little intimidated by the assertive woman, that was hardly a reason to dismiss her.

"Well, it's up to you, of course. As long as I'm not embarrassed again in front of Mrs. Bolton."

For a woman who didn't care a whit for what the lower classes thought of her, his mother seemed overly concerned with her companion's opinion. "Tell me, what else does Mrs. Bolton advise."

His mother's face brightened. "Oh, I'm so pleased you are ready to listen now." She patted his hand where it lay on the arm of the chair. "I know you have been heartbroken over Lady Amelia turning you down, but now that you are over it, I can tell you about the changes we need to make."

"Changes?" He hoped she didn't plan to dismiss their loyal staff.

"Oh yes, Mrs. Bolton says that our parlor is very outdated. I thought a lovely rose color would do well in there. Also, you have Mrs. Bolton in the attic, which for a woman of her age is just too much. I thought we could move her down a level?"

It was beginning to appear that he'd left Lyonsmere for far too long. "Really?"

"Yes, oh, and we must purchase a better coach, one with a better ride." She leaned forward. "Also, Mrs. Bolton says we must not eat any more blancmange as it plays havoc with our moods."

That was it. It was time for him to have a talk with Mrs. Bolton or she'd find herself dismissed. "We are not eliminating blancmange from our menu. It is my favorite dish. As for the carrots, the weather has made it impossible to grow the usual quality vegetables this year, so we will make do. And there will be no redecorating or purchasing of a coach. And lastly, Mrs. Bolton will remain in the attic and if that does not suit her, she can move to another room far away from Lyonsmere."

His mother just shook her head at him and patted his hand again. "You're just testy because you were thrown over. Don't worry, dear. We can talk of this in a few days after you meet your prospective wives."

His blood ran cold and his throat closed. Swallowing hard, he took his mother's hand in his. "What do you mean, prospective wives?"

His mother gave his hand a squeeze, though it was so light, he may have imagined it. "You didn't think I'd let you moon after some woman who can't see what a wonderful husband you would make? I sent invitations to all the families in the area, letting them know that you were looking for a wife and to please call." Her prideful smile made it hard not to grimace and he clenched his jaw to keep from yelling.

Carefully setting her hand back on her lap, he rose. "That was very thoughtful, but I will be very busy and will be unable to meet them. I will be happy to resume my search during the season."

His mother rose as well. "Andrew, you can't hide all winter. There can't be so much to do that you can't spare a few hours to chat with these ladies. Mrs. Bolton has agreed to review each one and make recommendations."

He opened his mouth to ask what possible qualifications Mrs. Bolton would have to make such a determination, but snapped it shut. It was definitely time to talk to Mrs. Bolton He glanced at the clock and dread crawled up his spine.

Taking his mother's arm, he walked her toward the door. "You had best get ready for *your* callers. Please give them my regrets, but I must meet with a tenant today."

"Must you really?"

His mother's disappointment hurt, but he was aware of his own limitations. "Yes, I must."

Her smile returned. "Then Mrs. Bolton and I will be sure to discuss our visitors and I'll give you a full report over breakfast tomorrow."

He opened the door, not making any commitment. "Have a lovely afternoon." As soon as she was gone, he closed the door and leaned against it. What else could possibly go wrong?

Movement outside the window caught his attention and he cautiously moved to it. The coach of their neighbor, who last he'd heard, had two unmarried daughters, pulled up. And there was his answer.

Looking past the drive to the snow-covered fields, his itch to be outside became unbearable. He moved back to the study doors where his mother just exited and slipped out, taking the servants passage to the back door. He grabbed a cloak off a hook nearby and settled it on his shoulders. Yes, he was a coward. Yes, he was escaping.

And yes, he couldn't bear to look into anyone's eyes that didn't twinkle with blue amusement.

CHAPTER TWENTY

AMELIA RAISED HER hand to knock on her mother's bedroom door, then dropped it. Her mother was the only one who might understand what it was like not to be able to paint for three long weeks, but that could mean having to confess she'd had Andrew to her studio unchaperoned. If she revealed that, she wasn't sure what her mother would do. She could possibly force her to marry him. If anyone knew how wonderful he'd made her feel, they'd definitely insist on the marriage.

She was too confused. There was an ache in her chest at his betrayal, but she also missed him. It didn't make sense. Even now, whenever she thought of how he needed her money, all the time pretending to enjoy her company, she felt as if bees buzzed in her stomach. When she thought about his profession of love, it made her sick. *I love you. You are more than I dreamed I could ever have in a wife.*

But when she thought of his playfulness, his smile, and his touch, her heart ached to be in his company again. His words at the masquerade when he'd known it was her still haunted her. *You work hard and seek perfection, but don't feel your work is worthy. I believe you are afraid that without your work, there is no point in life. I believe you are afraid that in anything else in life, you will be mediocre at best, but I know that cannot be.*

She clasped her hands together as her eyes watered. Mariel

227

had thought her wrong to reject Andrew and was not happy with her. But Mariel was a romantic.

She stared at the door, undecided, when it suddenly opened and her father, wearing his dressing gown, halted.

"Amelia, what are you doing up and about so early?"

Caught now, she had no choice. "I wished to speak to Mother."

Her father looked over his shoulder, keeping the door mostly closed. "Ruthie, Amelia wishes to speak with you."

Her mother's voice came from inside the room, but she couldn't hear what she'd said.

Her father stepped out into the corridor, his bare feet making no noise on the wood floor. "She'll be but a moment. Is anything wrong?"

Yes! But she knew better than to involve her father. "I just need some womanly advice."

His bushy brows rose. "Yes, well, your mother is quite good at that. I'll be off then and leave her to it." With that, he brushed by her, his robe flapping about his hairy calves.

Now what was that about? Why would her father have needed to talk to her mother in such undress? Surely her parents hadn't slept in the same bed last night. They were far too old for any of that. She frowned as she contemplated the door.

The door opened and her mother, in her own dressing gown, opened her arm. "Come in, dear. What is it? Is a painting giving you trouble?"

She walked in and slumped in one of the chairs at the small table near the fireplace where two dirty teacups and plates made it clear her parents had already eaten. And her father thought *she* was early. "Yes and no."

Her mother closed the door and joined her. "I know that feeling." She chuckled. "I had many days like that, especially if I attempted images far beyond my skill. I was just too stubborn to accept that. What is it you're painting?"

"Nothing."

"Nothing?" Her mother frowned. "You mean nothing of great import or that you are not painting at all?"

"I'm not painting at all."

"Oh." Her mother studied her then reached her hand up and laid it against her cheek. "Are you not feeling well?"

She rose, walking away. "I don't know what I'm feeling." She turned back, throwing her hands up. "I open my sketchpad, and nothing comes. I take out my paints and stare at a blank canvas. I don't *see* anything."

Her mother cocked her head as she contemplated. "Is it that you don't see anything or that your mind is filled with a certain lord?"

How could her mother know? Mariel had promised not to say anything. She crossed her arms over her chest. "What do you mean?"

"Joanna told me of Lord Sommerset's proposal, and I think it affected you more than you care to admit."

Joanna, of course. She forgot that her sister had gone for her father, who luckily had been indisposed. "Does Father know?"

Her mother shook her head. "I wanted to wait until you told me why you rejected his proposal. Joanna was pleased that you had, but she simply didn't like that he appeared to have suddenly found an interest in you. But my instinct told me he's been interested in you for a while, correct?"

Somewhat relieved now that her mother knew that much, she dropped her hands and returned to the table, lowering herself to the chair in a more ladylike manner. "Yes, he has. Ever since he came to call for my expertise on his paintings last season."

She shot up from the table. He wanted to sell his paintings for more funds! "That's why."

Her mother looked up at her expectantly, and she slumped back into the chair. "I thought Lord Sommerset was interested in me, but I discovered he only wanted to marry me for my dowry. His father left debts when he died."

Her mother grimaced, even as she took her hand across the

table. "I'm sorry that he was motivated thus. He seemed rather smitten with you."

She pulled her hand back. "Well, he wasn't. He just needed the money." Even saying the word aloud had her stomach buzzing.

"I understand. A man who cannot manage his family's wealth is not very stable. Thank the lord we have Joanna."

"No, I think it was his father who didn't do it well. He said he'd paid all the debt, but that this weather has caused his tenants hardship."

"Oh, yes. I heard the duke mention something about that. So you think he could manage his family's wealth?"

"Of course. That is not the issue." She stood again, the buzzing in her belly starting. "It's that he purposefully kept it from me because he knew I wouldn't want to marry him if he needed my dowry."

Her mother nodded as she poured more tea into her cup and took a sip. "I understand now. You are afraid that he will always withhold information from you that you wouldn't like, such as if he took a mistress. I told your father that if he ever intended to take another woman to his bed that I wouldn't marry him."

"A mistress? No, he already promised he wouldn't." His words in her studio floated through her mind. *I would be loyal to you.* At the reminder of his pledge, her heart started to ache again, deadening the buzzing in her stomach.

"Then is it that he's cold? Does he expect and receive adoration from all women? He is quite handsome. I can see where that would make him quite unbearable."

She shook her head, on the verge of tears. "No. He doesn't think about his appearance at all. He's warm and kind and even told me he loved me."

Her mother's teacup hit the saucer hard. "He said he loved you?"

"But only after he told me he needed my dowry, and I was appalled. How can I be sure he means it?"

Her mother rose and took her hands. "Amelia, what I'm hearing are excuses, not reasons. What truly keeps you from accepting this man?"

To admit the truth was to prove she was the least perfect daughter. But she'd never live up to Belinda's quiet strength and caring, so it would be no surprise. Taking a deep breath, she looked into her mother's eyes. "He seemed perfect and now this. I feel like a fool."

Her mother chuckled. "You are not the only one to think like that. You don't want to know what I said to your father when he explained what happened with our old solicitor. I had depended on him to take care of all of us, and he failed. I love him dearly, but his head is in the clouds even more than in his books."

She clasped her hands. "But you were already married more than twenty years. You had no choice but to accept that. Besides, with Father it was only that one time."

Her mother laughed this time, a full laugh that filled the room. "Oh, Ames, your father made more mistakes before we were married than he did things right. He was so far from perfect that I hadn't even considered him as a husband."

Not a little confused, she walked to the window of her mother's bedroom, the view of Thornwood truly spectacular with the grounds behind the house laid out, her own studio in the middle past the gardens. But she didn't truly see its beauty, her thoughts falling over each other. She turned to face her mother. "If Father wasn't perfect, then why did you marry him?"

"Because he was perfect for me. More importantly, he loved me as much as I loved him." She smiled softly. "Do you love him?"

"I don't know. I feel like he betrayed me, but he didn't. Not precisely. But he did keep the truth from me."

Her mother shook her head. "You can't expect anyone to be perfect like your paintings. We are all living, breathing flawed individuals, who will disappoint you on occasion. Everyone makes an error in judgment at some point or another."

She'd made so many errors herself, she felt the fool for expecting anything more.

"If he's willing to promise not to keep important information from you again, then he could make a good husband. I've always wanted my daughters to marry with their hearts. Just be sure you love him, and he loves you before committing to marriage." Her mother frowned. "I do not want you to go through what Mariel did."

"Do you mean with Lord Blackmore or Lord Beaumont?"

"Both."

Not entirely sure she understood about her older sister, since she'd been too young when Mariel had fallen in love, and was so grateful that her sister had married Beaumont to save them that she had never delved too deeply into Mariel's marriage. But she did understand that Mariel did not love George Walford, Marquess of Beaumont. And with Andrew, she didn't even know how she felt about him. All she knew is she missed him.

Her mother studied her from across the room. "Would you marry him if given another chance?"

"To be truthful, I don't think he'd accept me. We had made promises to each other. He kept his. I broke mine." And that was something she needed to do something about at the very least. It might help the guilt she felt and help her figure out how she felt.

A new plan formed and she was anxious to get started. "Thank you, Mother. I think I must first fulfill part of my promise." She strode across the room and kissed her mother on the cheek, then headed for the door.

"And then what?"

"I don't know." She closed the door behind her and headed downstairs. The first thing she needed to do is have a painting brought from her studio.

—

Amelia had three hours to decide what to say to Andrew when she saw him, but as the coach proceeded down the drive of Lyonsmere Hall, her words left her at the sight of three other coaches waiting before the stately home.

"It appears that Lord Sommerset and his mother are quite popular. Either that or they are hosting a special tea." Joanna's observation was on point.

If they had other guests, that made it particularly difficult to deliver the painting that sat on the seat beside her, across from James.

That gentleman sat forward. "Well, I for one will be happy to remove myself from this coach. As enchanting as it is to be accompanied by the two of you, spending hours couped up in here does have me anxious to stretch my legs despite the cold temperatures."

No one had a chance to comment as the door was opened and the steps set. The duke lifted the framed portrait wrapped in brown paper and handed it to the footman. "Bring this in and give it to the butler." He followed the painting out of the coach and extended a hand to her.

She took it and stepped down from the coach then waited as James helped Joanna down. The wind whipped across the drive, and they soon hurried forward followed by the footman with her painting. As soon as they were inside, James handed the butler his card and they waited. She clasped her hands together hard, her nerves threatening to make her visibly shake and she was determined not to. She was simply here to deliver a painting. That she hoped to talk to Andrew was of no import to anyone, and quite possibly, of no import to him as well. If that were the circumstance, then she would simply return home and continue as she had been.

Even she knew that to be the lie it was, but she held onto her belief anyway.

Though it was only a moment, it seemed like a whole season had gone by before the butler ushered them into the parlor where she followed behind Joanna and James, not sure how her reception would be with either Andrew or his mother.

"Your Graces." Andrew's mother curtsied. "What an unexpected surprise."

Joanna turned to her and motioned her forward. "Yes, my sister has told us so much about you that we wished to visit before returning to Burhleigh Park."

Andrew's mother gave her a cold stare. "Lady Amelia, this is even more of a surprise."

"Lady Sommerset, it is a pleasure to be here." She kept her smile fixed.

"Humph." Andrew's mother turned her attention back to Joanna and James. As she made the introductions to the three ladies sitting about the room, Amelia was keenly aware that Andrew was nowhere to be seen.

"They have come to call on my son, as they are quite interested in him as a husband."

At Lady Sommerset's statement, Amelia scanned the faces of the three women. One blushed, one smiled, and the last narrowed her eyes at her. Clearly, they all knew she had turned Andrew away and hoped to capture him themselves. At the thought of him marrying any one of them, her heart started to race and her chest felt as if the great Colossus statue in Italy had fallen on her.

"Unfortunately, Andrew is out with his steward." Lady Sommerset shook her head. "He cares too much for his people, I'm afraid."

Unable to stomach spending another moment inside, she spoke. "We only came to deliver a painting he commissioned. Please let him know it is here."

Joanna gave her a questioning look, but quickly confirmed her account. "Yes, I just couldn't resist the opportunity to meet you. Please tell Lord Sommerset that we are sorry we missed him and hope we will see him again soon."

Startled by what must have seemed like a sudden change in plans, Lady Sommerset curtsied. "I will be sure to tell him, Your Grace."

She couldn't wait for any more pleasantries. Turning around, she headed out of the room back to the entryway. As soon as the butler helped her with her cloak, she opened the door herself and ran for the coach, tears blinding her as attempted to enter, making it difficult to see the step. Despite the coachman's help, she tripped as she climbed inside, landing on the floor of the coach, but couldn't seem to gather the energy to get up.

She loved him!

The realization took her breath away for a moment as she struggled to breathe through the pain in her chest. She loved Andrew and she had lost him. No, she had tossed him away like an unsatisfactory canvas.

"Amelia!" Joanna's voice from outside the open coach door, made her cringe.

Strong arms lifted her and set her on the seat next to Joanna as her sister grabbed her hand. "Amelia, what is it? Are you hurt?"

The coach started to move. Was she hurt? Yes, she was. She'd hurt herself. Despite her tears, she looked at Joanna and hiccupped. "I love him."

Her sister pulled her against her and gave her a hug. "Are you sure?"

She nodded against her sister's cloak.

Joanna pushed her away to look at her. "My God, you do."

For some reason, she found the surprise in her sister's face amusing, and she smirked before another hiccup took her.

"How can this be? You hardly know the man. Tell me it is not his handsomeness."

She wanted to laugh at that thought. It was his handsomeness that had her avoiding him most of the season. "No, it's not that." She hiccupped again. "I know him well. He's kind and funny and caring and…he understands me."

At that, Joanna looked askance at her. "I find that difficult to believe. Does he know that when you feel there is a problem with your art, it's like the world is coming to an end?"

She nodded.

"Does he know you'll do anything for your art?"

She smirked. "He does."

Joanna thought for a moment. "Does he know that you wish to complete a masterpiece before marrying?"

Her heart squeezed, her throat closing. She nodded.

"Ames, does he know you underrate yourself in all things?"

Surprised that her sister would come to that conclusion, she widened her eyes. "Why would you say that?"

"Because you do. You don't accept how talented you are or how kind you are or even how proper you are." Joanna grinned. "You must admit you are far more proper than I."

That was true and she wouldn't deny it, but it was also one of her favorite traits about Joanna. "But being able to paint is not nearly as important as being intelligent or being able to run a household."

"Is that what you think?" The shock on her sister's face surprised her, and she looked to her brother-in-law to see if he agreed. James sat there shaking his head as if she were ridiculously naïve.

Stubbornly, she sat back. "Yes, and I know it to be true."

Joanna looked at her husband then back at her. "Francis Bacon said the job of the artist is always to deepen the mystery. Only someone like you can do that."

James nodded in agreement. "And Aristotle said, the aim of art is to represent not the outward appearance of things, but their inward significance. That is a significant contribution to humanity."

At their words, only four of her paintings came to mind, the three she'd done of Andrew and the miniature of Belinda. In those she could see what they meant, that there was something revealed about them when she painted.

"And William Blake says, art can never exist without naked beauty displayed. I believe—"

"Stop." Joanna's quote made her far too uncomfortable. "This does not negate the fact that I have ruined any chance of happiness with Lord Sommerset." Even saying his formal name caused her pain, as that was not what he was to her, but would be for the rest of her life. How could she have not realized, and worse why did she have to understand now, when three women, maybe more would gladly marry him? The thought started new tears.

James handed her a handkerchief and she stem the flow, but she had no hope.

"Well, we'll just have to figure something out, right James?"

At Joanna's question, the duke shifted in his seat. "Of course. What did you have in mind?"

Joanna looked to her, but she couldn't imagine Andrew wanting her, especially now that he said he loved her and she had turned him away. Now that she was aware how much she loved him, his rejection of her would destroy her.

For the first time, she finally understood what Mariel meant. "Mariel is right. Without love, nothing matters." Her heart ached for her sister.

"Yes, I didn't fully comprehend Mariel's feelings about Marcus until I lost James." Joanna reached across the coach and took her husband's hand almost as if she needed reassurance that she had truly had him.

"I don't know what to do. Even if he had been home, I doubt that he would see me. I don't think his mother would have allowed me in if you hadn't been there."

"I believe you are correct." Joanna squeezed her husband's hand and let go. "That means we have to find a way for you two to talk."

She looked at her sister, hope trying to get free, but her mind not letting it. "Even if I get to talk to him, he may not forgive me. He told me he loved me and I...I didn't believe him." She clasped her hands together hard, the pain of self-recrimination almost too much to bear. But she deserved it.

"I don't know what you can do, but I do know that I'm not traveling back to Bedford today." James gave his characteristic half-nod. "I've been cooped up in this coach far too long, and we passed a perfectly quaint inn as we drove through the village on our trek out here. My first suggestion, or should I say edict, is that we spend the night there."

Joanna pounced. "I think that a lovely idea. It will give us time to ponder a solution. We obviously cannot visit Lyonsmere Hall again. Not with all the local ladies calling. We need to lure him out."

James raised his brows. "We aren't hunting a fox."

Joanna winked. "We might as well be. I can see where the strategy could be the same."

Andrew was no fox. He was more like a lion and would be as likely to attack his hunter as fall to him. The only way she could see to entice him was if they could help him with his financial situation without mention of her or her dowry. "Oh, I think I know what would interest him. At Lady Dulac's season-closing ball, James offered to advise Lord Sommerset on the management of his estate after the unusual summer we had. Back then he was worried about his tenants and their ability to survive. Now, I understand why, his father left heavy debts when he passed."

"Really?" James frowned.

Joanna shook her head at her husband's lack of societal knowledge. "I can see that. The former Lord Sommerset enjoyed life to the fullest. He didn't gamble, but he did collect horses, paintings, um, women, and I believe he even sponsored a pugilist one year. I can see where he may have had debts."

She didn't like hearing that Andrew's father had collected women, but Andrew had pledged his loyalty to her and from now on she would take him at his word. "Lord Northwick, would you be willing to give Lord Sommerset advice on how to proceed?"

"I would." James contemplated the idea. "I could send a note from the inn and see if the man will meet with me. I'm sure they have some private dining rooms there." He looked her in the eye. "Understand that I can only do so much. A man's pride is a strong factor, and he may not be willing to meet with me, knowing that we travel together."

At his words, her chest constricted. It was a soft condemnation of her rejection of Andrew, and she deserved it. "I understand. Even if he won't see me, if you can help him, I would be grateful."

Joanna patted her hand. "Of course he'll help I will, too." She gave her husband a telling look. "I do keep the ledgers after all."

"And you do that quite beautifully." James smiled at Joanna.

Would she ever see Andrew smile at her again, or would he marry one of the many ladies anxious for his hand? The pain of that happening was too unbearable to contemplate. Those women didn't even know him. No doubt all they saw were his multi-colored golden locks and golden eyes and thought him perfect. They didn't know about his sense of humor, how he cared for his mother, or how exciting his touch could be.

Grasping her anger toward the local women like marble she was determined to sculpt, she kept herself from crying again for the whole of an hour.

CHAPTER TWENTY-ONE

ANDREW SAT OPPOSITE his mother at dinner, thankful to have peace and quiet for a moment. The day had been productive, but tiring. The cold had been especially harsh as he'd helped a tenant push his wagon out of a ditch. It had been a long time since he'd done any manual labor and it surprised him how good it felt to accomplish something. That his tenant was grateful would go a long way in letting his people know that he wasn't like his father.

Having already finished a plate of blancmange, he helped himself to another.

"Really Andrew, such an appetite." His mother's admonishment actually pleased him. She seemed to take so little interest in life unless it was something Mrs. Bolton said. In that instance, the lady companion had helped a little.

"You know how much I love blancmange."

"Yes, you and your father. Your love for that dish is at least something in common with him."

He forced himself not to grimace. He was nothing like his father beyond blancmange. The more he learned of his father's dealings with others, the more disillusioned he became with his parent. Deciding not to comment, he took another mouthful of food to avoid replying.

His mother set down her fork and waved over a footman

who took her plate. "It is unfortunate you weren't here for our callers again today. We had quite a few."

He took a sip of wine, glad he had been about. It was difficult making excuses to be away from the house every day, but his mother was enjoying the company, so he'd continue for a while yet. "Were you happy with them?" He took another bite.

"Oh, yes, well, except one. I was especially pleased to have a visit from the Duke and Duchess of Northwick."

The blancmange suddenly tasted like paste in his mouth, and he forced himself to swallow it. "How unusual." He grabbed his wine glass and took a gulp.

His mother watched him keenly. "Yes, unfortunately, Lady Amelia was with them. She brought the painting you commissioned from her. I didn't know you were having her paint your portrait. I don't think she captured your nobleness though. Your father was quite jovial, but his portrait is much more regal than yours. A portrait should be dignified befitting your station."

He sputtered on his wine, quickly wiping his face. "Did you see it?"

"Of course I saw it. Oh, it was wrapped in brown paper, but I had Mr. Pratt unwrap it. After how that woman treated you, I thought I should view it before you did. I really do think you'll need to have another done. It just won't do. I don't know what you'll do with it."

He rose. "Where is it?"

"It's in the study. Surely you aren't going to look at it now. Cook made green tea ice cream."

Striding toward the archway of the dining room, he did pause. "Tell her I'll have it in my study."

"Mrs. Bolton was right. I should have never…"

He didn't hear what else Mrs. Bolton had to say as he strode through the house to his study. Opening the doors, he scanned the room. It took him a moment to find where Pratt had set the painting. It lay on top of his desk.

Striding toward it, his heart beat erratically until the fully clothed figure came into view. "She painted another." A sense of awe filled him at her industry. Lifting the painting, he set it on one of the wingback chairs before his desk.

His mother had no idea how dignified this one was compared to the one he thought Amelia had brought. He was fully clothed in his usual colors, one hand resting on the back of a chair as he stood in front of a window. The scene beyond the window was snow and he recognized it from her studio. His breath caught at the sting of hurt that shot to his chest at the memory.

Ignoring the too familiar pang, he continued his perusal, smiling wryly as he found the painting of a friar on the wall. Intrigued, he looked for more clues and discovered a cloak that looked very much like hers hanging on a hook in the background and on a table beneath the friar painting was a bowl of fruit. A smile tugged at the corner of his mouth despite himself. She'd done it again, captured all of him, inside and outside with a nod to their time together.

Did she paint it before or after she decided his need for her dowry made him ineligible to be her husband? A flame of anger ignited deep inside him, and he picked up the painting, intending to smash it against the corner of his desk, but he halted. Why had she brought it to him after three weeks? Why not destroy it? And what did she do with the painting of him upon the acropolis?

He let the painting slide to the floor as he held one end. How could she think he would want it? Was it simply to fulfill their bargain? He sneered at the thought. A painting of himself was far from being his wife. He looked about for a place to put it and his gaze fell upon his father's portrait. He hadn't realized how much he disliked that portrait, but now that his mother had commented on it, he understood. The portrait was a fake vision of his father, just like he'd had a faulty opinion of the man.

Glancing toward the portrait of himself, he made his decision. Carrying it to the fireplace, he leaned it against a chair. "If Mother likes you so much, she can have you." He lifted the large painting from its place above the mantle where it had hung nigh on twenty years. Setting that one aside, he placed his own portrait on the wall.

Turning back to his desk, he sat behind it and took in the view. From across the room, the subtle reminders of his time with Amelia were not obvious, and he could simply gaze upon his figure. It really was very well done and much more pleasurable than staring at his father when he happened to look up from his work. He'd have his father's portrait added to his mother's bedroom or sitting area.

At a knock on the door, he called his man to enter, ready to have that ice cream his mother mentioned.

When Pratt entered, he didn't hide his surprise. His butler never served food, yet he carried in a bowl of green tea ice cream. "My lord, you just received this note from the Duke of North-wick." He held up the sealed paper in his other hand. "He has requested a response."

His heart started to beat harder in his chest. Had the man learned of his failed bargain with Lady Amelia? Or did he hope to warn him away from the Mabry family? That would be a waste of time as he had no intention of seeing any of them again.

Pratt handed him the note and he opened it quickly.

Dear Lord Sommerset.

I was disappointed we did not have the pleasure of your company upon arriving at Lyonsmere Hall and I hope your activities on your estate were successful. Your mother's mention of these brought to mind that I have been remiss in my promise to you to share my strategies for managing my tenants' current trials after this past summer's unprecedented weather and subsequent harvest. I have taken lodgings at the Owl's Nest Inn for an additional night on the chance that I could be of some assistance to you. If you are able, I am free for afternoon tea upon the morrow. A favor of your response is requested.

Lord James Huntington, Duke of Northwick

That was not what he'd expected, especially after his failed attempt to take Amelia as his wife. Why would the duke want to help him? Had she told the duke of his current troubles or was it simply the duke being in the area and wanting to, as he said, follow through on his offer? Part of him wanted to refuse outright. He didn't want to have anything to do with the Mabry family and knowing that the duke, his duchess, and Amelia were traveling together meant he could risk seeing *her*. He wished to avoid that for a very long time. His heart still hurt at her rejection of him and as he reasoned, their entire time together.

The duke mentioned afternoon tea, specifically. That might mean it was the best time while the ladies were otherwise engaged. He doubted very much that Amelia would wish to see him any more than he wanted to see her. The fact was, he did need advice and Lord Northwick was offering. Turning away such an offer when the man was in such close proximity bordered upon rude. He shook his head. There was much to be gained by accepting the invitation.

"Is that a no, then, sir?"

"What?" He lifted his head. "No. Tell the messenger I will attend upon the duke."

"Yes sir." Pratt started for the door then halted. He turned. "If I may sir. I believe that portrait suits this room much better. Would you like me to find a new place for the old one?"

He looked up at his own face above the fireplace, an amused smile curling his lips in the painting. "I was just trying it out, Pratt. But I think I agree with you. Yes, please find an appropriate place for my father's portrait, perhaps somewhere where only my mother can view it."

Pratt gave a short bow. "It would be my pleasure, sir."

As Pratt exited with the portrait of his father in hand, he moved the bowl of ice cream closer and dug in his spoon. Now that he thought on it, he had at least a dozen questions to ask the duke, unfortunately, all of them meant admitting his current financial situation and the reason for it. If he did so, he risked the *ton* discovering the truth, which would mean marrying before the season. Even at that thought, his stomach recoiled. He released the spoon, sitting back. But to not do all in his power to help his people and keep his mother from knowing the precipice they resided on was also foolhardy.

Also, if the duke had advice that he could use, he wouldn't need a wife...forever. He did have a younger brother. Christopher could always marry and have children. He'd obviously been practicing. His brother had received his letter about curtailing his spending on his mistress with much complaint, most likely because he couldn't bring himself to explain why.

His appetite returned with his new plan and he sat forward again, pulling out a spoonful of green tea ice cream. He closed his eyes as he savored the unique flavor. Opening his eyes, he found himself looking at his portrait. He was nothing like his father. Now he just hoped who he was would be enough to save his family.

—

Andrew walked into the private dining room at the Owl's Nest Inn and halted. The duke rose from the small table in a space no larger than his coach. The confines of the room were not what startled him. It was the duchess sitting at the table that had him rethinking his decision to accept the invitation.

"Lord Sommerset, I'm pleased that you were able to come."

He gave a short bow. "Your Grace, I could not refuse. It is a great boon you grant me." He turned to Amelia's sister. "Lady Northwick, I did not realize you would be joining us."

She waved off his comment even as she smiled warmly. "I'm only here to pour tea and be sure my husband has the numbers right. I keep our ledger, so I want to be sure he is correct in his advice."

The duke gave a short shake of his head. "I'm always right. Please." He opened his hand to the chair next to his own.

Andrew used this very room a few times when meeting friends and was familiar with the burgundy and gold pattern on the walls and furniture. It had been the birthplace of a prank or two with Harewood as well. Moving to the chair indicated, he silently hoped that Amelia would not join them. "I appreciate your experience. Mayhap you can tell me what you have done and if it has been successful."

The duke steepled his hands. "You must know, my management of my estates this winter may sound rather radical compared to what you've been taught, but it has been a most unusual year. Unlike the years when the Thames froze, this past summer has decimated our harvest."

"Ours as well. I also hear this same fate has been visited upon both Europe and America." He accepted the cup of tea Lady Northwick passed him.

The duke raised his brows. "That is correct. Am I to assume, then, that you have some investment in trade?"

"I do." He held his breath for the man's reaction.

"Good. That's good. Things may have ground to a halt at the moment, but they will pick up soon as countries search out necessities they don't have. Do not shy away from trade. It is part of a diversified strategy that allows us to weather any storm."

The duchess groaned. "James, must you use puns?"

One corner of the duke's mouth twitched. "You noticed that, did you?"

She rolled her eyes. "Please excuse him. He can't help but show off his intelligence."

"I can't help that my intellect is so obvious." The duke actually grinned.

Lady Northwick ignored her husband. "The first thing James did was to allow our tenants to keep their rents. They were shocked, of course, but it sets them up for the winter and the coming spring."

A feeling of relief flowed through him that his idea had been a good one. "Yes, I have done that as well."

"You have?" The duke raised his brows. "That's excellent. When I suggested it to others, they were appalled." He took a sip of his tea.

"I cannot see how starving my tenants and forcing them to move will help my estate." He didn't mention that he would be going into debt soon because of it. "What else have you done?"

"I have stockpiled feed for the animals. I don't believe there will be much available soon."

He hadn't thought of that. Blast.

"I have also ordered numerous necessities such as coal and foodstuffs, which are due to arrive soon."

And there it was, another expenditure that he could not make. He shook his head. "I'm afraid I cannot do that."

"James, could Lord Sommerset purchase some of what you have ordered? From what I remember, you did plan on both Burhleigh Park and Silver Meadows, but Silver Meadows won't need much with the fields we plan to leave fallow."

"I will not need to infringe upon your purchases." He curled his fingers into the palm of the hand he had beneath the table.

"Your estate has enough?" The duke's voice sounded almost affronted.

"No, I simply cannot purchase them." He unclenched his right hand and ran it through his hair. "I was sure Lady Amelia would have told you. My father left significant debts when he passed. While I was able to satisfy them all, I had counted on the yields from my tenants. That obviously didn't happen."

"That's why you wanted to marry Amelia this winter." Lady Northwick's eyes rounded.

Her realization surprised him. Had Amelia not told her family? Had Lady Beaumont not told them? Shocked himself, he didn't know what to say.

The duke spoke into the awkward silence. "Do you have property you can sell? Perhaps your London home?"

"I thought about it, but…"

"But what?" The duke took another sip of tea as if the topic they were discussing was the latest gossip and not the future of his estate.

They already knew more than he preferred, what was a bit more? "My mother doesn't know the state of our affairs. She idolized my father and had been so frail since he passed, I didn't wish to add to her burden."

Lady Northwick's gaze softened for the first time since he'd entered the room.

He didn't want her sympathy. What he needed was a bloody miracle. "I'm afraid I have wasted our time. There is obviously nothing else for me to do." He started to rise.

"Wait." Lord Northwick frowned. "If you can come up with an excuse to skip this coming season, you could keep your London home and rent it. I understand many of our peers rent during the season."

He sat back down. "That is a possibility." He was well aware that even the Enderlys rented a home for the season. He silently calculated what it would add to his coffers, and it could work, except it would be too late. He shook his head. "I'm afraid I will need the added cashflow before then."

"Then it appears you have only one option."

He stared at the duke in surprise. He didn't see any options and hope reared its fickle head. "What is that?"

"Marry a woman with a significant dowry immediately."

"James, no." Lady Northwick's reaction to the suggestion seemed odd.

"There's no hope for it. He must if he is to save his estate." The duke pierced him with a penetrating gaze. "Would you be willing to marry for a dowry?"

As his chest constricted at the idea, he rose. "No." Lord Northwick opened his mouth to say more, but he refused to listen. "No. I will not tie myself to a woman for life, just to solve a temporary and inconvenient disruption in my family's lifestyle. I would sell our London house and all my paintings before doing that." He gave a short bow. "I am sorry I wasted your time." He thought about asking them to keep his financial situation a secret, but dismissed it. They would do whatever they chose, even if he did ask.

Seeing that he was intent on leaving, the duke and duchess rose as well and moved between him and the door, Lady

Northwick laying her gloved hand on his arm. "I hope you will reconsider."

He started to shake his head, but the door opened and Amelia walked in. He sucked in his breath at the sight of her. After three weeks of absence from her presence, he felt like a thirsty man being offered water, but in this case that water was frozen. Still, he couldn't help staring. She was a vision in a pale pink dress, the wisps of her hair softening her face. He steeled himself against her beauty, reminding himself that she had different priorities than he.

Lady Northwick spoke to her sister. "We'll be right outside."

Amelia nodded and the door closed, leaving them alone.

Immediately, he moved to the door. "This is improper." The last thing he needed was to be forced into a marriage neither of them wanted.

"Please, they won't say anything to anyone. They are not Lady Garmoyle."

Part of him wanted to believe they were, but his instinct said otherwise. Still, he stayed near the door, as far away from her as he could. "Did you wish to speak with me privately, then?" He was lost as to what else she could say.

"Did you see your portrait?"

Was that all? Did she once more worry about her talent? Though he tried, he could not complement her work, even though it deserved it. "I did. Thank you."

She clasped her hands in front of her, a sign of her nervousness. "I need to apologize."

He almost broke out into laughter, but choked it back. An apology would hardly repair his heart. Only distance from her would do that. "I accept."

She blinked. "But you don't know what I'm apologizing for."

He raised his brows. "I would hazard a guess that you are apologizing for breaking our bargain and turning away my proposal of marriage."

She flushed, the red starting at her neckline and rising. She was truly embarrassed? That was too odd to ignore.

"Yes and no." She licked her lips. "I want to apologize for my reaction to your need for my dowry. I didn't realize my response was due to my idealization of what a husband should embody, but I understand now that I was incorrect."

He frowned, not a little confused. He shook his head. It didn't matter. "As I said, I accept your apology. Now, I should go."

"No, wait." She unclasped her hands and stepped closer.

The damn scent of violets teased his nostrils. He stepped back. "Why?"

"I'm not doing this right."

He almost laughed at her, but swallowed it down. Did she not realize that whatever she had to say to assuage her own guilt only made his pain worse?

"Andrew, I made a mistake. I do want to marry you."

He stiffened. What game did she play now? He swallowed hard, anger now making his voice harsh. "Why?"

She attempted to smile, but it faltered. "I want to help your family. I want to help you."

So she would sacrifice herself like her older sister only for his family and then be forever the martyr. "I don't need your charity."

"It's not charity." She stepped closer, the small room making it impossible to step away again. "I missed you. I missed your smile and talking about art. I missed your kindness. And I missed touching you." Though she blushed, she didn't look away.

That fickle flame of hope once more ignited, and he tried to snuff it out. "I'm sure you can find someone else to pose for you."

She shook her head, her smile genuine and unwavering. "No, I can't, because I love you. I didn't realize it until I'd let you go."

His heart started to race and sweat formed on his brow. "You rejected me." Saying it out loud seemed to take some of the sting away.

"You're right, and I was wrong to do so, but I knew no better." She touched his cheek, her hand soft against his skin. "I know better now. I want to be your wife in all ways. I want to be your companion, your hostess, your artist, your dance partner, and your mistress."

Breathing in her scent, losing himself in her sky-blue eyes, hearing her profess her desire to be his in all ways was too much to resist. He grasped her to him. "How can I believe you?"

Her smile widened. "Because I know now that even if we had to sell my paints and move into a small home with nothing more than a single maid, I would be content as long as I'm with you."

His chest filled at her willingness to be with him, come what may. It was more than he'd expected. He tried to imagine her in such a setting and chuckled. "Just a maid, you say?"

She cocked her head. "Perhaps a cook as well. I don't know how to make blancmange."

"Do I hear correctly?" He gave her a doubtful look. "Are you asking me to marry you?"

Her eyes lit with amusement. "I do believe I am."

Happiness filled him, spreading from his chest to the tips of his fingers. "Then, my answer is yes." Cupping her head with his hand, he lowered his lips and kissed the sweet mouth he'd missed for too long. With her by his side, he could do anything.

Her tongue nudged his lips, but he pulled away, not willing to have any impropriety before they were wed. "You must wait."

She pouted, her lower lip slightly further out than her upper.

"I know, but we must do this right. First, I must ask your father."

Her hand rifled through his hair, making it hard to concentrate. "Couldn't you just ask the duke for now and we can run away to Gretna Green?"

Taking both her hands from his person, he forced her to step back. "No. You can wait three weeks." Though how he would, he wasn't sure.

"Fine." She crossed her arms and gave him a sly smile. "I just hope my bowl of fruit isn't rotten by then."

As his laughter filled the room, the door opened and the duchess stepped in. "Am I to assume we have a wedding to plan?"

Amelia flew into her sister's arms. "Yes!"

CHAPTER TWENTY-TWO

Late February 1817

ANDREW SQUEEZED HIS new wife's hand as she watched the snow fall from the coach window. "We're almost home."

"Home. My new home."

"Yes, Lady Sommerset." He smiled, hoping to make her as comfortable as possible settling into Lyonsmere Hall.

She held up her other hand to view the ring he'd placed upon her finger just hours earlier. He'd commissioned it, not wanting to take his mother's since his father was yet a year in the ground.

Her ring was a classic band with a unique design, the grape vines running round it a nod to their favorite source of amusement—he as her bowl of fruit. "Yes, I'm a countess now. I do hope I remember that." She smirked as she turned her hand this way and that. "This should help. It's so beautiful."

"I think it will take my mother time to become used to being the dowager countess. She still forgets that I am the Earl of Sommerset now."

Amelia lowered her hand to hold his between her two. "I won't mind if she forgets. I'm just grateful that she forgave me for my poor judgment in rejecting you. She thinks you are infallible, which was my mistake as well."

He chuckled even as he shook his head. "That is not what she reveals to me."

"You are her son. She should believe in you. You give her a lot to be proud of."

And if the truth be told, he'd given her many worries growing up. "Your father and your sister, Lady Northwick, believe in you even more." He shook his head. "Your sister is a formidable negotiator with the bridal contract."

"I do hope she was fair. I did tell her to be so."

"Fair? The woman was far more generous than I wished, but made it seem as if it was all my idea in the end. I am quite good with numbers, but I do think I've met my match with Lady Northwick."

She grinned, so proud of her sister now. The old resentment melted away with the realization that she would have never considered Andrew as a husband if her Aunt Mabry had left Silver Meadows to her instead of to Joanna. "So we and our tenants will be fine until spring?"

He pulled his hand from hers and stroked her cheek with his finger. "I love hearing you say 'we' and 'our,' and yes, we all will be fine for years with just your dowry." His brows lowered. "Though I do worry about supplies being available."

"You can always consult the duke on that. He is highly connected. So you see, I bring more than just money with me." She smirked to be sure he would understand she jested.

"I know that. You bring warmth and light, laughter and companionship—"

She put her finger over his lips. "Please, no more listings of my qualities. I fear they will turn my head and Belinda said ego was the worst of all faults."

Unable to resist, he opened his mouth and sucked on her finger.

"Andrew!" She pulled her finger away.

He laughed, loving her reaction and anxious to see more as he introduced her to the marriage bed. "I cannot promise to save you from my compliments. I fear your sister may not approve."

Amelia's smile disappeared. "Belinda never expected us to be perfect. She loved us, faults and all, and I know she would have approved of you."

"I'm humbled that she would because I too have many faults. But you have gone far beyond my expectations for a wife."

"I have to assume, then, that you did not reach very high." She held up her hand as he opened his mouth to argue. "And there is one expectation I have to be more cognizant of, not to minimize my own qualities. If you can refrain from listing them, I can attempt to stop minimizing them."

"I can agree to that." He looked past her and out the window as the coach turned into the long main drive of Lyonsmere, the bushes lining the lane covered in powdery snow. Soon he would have his wife all to himself. "It was kind of your parents to invite my mother to stay for a few days. She does enjoy socializing and hasn't done much since my father passed."

"Was she quite upset that you released Mrs. Bolton from employment?"

"At first, she did seem put out, but when I explained that you would be here, she brightened considerably. I believe she plans to show you how to run everything." He held his breath, not sure how his wife and new Countess of Sommerset would feel about that.

She cocked her head. "You did tell her that I would appreciate that, having never run a household before. Unfortunately, though I learned the basics, I rarely helped as I was closeted in my studio. With Mariel and Joanna about, Mother didn't need me."

He let out his breath in relief; navigating two women in his house was a new experience. "I didn't, but you can. Though Pratt and Mrs. Ridley cover all the details and the assignment of work, my mother does give direction."

"And don't forget, you promised me a studio of my own. I only sent a few paintings ahead until we decided on a room. So I will need your mother's help for as long as she wishes." Once again, he was struck by how warm her smile was and how generous her heart. His misgivings about the two women slowly dissipated.

The coach came to a stop and Amelia quickly pulled her gloves back on.

The footmen put down the steps and opened the door for him. Stepping out, he gave her his hand. As his wife came to a halt before his home, he felt a new sense of pride and contentment. This was their home, where they'd raise their children and where she would fill the walls with her art. He would no longer need to determine the authenticity of his paintings, as he'd be able to witness their creations.

"Oh, Andrew. Lyonsmere looks like a dream in the snow. I wish I could paint it right now."

Her breathless comment had him looking at her and in that moment, that mystic moment, he knew he'd never forget her coming home with him. Her eyes shone with happiness as snow fell upon her blue spencer and bonnet. She raised her head and stuck out her tongue.

"What are you doing?"

She looked at him as if he was a simpleton. "I'm catching snowflakes on my tongue. Surely you did that as a child."

He shook his head, bemused by her assumption. "No. I didn't know anyone did."

She pulled her arm from his and faced him. "Oh you poor thing. You must try it. Just stick your tongue out and try to catch the flakes. They don't taste like much, but when the cold hits your tongue it's just, well, it's triumphant!"

After smiling at him, she tilted her head again and chased after the snowflakes with her tongue.

He looked at his footman, who was better trained than to watch the sight of his wife looking into the gray sky. Shrugging his shoulders he tilted his head and stuck out his tongue. He didn't exactly chase after the white powder, but when a snowflake landed on his tongue, he understood what she meant. There was a ridiculous sense of accomplishment in the small achievement and before he knew it, he was counting how many he caught.

So intent on his count, he didn't see the ball of snow coming until it hit him on the side of his hat, knocking it off. "What?" He looked about to see his wife grinning at him.

"Surely you've thrown snowballs before." Her arm lifted and another came his way.

He ducked, then turned with a grin of his own. "I am by far the best snowball thrower of this family."

She laughed. "You mean you *were*."

Another snowball hit him on the shoulder, half the snow sprinkling his face as it burst on contact. "You imp!" He should have known. Quickly, he gathered up a snowball, but another of hers hit him on his arm. She must have created them while he was catching snowflakes. With her head start, there was only one way to win this.

He headed for her, and she laughed as she threw another, hitting him squarely on the chest. She was less than twenty feet away and started pummeling him with snowballs. When he reached her, he knocked her over, to keep the next snowball from hitting him.

She shrieked as they fell to the snow-covered ground, and he twisted in mid-fall, so she lay on top of him.

"I win." He smiled at her rosy cheeks and the touch of cold upon her nose.

Her laughter filled the air even as their clouds of breath mingled together. "You certainly did."

Yes, he'd won her heart and his happiness. Cupping the back of her head, he kissed her. This time it wasn't the chaste kiss he'd given after the ceremony as they signed the parish registry. He wanted to warm her from the inside out until she wished to be as naked as he had been in her studio. His tongue demanded entrance into her sweet mouth, and she opened willingly, her hands in her gloves holding his head as if she were afraid he would stop.

As their tongues entwined, a small moan came from deep in her throat and he felt himself growing hard. He grabbed her rounded arse and pulled her tighter against him, oblivious to everything but the woman in his arms who squirmed to get closer.

It wasn't until the snow beneath his uncovered head began to melt down the nape of his neck that he recalled where they were and the dangers of the cold to his new bride. Forcing himself to retreat, he broke the kiss, only by turning his head.

She proceeded to kiss his neck, causing ripples of excitement to run up his spine. He whispered in her ear. "Amelia, we must go inside if you wish to take your clothes off and sate the fire building inside you."

She stilled as if she too suddenly recalled where they were. She jerked her head up. "A fire? That's an excellent idea." She rolled off him to sit in the snow.

Quickly, he gained his feet and helped her stand. Then as if nothing untoward had occurred before the coachman, footmen, and no doubt some of his house staff, he escorted his wife up the steps to her new home.

His wife. Just those two words had his heart beating harder.

The door opened before them. "Welcome home, my lord and lady." Pratt stood to the side as they entered and helped Amelia with her outwear.

The butler then assisted him with his great coat, looking pointedly at his head for his hat.

"It's outside."

Pratt raised one eyebrow at that news, but refrained from further comment on it. "The staff have been given the day off as you requested. The stable master will inform the coach attendants."

"Very good." He wished to have Amelia alone as soon as possible.

Amelia smirked at him, amusement glittering in her eyes. Pleased that she found his decision acceptable, he started to lead her past Pratt.

"Excuse me, my lord."

He halted and turned. "Yes."

"I had cook put together a cold dinner for you. You'll find it in the kitchen if you so desire it." The older man didn't exactly smile, but his usual stoic countenance had disappeared. "I think you may require it later."

"Very forward thinking of you, Pratt. That will be quite acceptable." Pleased that his butler had thought further ahead than he had, he led his wife up the stairs.

When they reached the landing, she finally spoke. "If we are not to need the servants, whatever will we do?"

"I will show you where your bedroom is and then we will make full use of it."

She halted, pressing her hand to her chest. "During the day?"

At first, he thought she jested, but her gaze revealed she hadn't thought making love normal in the afternoon. It reminded him of exactly how innocent she was. "Yes. There is no inappropriate time of day for me to show my wife how much I love her."

A pretty blush colored her cheeks. "And is this any day or just for our wedding day?"

He let his need to make her his show in his gaze. "Any day."

"Oh." Her breathless excitement was all he needed to hear.

He turned down the hall and pointed to his bedroom. "This is where I sleep, and right next door is your bedroom." He halted before the door and turned the knob, letting the door swing open.

She disengaged her hand from his arm and took a step inside. "Oh, it's perfect."

The walls were covered in lavender wallpaper, the bed and bed curtains though were a pale green. The color theme was carried throughout the room from the settee to the rugs. The room had originally been decorated in all lavender, but over the last weeks, he had a sense of what she would like and had the green accents added to the room. Hearing her genuine pleasure, he grinned, quite happy with himself.

She scanned the walls, turning as if looking for something.

He studied them as well, wondering if he'd forgotten something when his gaze came upon a new painting. His heart stopped and emotion closed his throat.

"Do you like it?" Her voice whispered through him.

He couldn't take his gaze from it and strode toward the nude portrait she'd done of him in her studio. She made him appear like an ancient Greek hero, standing proud with the acropolis behind him and his hand resting on the neck of a large lion who stood slightly across him, hiding his male parts. Almost everything was painted in a golden or brown shade except the bright sunset glimpsed in the top corner of the piece.

He walked closer to it, his chest swelling with pride at her accomplishment. "This is a masterpiece."

She came up next to him, her violet scent announcing her presence before she spoke. "I arranged to have Pratt hang it for me when I sent some of my belongings. You are pleased then?"

He couldn't believe the painting was him, yet it was. She'd added much to it besides the background since he'd last seen it. His hair was longer in the painting than he usually wore it and filled with lights and darks. His face had more beard growth than he sported, but every nuance of his physique and features was exact. In the portrait, he gazed into the distance like a king surveying his realm and a soft smile played about his lips.

He forced himself to look away from the creation to gaze at the creator. "It is perfect. Far better than I could have imagined. It's as if you have caught a mystic moment, even though such a moment never occurred."

Color rose in her face, but she didn't look away. "I thought so as well, but never sought such an epitome of talent." She looked at the painting and back at him. "I think it was my subject. You brought this out in me. I could not have achieved such genius without you. To be honest, I am a little in awe of it."

Seeing how she truly felt, he decided to put off his own need to make her his wife in truth for just a bit longer. He'd known she had talent in addition to all of her other qualities, but seeing this now, he felt confident in his decision to transform one other room. "Come, I wish to show you something."

She gave him a shy smile. "But I thought you wished to consummate our marriage."

"I do, but there is something as important to you, to us." He took her hand, his excitement growing as he led her back into the corridor and to the room next to hers. Without preamble, he opened it and allowed her to precede him.

She scanned the space in an instant before her eyes widened as her gaze came to rest on him. "A studio?"

"*Your* studio." He opened his arm to allow her the pleasure of discovering everything. He'd enlisted the aid of her sisters to furnish it with not only all the furniture and supplies from her studio at Thornwood, but also to add additional items they suggested.

She began to walk around the circumference of the room, her hand touching first an easel, then a table, and finally stopping at the settee across the room from him. Even from where he stood, he could see the glistening in her eyes.

"Is it sufficient?" He found himself holding his breath.

Instead of answering, she wound between the tables and two chairs coming to stop just inches from him. "It's more than I dreamed of. You really do wish me to continue painting." The wonder in her voice was unmistakable.

He pulled her into his arms. "Of course I want you to continue painting. You are welcome to as long as you wish. It is a part of who you are. And I love who you are."

A tear slipped down her cheek as she wrapped her arms around his neck. "And I love who you are, Greek hero or peer of the realm."

"Or bowl of fruit?"

Her laughter filled the room and sent a feeling of contentment deep into his soul.

"Yes, that as well." She gave him a sly smile. "After all, you do taste so sweet."

Now that definitely deserved a kiss. Lowering his head, he captured her mouth and shared his happiness with her as their tongues entwined.

When a quiet moan escaped her, he forced himself to pull away. Her studio was not the place to take his wife when a perfectly good bed was right next door.

Her blue gaze focused on him. "With this room, I think I'm going to need to paint many more portraits of you." Her teasing light faded, and her brows lowered.

"What is it?"

She glanced toward the paintings she'd completed that were leaning against the walls in one corner, awaiting her choice of placement. She shook her head. "I don't understand a criticism that was leveled at one of my paintings at my exhibit this past summer."

"Criticism?" He stiffened, ready to call out whomever dared to think his wife's work imperfect.

"Yes." She stepped out of his arms. "Maybe you can help me pinpoint the problem."

Before he could react, she headed for the corner and rummaged through the paintings. "Here it is."

He walked over and lifted it from her.

"Put it on that easel, please."

He did as requested. It looked to be after a hunt with three gentlemen talking while the dogs frolicked about. One man was almost facing front, another faced directly forward, and the third was positioned facing the first somewhat. It was a fine painting. Not nearly the caliber of what she'd done of him, but still well done.

He turned around to see what she was about, and he found her bent over the chest from her old studio.

"Here it is." She moved toward him. "Can you move that easel next to this one?"

He did, and she promptly set her book on the tray at the

bottom. It was open to a picture of a man and a woman in a similar position as the painting except they were naked. He whipped his gaze to his wife who stood back comparing the two. Was she not affected by the drawing?

"I just don't see the flaw." She crossed her arms. "Do you?"

Not sure what she was looking for, he walked over to stand beside her. "What flaw?"

She uncrossed one arm and pointed to the book. "I used that sketch to paint that scene." Her finger moved to indicate the painting of the men and dogs. "I didn't feel confident in my male figures. So with no male model, I used the next best option, a sketch of a nude. But during my exhibition, while I spoke to my very good friend, Lady Spencer, two gentlemen were viewing my painting and said in a matter-of-fact tone that the artist had obviously never seen a naked man. Then they laughed at it. But I don't see anything wrong. Do you?"

He moved forward and studied the sketch, avoiding the female in it, and then studied the painting. There was no flaw at all. She had copied the male form perfectly, only adding clothes. A suspicion began to form. "Did these gentlemen know you were nearby?"

"Yes, but they didn't know I was the artist."

He tried not to smirk, but he failed. "Then I believe they were simply trying to catch your attention."

"What? By pointing out a flaw in my work when they didn't know I was the artist? I think not."

Grinning, he pointed to the fall of the pantaloons she'd painted. "There is no flaw. They were simply inferring that they have a bulge here because they are well-endowed. If you had suddenly looked at them, they would have thought you an experienced woman and possibly interested in what they had to offer."

She scowled at him before joining him at the painting. "Are you saying that they only said that to brag about what was in their pantaloons?"

He nodded, still grinning though he shouldn't.

"You mean I didn't need you to pose for me after all?"

At her question, he lost his grin. "What do you mean?"

She lifted her brows at him. "The conditions I set upon your abrupt proposal were meant to accomplish either one of two outcomes. Either you would say yes and model nude for me so I could paint my male figures accurately or…"

"Or you expected me to rescind my proposal."

"Exactly." Her eyes sparkled with pride.

"You little minx." He grabbed her to him. "I was but a means to an end."

She cocked her head, amusement playing at the corners of her very fine lips. "As was I to you, correct?"

How had he ever thought her topics unusual and unimportant? But he'd been right on the mark to think of her as an imp. "I must agree. It would appear that whatever our motivations were, they led us in the right direction."

"Right into each other's arms."

He tightened his hold around her. "My wife." Lowering his head, he showed her with his kiss all the feelings he couldn't seem to put into words.

CHAPTER TWENTY-THREE

A MELIA WRAPPED HER arms around her husband, wanting him to know how happy she was, but not sure how to explain it. She could feel his love in their kiss. Did he feel hers?

She broke away, wanting to say something but not sure what. How did a person tell their spouse how they truly felt?

"You look puzzled."

At his observation, she gave him a nod. "I am." Though she felt she could tell him almost anything, it didn't feel very complimentary to explain that she didn't know how to show him what she felt. She looked away to think and her gaze fell upon the book. Of course, *The Illustrated Pleasures of Seduction*! There was a page, *the* page that had fascinated her and had her wanting to touch Andrew so much. She really could show him how she felt. "I think I need you to undress."

His eyes widened before a slow smile moved his lips and a golden shine sparkled in his eyes. "I was thinking the same thing. Would you like to return to your bedroom?"

She stepped out of his embrace. "No. I would like very much if you would undress in here."

His Adam's apple moved as he swallowed hard, his smile freezing on his face. "You want me to pose again?"

Not willing for him to know her true purpose, she stepped back toward the easel with the book. "Well, I never did get to paint your backside."

"Don't you think we could do that another time? After all, we can come in here any day we want with no fear of others thinking ill of us." He held his hands out, palms up as if hoping to move her.

She bit the inside of her cheek to keep from laughing aloud, thrilled that he had the same thing on his mind as she did. "Oh, I plan to take full advantage of that fact, starting right now."

His quizzical look had her turning toward the easel to avoid letting him see her grin. Lifting the book, she turned to the page she remembered, the one where the man sat upon a chair. Not only did the position appeal to her on some instinctual level, but somehow, she *knew* Andrew would like it.

His hands on her shoulders startled her. "What are you looking at?"

She set the book on the easel. "That." She glanced at him over her shoulder. "I want to do that."

His fingers tightened and his breath whooshed by her ear. The tension in his body where it touched hers communicated his agreement before he even spoke. "Are you sure?"

Why wouldn't she be sure? She turned to face him, dislodging his hands. "I'm not sure of anything but my painting." She pulled on the white cravat he sported that made his skin look so tanned despite the season. Untying it, she tugged it from around his neck and draped it around hers. She couldn't resist touching his chest where the opening of his ruffled shirt revealed his skin. Leaning in, she set a light kiss there. Inhaling, she breathed in his clean scent that just made her wish to touch him more.

Without hesitation, she undid the buttons on his tailcoat, pushing it off his shoulders and throwing it on the table next to them.

"My turn." His voice seemed deeper as he turned her around and untied her blue dress.

She faced the sketch, which made her all the more anxious to disrobe and feel Andrew's hands upon her again. As he lifted her dress over her head, she pulled her arms down, happy to have the suddenly heavy gown gone. Spinning around, she quickly unbuttoned his waistcoat, allowing him to shrug it off before tugging at his shirt tucked into his pantaloons.

His hands grabbed hers. "Wait. Slow down. I promise it will be just as good if we take it slower. Maybe even better."

He just didn't understand her need to be touched and to touch. "Then, could you help me with my stays?"

"That will no doubt become one of my favorite things to do." Grinning, he had her turn around and untied the lacing in the back.

As soon as they were undone, she pulled them from her throwing them on the table.

"Is that better?"

She faced him. "Very much so. Now would you not feel better without these on?" She'd unbuttoned the top buttons of the fall of his pantaloons before he once again stopped her. Did he not see how frustrating he was being?

"Amelia, look at me."

She brought her gaze from his pantaloons to his face.

"You must be gentle around a man's male parts. They can be damaged easily."

Her cheeks heated that she hadn't known that. It was probably in the writing in the book, but she never read it, only studying the images. "Did I hurt you?"

"No, but if you continued as you were, you may have. Will you allow me?"

She gave him a nod, embarrassed that she'd been so intent on seeing his nude body again that she hadn't considered what it was like for him. She didn't think she had any parts that could be hurt simply by undressing, though as she watched him continuing the chore of unbuttoning, the tips of her breasts felt extra sensitive to the fine linen of her shift. Seeing no need to wait to undress, she pulled her shift over her head and dropped it on the table. Finally, she found some patience as she stood in her stockings and shoes and nothing else. How odd that it didn't bother her.

"Amelia."

At his breathy word, she looked at Andrew to find him studying her from the tips of her toes to the tips of her breasts. His pantaloons were finally off, and his gaze had darkened.

"Yes?"

"You would make a far better portrait than I."

Paint herself? It was an interesting challenge. "I'd never thought of doing a self-portrait. I suppose I could if I had a mirror in here."

He groaned.

Looking askance at him, she noticed his shirt was held out from his body by what could only be his manhood. She reached out to touch it, but snapped her hand back. She didn't want to hurt him. "Are you sure you aren't hurt?"

He closed his eyes for what had to be at least ten seconds then opened them. "I am not hurt. I am excited to make love to you, but I want to go slowly so that you enjoy it as much as I will."

She cocked her head. "If it is anything like what you did to me in my studio, then I know I will." The shirt jerked in his groin area. "But I do hope you plan to take that off." She pointed to his shirt, tired of waiting to see all of him again, especially now that she could touch him freely as his wife.

"You really don't understand slow, do you?"

She was saved from answering by him lifting his shirt and dropping it on top of the rest of their clothes. Oh, it had been a long three weeks. Without preamble, she ran her hands over his shoulders and down his chest, fascinated by the puckering of his nipples. Tiny sparks of excitement seemed to pop throughout her body, causing her own nipples to harden.

He pulled her against him, trapping her hands between them. "Has anyone ever told you that you look at things differently than the average lady?"

The shock of his naked body touching her naked body took away all thought at first. His was warm and hard, and her own soft curves seemed to accommodate him. She felt his hardness against her abdomen and rocked her hips toward him.

"Amelia!"

Startled, she pushed back, and he let her go, but he grabbed her hand, keeping her from going far. "What's wrong?"

He ran his free hand through his hair. "Nothing is wrong. In fact, everything is right. You'll understand better after. It's just that seeing you like this, touching you, having you touch me, makes it hard for me to go slow."

Her heart thumped in her chest. "You mean you want to consummate our marriage as quickly as I do?"

He grimaced, but nodded. "Yes, but as I said, if we go slowly, we can enjoy it more."

She wasn't sure it would be worth the wait. "Cannot we simply do so again and go slowly then?" She doubted she'd want to, but maybe she would.

His body reacted to her comment, and she grinned. "Maybe we should just get to it."

"I...We...hell." He pulled out the chair from the table next to them and sat, pulling her toward him. "I'm all yours."

Though he meant it in the vein of copulation, his gaze told her there was far more meaning to his words.

It made her heart ache with happiness, but it also heated her to know he'd allow her free rein of his magnificent body. She walked around him, pulling her hand from his grasp and placing both on his shoulders. Running them down his torso, she kissed his neck, in the same spot he'd kissed her before.

As her hand roamed lower to his abdomen, she could feel the tension in his body. Finally, she got to the place she wished most to touch, and gently grasped him in her hands. The smooth texture and heat of it surprised her. It was a wonder that he could grow so much.

Her own body heated with the knowledge that she was capable of doing this to him. Anxious for what was to come, she straightened and walked around the chair to face him. His eyes were closed and his jaw tight. She thought to step between his thighs, but that didn't seem right. Glancing over her shoulder, she studied the sketch. Of course.

When she turned back, he was staring at her, his pupils large and his breathing short. More signs that he wanted her? She moved forward and straddled his lap, careful to keep him between her legs. Immediately, he looped his arms around her.

His head moved forward and he licked at her breasts, first one, then the other, before blowing on her wet tips. They felt as hard as the stone of the ancient statues. Tingles of pleasure raced through her body and moisture started to gather at the juncture of her thighs.

He looked up at her as one hand came up to cup her head, and she eagerly kissed him. There was no softness in the kiss. It was pure passion, his own want connecting with hers.

She finally broke the kiss, breathless and with an ache starting in her core.

He immediately switched his kiss to her breast and sucked. Need like she'd never known shot through her, making her grind into him. He didn't stop her this time though. Instead, his mouth kept up its pleasurable torture until she half-raised from his lap. It was then she felt him at her entrance and instinct took over.

Positioning herself, she started downward, but his hands on her hips stopped her.

"Only do what is comfortable. If you wish to stop, we can."

Confused, she just nodded and started again. There was pressure she'd never felt before, but the need inside her insisted and she pushed through. Slowly, she lowered herself, taking him in, at first finding the feeling odd, but she closed her eyes and relaxed into the sweet slide that brought her down onto his lap. He filled her and for the first time she understood what she'd craved. This. A oneness with him. To be a part of him and he a part of her.

"Amelia?" His whisper had her opening her eyes.

"Yes?"

"How do you feel?"

She smiled. "I feel full, excited, happy."

"Do you know there is more?"

She frowned, confused. Was this completeness not what they sought? "There is?"

His gaze softened. "Let me show you."

His mouth returned, this time to her other breast and took her peak between his teeth and rolled.

The jolt of pleasure shot through her so fast that she lifted. Quickly, she lowered herself again only to discover more pleasure at the movement. Anxious to experience everything, she pulled up again and came down.

"Yes. Like that."

His encouraging words were all she needed, but his hands grasped her hips to set a rhythm. Soon she was panting, the need to continue impossible to ignore, but she felt as if she were on the edge of something miraculous, like last time with him, but more spectacular.

His hands on her hips moved, pressuring her to change her angle. Accommodating his silent direction, she did and as she slid down, her body felt as if the sun burst inside her, splintering into thousands of colors. With no control, she rode the feeling, gasping for breath as Andrew's shout rang out and warmth filled her. Pure joy took over, floating her on a cloud of contentment.

Tired, her breathing beginning to slow, she opened her eyes in wonder at the man before her, his golden gaze filled with love. She swallowed to get her voice to work. "That was mystic."

She felt his silent chuckle in all places, sending tiny sparks through her. Surprised that she could want him again so soon, she tried to ignore it. That surely couldn't be normal.

"It is only mystic if you love someone." His gaze complemented his sentiment.

She grasped his head and tilted it before kissing him with gratitude. Breaking the kiss, she let him see how much she loved him. "Thank you for being my muse and my heart."

He reached up and unpinned her hair. "Thank you for being

my love."

She placed her hand on his chest to feel his solid heartbeat, the vibration calming her body and seeping into her soul. She started to rise, and his hands tightened on her hips.

"Not yet."

That suited her fine. She wasn't sure if her knees would hold her.

He brought her hand to his lips and kissed it. "Why do I have the feeling that you will never want to go slow."

She chuckled that he knew her so well. "Because I won't?"

His smile turned sly as he licked her palm then sucked one of her fingers into his mouth.

The sudden spike of excitement caught her unawares. "Oh." The feeling continued as he slowly pulled her finger out.

"Now, are there any other pages in that book of yours that you wish to explore?"

How could just his words set her fairies to dancing again? "As a matter of fact, there are. Shall I show you?"

"Yes." Andrew gazed at her. "I want to fulfill your every wish."

She cupped his chin. "You already have and more."

As he pulled her head down for a kiss, she had to admit that painting the earl had been her smartest proposal yet.

$$\text{\Large \textasciicircum}$$

EPILOGUE

March 1, 1817

AMELIA WALKED INTO the dining room of Lyonsmere to find her husband at the sideboard and her sister and the duke reading the newspaper. She could just imagine how quiet it must be at breakfast at Burhleigh Hall where they resided when Joanna's school was not in session.

Andrew turned with his plate and smiled at her. "Here she is."

Both Joanna and James looked up from their paper, but Joanna spoke. "Whenever did you paint that portrait of Belinda? It captures her very soul. I must have one for the school."

She moved her gaze to her latest effort. Even she admitted it was an outstanding piece. She was quite pleased with it. "I finished it yesterday before you arrived. It didn't take long. I find that the more I love my subject, the easier it is to paint it."

James looked to Andrew who sat at the head of the table. "Will you have a portrait of yourself in every room then?"

He took a sip of tea and grinned. "If that's what my wife wishes, that's what will be." He winked at her. "I find I'm quite good at posing."

She felt her cheeks heat and stopped by the sideboard to fill her plate to hide her blush. By the time she turned and joined them at the table, sitting next to her husband, her embarrassment was under control. "Is Mariel still out riding then?"

"She is." Joanna studied her. "You haven't said yes to a painting of Belinda."

"Oh, of course I will." She paused, cocking her head. "Do you think Lord Harewood would wish to have one?"

James and Andrew shared a look, and she pounced on it. "What is it?"

Andrew clasped her hand. "I know your thought is to be kind, but it would be best that he is not reminded of her. He will need to find a wife one day and I fear he won't find someone to love as I have if he still pines for your sister."

She understood what he said, but her chest hurt that she couldn't provide a painting to the man who brought her Andrew. She gave a short nod. "I understand. I will have Pratt move this one before Lord Harewood visits next week."

"Are you not going to Town?" James asked the question as if he were hoping that were the case.

She found that odd, though in fact, perhaps it wasn't. He was not overly fond of London. "I believe we may miss the whole season. Andrew has insisted I meet all the tenants and then we must make the rounds."

"Not to mention a trip up to Scotland so my lovely wife can paint the rugged highlands."

Andrew's announcement of their honeymoon had Joanna's eyes rounding. "But I thought the two of you would prefer to travel to the continent where all the great masterpieces reside."

"You mean besides the ones here?" Andrew raised his brows.

Joanna didn't miss a beat. "Well, of course. These masterpieces," she waved toward the painting of Belinda that reigned over the fireplace, "you can see every day."

Her husband opened his mouth to respond, but she jumped in. "We would very much love to return to the continent, this time together, but with the famine and sickness after last summer, we thought to stay closer to home." She gave her husband a meaningful stare. "I'm sure we will return to the continent another year."

He nodded, and she breathed easier.

James set down his newspaper and spoke to his wife. "Without Lady Sommerset in Town, is there really any reason for us to venture there?"

Joanna grinned. "Of course there is. I can give you the most important reason."

His eyes narrowed. "If you say mascarpone ice cream, I will personally have Sir Armand send enough to last you the entire summer at Burhleigh Park."

Joanna, who had opened her mouth, closed it quickly.

Amelia couldn't help her chuckle. "Surely you can think of another reason, Joanna."

As usual, her sister recovered quickly. "I can. James, I don't know why you would think I was going to mention ice cream. Actually, we need to go because our students are expecting outings and discussions during the season. We've already missed the first month because of Amelia's wedding, and I heard from Elsbeth just yesterday that there is a new scene at the panorama."

James frowned. "You didn't tell me you heard from my cousin."

"Well, there are only so many hours in a day."

Amelia's concern for their cousin on the continent had her speaking up. "Speaking of Elsbeth, have you heard anything from Teddy?"

"I did." Joanna finished the last piece of her toast and took a sip of tea before elaborating. "He's enjoying himself far too much. I don't think he even remembers Elsbeth."

"And he's safe?"

Joanna waved her hand as she lifted the paper once again. "He's in Paris enjoying the pleasure of Montmartre."

Amelia exchanged a look with Andrew, who started to grin. He obviously thought Teddy was enjoying the women and wine of the quarter. He could be right, but she still couldn't think of him as a man grown. Before he'd left, he'd become so melodramatic.

She actually didn't mind if she missed the season this year. She was still learning her role as Countess Sommerset, getting to know the staff and she'd already met two tenant families, who praised Andrew with heartfelt gratitude. It had given her a feeling of pride in him that she hadn't experienced before. He really did care about his people, or rather, *their* people as he insisted.

There were also fewer distractions at Lyonsmere, which allowed her to paint. In just a week, she'd—

"Oh, my Lord!" Joanna exclamation from behind the newspaper had them all staring at her.

She was the first to recover. "What is it?"

Joanna looked at her over the paper. "I…it's…"

James leaned over and Joanna pointed. He read. *Marcus Stratton, younger brother to Lord Jacob Stratton, Viscount of Blackmore, who inherited the title after the sudden death of his older brother and wife last winter to open Ravenridge in Northampton Parish this week.*

Her own heart stopped, and she stared at Joanna. "Mariel's Marcus? Alive?"

Joanna nodded.

At Andrew's warm hands on her shoulders, she breathed deeply before looking up at him. "What should we do?"

"I believe you must tell her."

Joanna shook her head. "But he died on the battlefield. I myself was with Mariel when we checked the scrolls. It must be an imposter."

"Not necessarily." Andrew squeezed her shoulders. "Battlefields are messy. Surgeon tents are chaotic. If the man was unconscious and moved to a hospital, no one would be the wiser. If anyone saw him fall, they would have listed him as dead."

Joanna looked to her husband. "Is this true?"

He held his hand out to Andrew. "I have little knowledge in this area."

Amelia looked up at her husband. "How do you know so

much?"

"While I traveled the continent, I became friends with a former officer from Portugal. He was collecting paintings of the battles, which is how we met. He explained to me the realities of war and which painters truly captured them."

She laid her hand on his and he grasped hers. She was thankful that he had never actually experienced battle. "But why would he have not sought out Mariel?"

No one answered her question.

Her heart ached for her oldest sister. She'd lost so much, sacrificed so much. Was this perhaps her reward or a new punishment?

"Your husband is right." Joanna set the paper down on the table, the small announcement facing upward. "We have to tell her."

They all nodded, but Amelia couldn't help wondering what Mariel would do. "Yes, she needs to know. If this is a chance to find the happiness we have, we can't keep this information from her." She squeezed Andrew's hand, thankful for his support.

Pratt entered the dining room and bowed to them. "Pardon my interruption, my lord, but there is a gentleman who insists on meeting the countess. I told him to come back this afternoon, but he will hear none of it. Here is his card. Do you wish me to have him removed?"

Andrew took the card and grinned. "No. If my lady is willing, I think we will see him in my study."

Pratt didn't bat an eyelash before heading back to the entryway.

"Who is it?" She frowned at her husband. It was hardly an appropriate time to call.

He didn't say anything, just handed her the card.

Ansel Bartleby, Art Dealer. 18 James Street, London.

"Who is it, Amelia?" Joanna craned her neck as if she could read the card from across the table.

She rose, raising her brows. "It's an art dealer."

"An art dealer? Why would—"

Andrew interrupted Joanna. "It would appear that my wife's art is requested."

"Do you think so?" Her heart started to pound.

"I do." He gave her an encouraging smile and placed her hand on his arm. "Shall we meet him and see if I'm correct?"

She nodded, still too surprised to understand what it meant. But once out of the dining room, her curiosity came to the fore. "Do you know this Mr. Bartleby?"

"I do. He has an excellent reputation." Andrew led her past the stairs to the upper floor.

"Then he may be here to see if you are willing to sell one of the paintings in your collection. You do have a stunning collection." That had to be why the man was here.

"Did you not hear Pratt? He is here to see you."

That was true. He did say that. "But he could be here because he heard I have knowledge of classical painters and he wished another opinion on a piece."

Andrew halted, still feet from his study and stepped in front of her. "Mr. Bartleby is here to inquire about purchasing one of your paintings. Why is it hard for you to believe that?"

She shrugged her right shoulder. "There are so many other skilled artists. Why me?"

His gaze turned soft and he took her hands in his. "My beautiful, talented wife. You are one of those skilled artists, and I have no doubt that you are far better than most."

She started to shake her head, but he dropped her hands and cupped her face. "I'm an art collector. You are more skilled than most. Now I want you to accept the fact, before we walk in there, that someone wants to buy one of your paintings."

"They do?" She had so many questions, like how did they even know about her, who wanted a painting, and why her?

"Yes, they do. Now shall we find out which one?"

She nodded, still not quite believing it and half expecting the dealer had the wrong artist.

Andrew placed her hand on his arm again and took them to the door, as he opened it, she could feel the tension in his arm. "Mr. Bartleby. You insist on seeing my wife at a most ungodly hour. I trust there is something of great import that you must communicate then?"

Having never heard Andrew use such a tone, she found herself distracted by him. He was her Greek hero come to life.

The man, dressed in the fine clothes of a wealthy merchant, spun away from the painting of Andrew that hung above the fireplace. "My lord, my lady. I do apologize for my strong insistence, but my mission is of great import to the Duke of Marlboro."

Andrew gave the slightest of nods. "And what could we possibly do that would be of assistance to the duke?"

Mr. Bartleby didn't cower at Andrew's tone. Instead he pointed to the painting. "It is artwork like this that the duke is searching for."

Andrew walked her to his desk before responding. "Mr. Bartleby, I highly doubt the duke would appreciate a portrait of me in his home."

The man strode forward, anxious to convey his true mission. "No sir. Of course he would not, but he is looking for such talent." The man moved his gaze to her. "My Lady, I know this is most unusual, but the Duke of Marlboro was quite taken with your painting of the Tower of London."

"The one at Lady Spencer's in Town?" It wasn't one of her best works, having been accomplished over a year ago.

"Oh yes. The duke is having a new home built in Mayfair, and he has very specific requirements for the artwork. It must be by someone trained in the classic style, but not an old master. It must be original. And it must have as its subject London specifically. He wants his home to reflect his home country, not some idealized version of Paris or Rome."

The man recited the duke's requirements as if he'd done so a hundred times.

"And most importantly, the artwork must be well done, and

the Tower of London is most exceptional."

Something was wrong, as she suspected. The painting Mr. Bartleby mentioned was in Lady Spencer's ballroom, but she hadn't hosted a ball yet this season. "How did the duke come upon Lady Spencer's painting?"

"Yes, I don't believe I've seen that one." Andrew looked at her in question.

Bartleby was quick to answer. "It was Lord Harewood who told the duke of the painting. Upon which the duke called on Lady Spencer who, of course, had it brought out for him to view. He wished to purchase it from her, but she refused, at which point he asked the artist's name. You can imagine what a surprise it was to him to hear it was a lady of the realm who had created such beautiful work."

"Harewood." Andrew grinned.

"Lady Spencer." She shook her head, still finding the entire story difficult to believe.

Andrew motioned for Mr. Bartleby to sit and pulled out the chair at his desk for her. After she sat, he stood at her shoulder. "So how can we be of help?"

"My lord, I came at once on the duke's bequest to discover if perhaps your wife had any other paintings of London. The duke would be interested in purchasing at least five or six, if they were available."

She thought to the ones she had in her studio. "I have three, possibly four, though the fourth is set in the middle of Hyde Park with no distinguishing markings to show it's there. Just a couple of ladies at the water's edge."

Mr. Bartleby scooted forward on the chair and leaned toward them. "I would very much like to see them."

Andrew's hand came down to rest on her shoulder. "I'm sure we can make those arrangements, but as we did not expect you and have other plans for our day, I hope you will excuse us now. Where should we send for you?"

Mr. Bartleby rose, looking contrite for the first time since arriving. "Of course. I apologize. I will await your leisure at the

Owl's Nest Inn. I dare not return to London without at least one piece of artwork for the duke's approval. He was very insistent on that."

Andrew lifted his hand from her shoulder and motioned for Mr. Bartleby to precede him to the door. Suddenly, Mr. Bartleby halted and turned to look at her. "My lady, would you be willing to paint the duke's portrait? I'm sure he would be most delighted—"

"No!" Andrew's voice reverberated through the study, causing their guest and herself both to jump. "She does not paint anyone's portrait."

Mr. Bartleby pointed to the one of Andrew over the fireplace and opened his mouth to argue, but her husband was having none of it.

"No one's outside of her family. Do I make myself clear?"

The man was intelligent enough to realize he would get no further on that front. As the two continued toward the door, she grinned. No doubt her husband was thinking of exactly how he had posed for that particular portrait.

After seeing that Pratt showed Mr. Bartleby out, Andrew closed the door and faced her from across the room. "Do I need to reiterate now that your talent far surpasses others?"

She shook her head. "I don't know what to think. I'm still so surprised." But it was more than surprised. Satisfaction, triumph, and excitement also filled her, the fairies in her stomach dancing for joy. "I did it." The wonder of it was almost too much to comprehend. "I'm an artist."

"Not just an artist, but a sought-after artist."

His face was full of pride in her, and it was that which had her accepting the truth. Her skills were exceptional. She'd always hoped, but a niggling doubt never expected her dream would be fulfilled. And it was all because of him, a man she'd thought to dissuade. She smirked. "Whyever would you not want me to paint portraits then?"

He narrowed his eyes at her as he stalked toward the desk. "You know quite well why I'll not have you painting other men."

She rose from the chair. "No, I don't believe I do. Is it that you don't wish me to be alone with a naked man? After all, the human form is nothing more than another object." She gave him a sly smile. "Like a bowl of fruit."

At the desk now, laughter in his eyes, he set his hands down on its empty surface. "I'll show you a bowl of fruit, madam." Even as he said the words, he jumped over the desk.

With a high-pitched squeak she didn't know she could make, she jumped back and took one step to run. His arm wrapped around her waist, pulling her tight against him. He had her pinned between him and the desk, the rumble of laughter in his chest stimulating her own. "Really sir, such brazen liberties you take of my person." Though she tried to appear stern, she couldn't keep her lips from twitching.

His whisky-brown gaze seemed to darken, making her heart skip a beat. "You are my bowl of fruit, and I plan to investigate and taste every last piece right now."

Alarmed, she looked over her shoulder at the door. "We can't. We have guests. The door."

His mouth quirked up into the most seductive smile she'd ever seen on him. "I locked the door."

Suddenly, her knees felt weak, and a thrill of excitement raced from her chest to her core as she turned back to meet his gaze. "Then by all means, I am happy to allow you your tastes. Enjoy, my lord."

His breath caught and his face tensed before he lifted her to sit on the desk. "My Lady Sommerset, I will most definitely enjoy."

As Andrew untied the back of her dress and pulled it down to do just that, her heart filled with love. A deep knowledge that her life was now its own masterpiece overwhelmed her with happiness, until Andrew's mouth touched her, and they soared to new heights together.

The End

About the Author

Lexi Post is a New York Times and USA Today best-selling author of romance inspired by the classics. She spent years in higher education taking and teaching courses about the classical literature she loved. From Edgar Allan Poe's short story "The Masque of the Red Death" to Tolstoy's *War and Peace*, she's read, studied, and taught wonderful classics.

But Lexi's first love is romance novels so she married her two first loves, romance and the classics. Whether it's dashing dukes, hot immortals, sizzling cowboys, or hunks from out of this world, Lexi provides a sensuous experience with a "whole lotta story."

Lexi is living her own happily ever after with her husband and her two cats in Florida. She makes her own ice cream every weekend, loves bright colors, and you'll never see her without a hat.

Website: lexipostbooks.com
Lexi Post Updates: app.mailerlite.com/webforms/landing/c1w1g3
Facebook: facebook.com/lexipostbooks
Twitter: @LexiPost
Instagram: instagram.com/lexipostbooks
Amazon Author Page: http://amzn.to/1IEL2cc
BookBub: bookbub.com/authors/lexi-post
D2D: books2read.com/author/lexi-post/subscribe/1/16171
Goodreads: goodreads.com/goodreadscomLexiPost
Instagram: instagram.com/lexipostbooks
Blog: happilyeverafterthoughts.com
Pinterest: pinterest.com/lexipost77
Email: lexi@lexipostbooks.com

www.ingramcontent.com/pod-product-compliance
Lightning Source LLC
Chambersburg PA
CBHW071423200726
48294CB00002B/496